THE TWO KINGDOMS

Books by Mark Saxton

THE TWO KINGDOMS
THE ISLAR
PAPER CHASE
PREPARED FOR RAGE
THE YEAR OF AUGUST
THE BROKEN CIRCLE
DANGER ROAD

THE TWO KINGDOMS

A NOVEL OF ISLANDIA

MARK SAXTON

HOUGHTON MIFFLIN COMPANY BOSTON

1979

To my friends
Martha and Russell
with love

Library of Congress Cataloging in Publication Data

Saxton, Mark.
    The two kingdoms.

    I. Title.
PZ3.S2736Tw   [PS3537.A979]   813'.5'2   79-10771
ISBN 0-395-28152-0

Printed in the United States of America

V 10 9 8 7 6 5 4 3 2 1

"The whole psychological analysis of historical thought would be exactly the same if there were no such thing as the past at all, if Julius Caesar were an imaginary character, and if history were not knowledge but pure fancy."

R. G. Collingwood
in *The Idea of History*

NOTE AND ACKNOWLEDGMENT

SINCE THE LINES of fact and fiction converging on this book are not entirely distinct, the reader may welcome an attempt at clarification.

Lang III, who appears in the ensuing pages as the translator of Frare's narrative, is the leading figure in my novel *The Islar*. He is also the grandson of John Lang, the American hero of Austin Tappan Wright's novel *Islandia*, who started things off by leaving America and eventually becoming an Islandian citizen.

In addition to *Islandia*, Austin Wright wrote a full scale history of his imaginary country, which was never published. He called this work *Islandia: History and Description* and attributed it to Jean Perrier, first French Consul to Islandia, himself a character in Wright's novel. The history does exist, however, and is the basis for events in this book. Everything Lang III has to say on the subject is quite correct, although he naturally sees the history from a different position.

Once again I want to thank Sylvia Wright Miterachi for reading a manuscript of mine and for her interest in my interest in Islandian affairs. My thanks also to the Houghton Library of Harvard for making available to me their manuscript of *Islandia: History and Description*.

M.S.
Boston

STORNSEA

BELTSEA

Storntock Hills

S T O R N

Storn

Thist Bay

Shores

A

Islan

Ardan

Ardan Hills

N I V E N

Niven

A L

Alban

B

Herntock Hills

MATWIL R.

Matwin

Camia

C A M I A

BEALSEA

H E R N

HERN R.

Beal

Steen

Brome

R O M E

Alwin

Deentock Hills

D E E N

Great Deen Wood

Deen

Monar

B R O M E

THE FR

MT. MATCLORN

MT. BRONCLORN

Miltain

MT. MATCLORN

Matclorn Pass

M I L T A I N

Alena

Bronclorn Pass

Sobo Pass

S O B O

ISLANDIA

Mobono

Sulliaba

K A R A I N

St. Anthony

KARAIN R.

The KARAIN CONTINENT

0   600 Miles

C A R R A N

Carran

Madley

Madley Pass

Sea Pass

MOBONO R.

Sobo Pass

Mobono

C O N T I N E N T

SHB

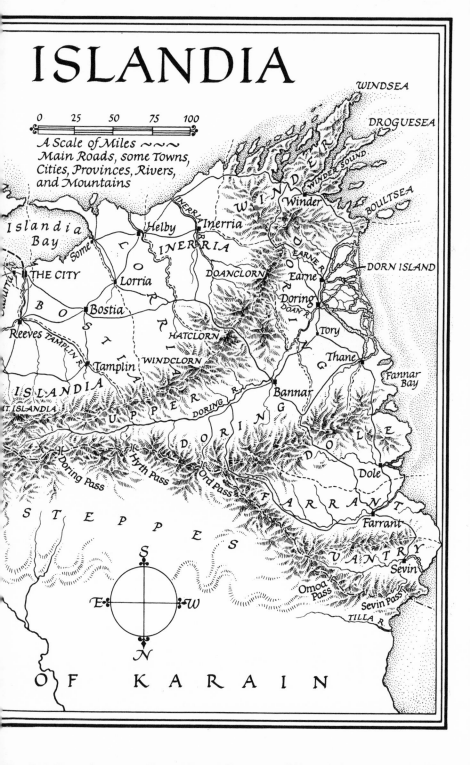

ISLANDIA

0   25   50   75   100

A Scale of Miles ~~~
Main Roads, some Towns,
Cities, Provinces, Rivers,
and Mountains

WINDSEA

DROGUESEA

Islandia Bay

THE CITY

Helby   Inerria

INERRIA

Lorria

DOANCLORN

WINDER

Winder

WINDER SOUND

BOULTSEA

DORN ISLAND

EARNE R.

Earne

Doring

DOAN R.

DORING R.

BOSTIA

Bostia

Reeves   TAMPLIN R.

Tamplin

WINDCLORN

HATCLORN

Tory

Thane

Fannar Bay

ISLANDIA

T. ISLANDIA

UPPER

DORING R.

DORING

Bannar

DOLE

Dole

Doring Pass

Hyrth Pass

Oru Pass

FARRANT

Farrant

S   T   E   P   P   E   S

VANTRY

Sevin

Omoa Pass

Sevin Pass

TILLA R.

S

E   W

N

O   F   K   A   R   A   I   N

THE TWO
KINGDOMS

FOREWORD

DURING THE TEN YEARS since the divisive events I recorded in *The Islar,* Islandia has recovered much of its old skeptical pragmatism and with it a measure of poise. Not without considerable dissent, the country has decided to go its own way once again. We have taken advantage of the escape clauses in our American agreement with the result that there are still no automobiles on our roads, no tractors in our fields, no earth-movers taming our rivers, and, most important, there is no tanker terminal in Islandia Bay.

In declining to climb on the world treadmill, we know we are a precarious anachronism, but it is only the terms of the condition that are new. We have always been in peril from one or another refusal to join or acquiesce and our attitude now is that we were right in taking the risks. Accompanying this national sang-froid, there has appeared a renewed interest in just what those risks were, what happened in the times of great crisis, and efforts are being made to uncover historical material.

The manuscript of the personal story that follows was found well, if fortuitously, preserved in Winder at the bottom of a chest full of old family carvings. Frare, the writer, appears once or twice in the meager official records of the fourteenth century and his own account suggests why he does not turn up more often.

Frare's narrative covers approximately six months in the year 1320, a time when Islandia had to decide — although it did not know it — whether or not it wanted to be. Frare tells how Alwina, Islandia's first Queen, came to the throne. He saw the plots against her life, her troubled fascination with King Tor, her attempts at reconciliation with Tor's kingdom of Winder, and the onset of desperate war with the Karain. Frare shows us a young woman of twenty, no more than a girl, eager, beautiful, untried — full of doubts and fears as well as courage and intelligence — who was called on for a task no Islandian woman has faced before or since. Frare offers less grandeur and more immediacy than we usually get.

The question of authenticity inevitably arises. Of course, there is no doubt that there was a man named Frare who lived at that time and who set down this record. But how reliable is he?

It is useful to compare his work with Jean Perrier's *Islandia: History and Description*, still by far the best of the general histories. Perrier can allot only a few pages to the half year in question; yet virtually all Frare's material gives body and presence to actions and events on which they agree, or is of a sort that was inaccessible to Perrier. On only two occasions are there significant differences between them, and these are silent not overt. Both concern the whereabouts of certain people at given times and in both the logic of events somewhat favors Frare. In short, where Frare can be checked he is trustworthy, and so presumably his evidence should be discounted only to the extent that it represents a definite point of view. That much is important, however, for Frare considered himself no mere witness, as he makes clear in a sharp exchange with Bodwin.

As with *The Islar,* I am offering this translation because of the continuing interest of English-speaking friends ever since my grandfather, John Lang, told his story in *Islandia*. With this long leap into the past, Frare shows in the making many of the qualities John Lang found irresistibly attractive.

Lang III
The City
Islandia

NOTE ON PERSONAL NAMES   It has not been Islandian custom to use given names, children being designated numerically. Some European and even a few American families have followed a similar practice: Primus-a; Secundus-a; Tertius-ia, etc. Thus in Islandia: Ek-Ekka; Atta-Attana; Etteri-Etterina, and so forth.

Trans.

IN THE BRIGHT SUN of a soft spring morning, the widely spaced trees forming open glades on all sides, I stood among the crowd at the funeral of Alwin the Good. The City, immediately below, lay partly hidden behind a small ridge, but the path of the river through it was in full view and the clear light drew tones of earth color from the roof tiles and even from the gray stone of the houses. Beyond, Islandia Bay stretched glinting to the horizon.

Alwin was in fact a good king and well loved, his principal fault no doubt being a certain carelessness in begetting a daughter but no son. There were rumors that some Islar found this omission disturbing, but in the crews of the ships I knew and among my friends there was no such feeling. While Alwin was alive there was some bawdy jesting on the subject up and down the land, but now, without words and without ceremony in the Islandian manner, only affectionate silence marked the end of his time.

After a while by unspoken agreement the gathering broke up, the mourners in their blue, brown, or tan wool clothes moving away singly and in twos and threes. All wore loose tunics or jackets, the men distinguishable by trousers gathered just below the knee and the women by skirts of the same length. Stockings were a matter of choice for both sexes. Following the greater number into the center of The City, passing handcarts and occasional pony carts returning empty from the market, I turned into the square in front of the Council chamber, an unusually light and graceful building made of a buff-colored stone with veins of rose in it. Here I chose a sheltered bench and settled down to wait for the end of such deliberations as the Council might feel proper for that day. A few years earlier I would have worried uncomfortably about why I was there, but by now I knew that the south wind was as likely to answer questions as Admiral Lamas was to give a reason for an order. There was no point in wondering. To pass the time I opened the new sequence of fables by my young cousin Bodwin. On the blue inked page the words appeared attractively in white, not having been copied but incised on wood and printed.

While the shadow of the arm on a nearby sundial moved an hour's worth, my cousin's efforts amused me greatly. This was not merely for the wit in them — though there was a good leaven of that — but also for the fact that so apparently ingenuous and naturalistic was the writing one could not determine what political principle the author favored, or even certainly that he was discussing such principles. This conformed to Bodwin's expressed belief that fables should embody the lessons taught by the natural world and no more. With what ringing and powerful rhetoric I have heard him denounce Aesop as a model for our own writers. And yet these of his, if one could read them right, were certainly Aesopian. Or were they not? Who here was salamander, who toad, and who again lizard? How to know without a key to his private bestiary of character traits? Or perhaps here was really nothing more than his view of the natural irony of natural history. He was indeed a clever young man, and would live long and safely.

I had just formed this opinion when there appeared on the steps across the way a man who, like Admiral Lamas, had little liking for explanations but at least was skilled in giving them. He was Lord Cabing, head of the Council and Commander of the Army. He beckoned me. I joined him and we set off briskly on foot for a destination left to my guesswork. Cabing was a personable man with the marks of his career on him. Nobility by blood, the inheritance of the rank of Isla, was abolished in Islandia more than a hundred years ago, after the conspiracy of the League of Nobles, and in that time Cabing has become the third member of his family to earn an Islaship by way of the military path to the Council. That is most unusual. Of middle height with thick gray hair, he had a narrow face, brown eyes and a wide, thin mouth below his mustache. He has always possessed natural physical grace and has acquired both force and subtlety by becoming stronger than his once notorious temper. The Army is still full of tales about him as a junior officer and I think he enjoys their echoes.

We crossed the downstream bridge of the Islandia River and continued westward, skirting the bay until I knew we must be going to Alwin House. This stands on the high tip of a point slanting out from the shore about a mile from the limits of The City. At the base of the point there is a guard post and then, beyond this formality, the Alwin land rolls away in woods and pasture to the big, heavy building overlooking the water. It looks like a fort.

Actually, whether any large Islandian residence is considered fortified or not is largely a matter of preference and past history. All such places are built of continuous stone with thick walls, deep round-vaulted arches, and massive buttresses. Windows are few and narrow. Any of them can be defended and many have been. The technical distinction between a manor and a fort lies in the location of the well and the kitchen garden and the number of people and animals that can be brought to live within its walls. By that standard the Alwin palace is not fortified, whatever its appearance.

As Lord Cabing and I approached the last broad meadow between us and the palace, the sheer mass of the gray building, high in the center and sloping down toward the shores, seemed so great that the whole pile must slide off the peninsula and down into the water. Cabing looked away from the palace toward me and asked, "Ever been in the Karain, Frare?"

"No, sir."

"Never seen any Saracen buildings?"

"On a voyage north I came within sight of Mobono, but not that close."

"They know how to handle sun and air and water. They could teach us something about building houses."

As he spoke, a lookout crow spotted us from a leafing tree on the edge of the meadow and rose squawking and flapping from his perch. In response to his danger signal a dozen of his fellows down in the field-grass joined in his croaking and lunged and scrabbled into the air. Cabing watched the routine frenzy of their exercise with a sardonic smile. "Now there's a subject for one of young Bodwin's fables," he said. "They'll teach me to talk treason. Ugly, noisy brutes. Remind me of Councilors."

The crows continued circling and did not return to their feckless business. The casual thought drifted across my mind that we might not be the only ones disturbing them. In that moment, out of the edge of my eye I caught a semblance of motion deep in the woods, like the lifting of a hand.

I dove at Cabing's knees, drove him to the ground, and rolled over and over with him to the protection of a tree trunk. As we fell, a throwing dart flashed through the space where his shoulders had been. While we rolled, a second dart struck quivering into the ground where we had fallen.

Leaving Cabing shaken and bruised, I scuttled, crouching from tree to tree, along the path of the darts. Soon, over the hiss of my own breathing, I heard the snapping of brush and the indistinct thuds of running feet. Quitting dodging, I stood up and began to run myself. Thirty yards ahead I saw two backs turning left into the easier going of the old forest. I was fast. I might at least be able to see them to know again. Just then something flat and narrow like a rod hit me hard across the chest. My feet flew out in front as I fell flat on my back, the wind driven wholly out of me, and struck the back of my head on something hard.

I don't think I went out completely, but it was some time before I stopped gasping and heaving and the red curtain lifted from my eyes. When I began to see, I realized that Cabing was kneeling beside me with an arm under my shoulders. "There's no hurry now, Frare," he said. "You're all right. Your head hit a root, not a stone. But take your time. Don't try to stand up yet. Thank you for knocking me down so neatly. A good job." He smiled and sat back on his heels. "That'll teach me to be patronizing about crows."

He showed me one of the darts, saying, "Made in this country." Like all weapons of the type, this dart was heavy for its three feet of length. It had a metal head, a roughened place for a grip at the balance point of the shaft, and three fledgings around the tail. The shape of the head, the size of the feathers, and the style of their lashings all did seem to make it Islandian.

Then Cabing stood up and rested his hand on a horizontal shadow, the cord I had met but not seen. Cabing drew his thumb across his throat and then snapped his fingers. "They didn't figure on a giant," he said. "Just the same, it stopped pursuit." He looked at the knot at one of the terminal trees. "This is a tie I don't recognize."

When I could stand without dizziness, we cut the cord away from the trees to leave the knots intact, picked up the other dart, and crossed the meadow, upsetting the crows again.

At the palace guardhouse we brushed and washed away the marks of rough usage — my hair hid the lump on my head well enough — and Cabing called the duty officer aside for instructions. "Send out a pursuit party," he said, "but be quiet about it. No word of any of this to the Queen. You won't catch the men, but you should be able to track them. Probably to a boat. I want a confidential report, along with this equipment, delivered to me in The City tonight."

Alwina received us in an open, sheltered court on the west side of the palace. Here warm sunlight and a light breeze from the water made a refuge from the damp chill of the rooms that were still full of winter. There were chairs and a large table on the grass and silver cups around a bowl of wine. Delicate, intricate carving formed a broad band around the top edge of the table, and I wondered which one of the many Alwins had done it. As we approached, the company surrounding Alwina withdrew. This was my first sight of her. She wore a deep shade of green, which set off her dark red hair and fair skin. She was tall for a woman, with good shoulders, and her hazel eyes had flecks of tan in them. She stood smiling, as we stopped in front of her and bowed.

At Cabing's introduction I bowed a second time and she said, "Welcome, Frare." And then, "What of the Council, Isla Cabing?"

"Your Majesty, I . . ."

She interrupted him crisply. "My name is Alwina. It always has been to you, Isla Cabing."

"Then I'm afraid my name has to become just Cabing."

"But I can't do that," she said. "I can't say it. Isla is part of you to me. It would be indecent to leave it off."

"Since yesterday, Your Majesty," Cabing said dryly, "I've had the same difficulty with you. No, if you want the substance, then I'm sorry but you'll have to stay with the form. Even in private."

"I see," she said flushing and looked down at her hands

working awkwardly at each other. "Then we'll do what we must — for a while." She dipped cups into the wine bowl and handed one to each of us. "Do, please, sit down. Now, Isla Cabing, what of the Council?"

Cabing took his time, moving from his chair, sipping from his cup. Alwina sat waiting, one hand in her lap, the other on the table. She seemed younger than I expected, perhaps younger than she actually was. She let herself appear rebuked and her posture said she was annoyed at herself for doing so. There was great beauty about her, but it lay scattered around as haphazardly as her arms and legs and the folds of her dress. There was also tremendous energy, but one was aware of it only in dispersal, in abrupt single gestures, in a kind of peripheral flickering, like heat lightning. In a little while, a day or a year, when she wanted or when some particular thing happened to her, the beauty would form and the energy would gather itself into a force that would fell a man. Now she seemed content to sit disassembled — embarrassed and impatient.

"Going to my father's funeral," she said to me, leaving Cabing in his silence, "I stopped in a House of Quiet. Om was there. I was very much surprised. I never thought He'd come for me."

"What did you have Him tell you?"

"He doesn't speak, you know," she said. "He just *is*."

"Yes, I do know, but I've never found Him," I said. "What was He like to you?"

"It's hard to describe," she told me. "It's true He just *is*, but He's more than that, too. I suppose it's different for everyone. I felt warm inside — and buzzing. Like a hive of bees. It was nice."

She laughed and then turned suddenly and sharply to Cabing. "If not the Council, Isla Cabing, what of the Karain! All through my father's illness reports from the north told of Mobono concentrating ships and building new ones. What of that?"

"The reports don't change," Cabing said.

"I'm sure they don't. Now then, will you tell me of the Council?"

"Of course, Your Majesty." He set down his cup and touched his mouth with a white cloth. "A sorry business and going to be sorrier unless we're fortunate. How much do you remember about the Council's action a year ago?"

"I remember what I heard," she said, "but that wasn't much. When the Council disapproved of me, Father was furious. He said it didn't mean anything and that I should forget it. He never spoke of it to me again."

"He was right in a way," Cabing said, "but I wish he'd discussed it. I don't know why the Council voted to ban you from the throne. I thought then, and I still think," and he smiled as though there weren't two throw darts in the palace guard room, "that many members found it an easy way to demonstrate their traditionalism without paying for it. We've never had a Queen! We don't want one! At that, the margin was very small. And in any case the vote was gratuitous and irresponsible. By that I mean there was no serious supporting debate and the votes were not recorded by name. That's not to take the thing lightly. I don't. Not at all."

"Yes," Alwina said, "just so. You refuse to tell me, Isla Cabing, so I must guess the Council did nothing today. You wouldn't be talking this way if it had."

"I apologize, Your Majesty," Cabing said, and brushed his mustache, relaxing his trim shoulders and the set of his clean-shaven chin. "You are correct. Today the Council did no business. Several members haven't arrived yet. We declared ourselves a rump and adjourned until tomorrow."

"That was clever of you, Isla Cabing."

"Not so difficult, Your Majesty. Hardly a case of unmeeting wishes. No one was eager to join the issue." He picked up a small portfolio from beside his chair and extracted a document. Handing it to Alwina, Cabing said that shortly before his death the King had asked him as head of the Council to use his customary delegated authority to bring the Council up to full membership. That meant naming members to any vacant appointive seats allotted to government departments. The provincial seats of course were another matter.

"This is the King's formal request to me," Cabing told Alwina. "I think you should write a similar one making reference to this."

Instead Alwina wrote a line of endorsement below her father's message, signed it, and gave the paper back. "Do you still have the power to do this?"

"We'll see," he said, and handed her another document. "No one is sure who has what power."

"Isla Cal," Alwina said to him. "Lord Sharp. My father used to call you that. You are being evasive with me. I can understand that up to a point. In fact I agree with it. I should be innocent on my path to the throne. But I won't see to get there if I'm blind. And that's what I am. Blind in the fog. Tell me. Suppose this faceless cabal succeeds. What then? Suppose it keeps me from the throne. That's not the end of it. These men have more on their minds than their objection to me as a woman."

"Perhaps not. I don't know yet."

"It's not as though there were a strong pretending line," she said. "There is none. And this isn't Dorn or Mora work. Vantry? Carran? The border Lords? I'm sure you've some idea, Isla Cabing."

"I don't like to speculate that way, Your Majesty. It's dangerous. It's too easy to be caught off guard looking where you're thinking."

"All right," she said. "As you wish," and picking up the second document turned to me. "Why are you in the Navy, Frare?"

Shocked and relieved to guess now why I was here, I was myself caught off guard by her question. I'd never actually thought the matter through. At bottom, I suppose, I went to sea because for me there were too many people at home. But I wasn't going to say just that.

For longer than anyone can remember we have lived by what we call *alia* — the devotion to place and countryside — and *ania* — the outgoing love for family and husband or wife. I do not know how these concepts were abstracted from our behavior, but it is certain they apply to what we were and are. We like to stay in the same locations generation after generation, putting down deep roots, and we add, if need be, to the homes we already have instead of building new ones, even nearby. These habits are part of us and provide us with stability and strength, but there has been a tendency in recent times to speak of them publicly as virtues and make them both fashionable and a duty. That surely is not good, for, other dangers aside, there are many useful people for whom the admiration of an anchored life serves better than the reality. Knowing myself to be one of these, and uncertain of the Queen's purpose, I said truthfully enough, "Going to sea came naturally, Your Majesty. I like hauling ropes better than grubbing weeds. We come from Niven and some of my family have always been fishermen and sailors."

"Well, sailorman," she said with a sudden, harsh edge on her voice, "do you support the monarchy in this crisis?"

"Yes," I said.

"You don't have to say that. You can leave here and nothing will happen to you."

Perhaps she believed that, but I didn't. Admiral Lamas and Isla Cabing didn't run their services that way. In this case it didn't matter. I gave an honest but question-begging reply. "I wouldn't be much good to you if I said yes because I thought I had to."

"You support me in spite of the fact that I'm a woman and Islandia has never had a Queen?"

"I don't see what that has to do with it. I'm loyal to the monarchy."

"Good enough," Alwina said, and gave me the small, square sheet.

Signed by Cabing and now with my name in Alwin's hand, the document appointed me to the Council as an Isla for the Navy. I looked from Alwina to Cabing and back to the thing in my hand. I could think of nothing whatever to say and said nothing. This didn't seem to be a moment for either gratitude or pride.

Cabing was sliding papers back into his case. "You're young for the post," he said over his shoulder, "but don't let it worry you. There have been many younger. Lamas chose you and I'd say he chose well. You're the last. The second and last. Now we have all the soldiers and sailors custom has ever allowed. All I have authority for. If I have that. I wish I had ten of you."

Alwina said to me, "I hope you don't mind the appointment too much, Isla Frare. It's a great help to me."

"It's not a question of minding it, Your Majesty. I'm afraid I won't be any good at it. This is a kind of duty I don't know anything about."

"Nothing to it," Cabing said. "Nothing at all. But don't call it duty. Just say yes when the time comes. That is, unless you feel moved to make a speech. There'll be plenty worse. Might not be a bad idea. Tell 'em how the Navy and Army would rather fight for a Queen than a King. They would, too." He closed his portfolio, keeping out only a single sheet of notes.

"Is that all for now?" Alwina asked.

"No, not quite, Your Majesty. One more thing. As I said, the

Council did no business today, but Tor spoke about Winder anyway."

"Aha!" she cried, her eyes lighting up and her face coming into focus as though an artist had redrawn the contours. "That problem! What did he say? What's he like?"

"That's true," Cabing said. "You've never seen him. For so large a man — he's as big as Isla Frare here — his appearance is neat and creditable. As for what he said, I didn't at all like it, but to be fair I have to admit that in his place I'd have spoken the same piece long since and been lucky to do it half as well. He went to the point and didn't waste any time about it."

"Tell me."

Cabing looked at his notes. "I tried to get some of it down. It came out of a clear sky. Everybody was still busy counting heads. He just stood up and told us he couldn't understand how his predecessors abided the job of being King of Winder and a member of the Council at the same time. He wasn't at all sure how the double position began, but he did know it had to end. He said he wasn't attacking anybody. Not the members of the Council. Not his predecessors. In other times things might have been different although he couldn't see how. But he was speaking for himself. After a year and a half of being both King and Councilor, he found the combination a perfect formula for humiliating and abusing the people and kingdom of Winder, for corrupting the Council, and for earning the hatred of Islandians. As a man of principle and conscience, he felt the situation was intolerable. Some other method of conducting affairs between the two countries would have to be found. Winder was no longer in any way part of the Islandian body politic. As for himself, he had cast his last vote in the Council. He was now King of Winder and that was all. In that capacity he was prepared to receive and make proposals for settling accounts between the two nations." Cabing looked

16

once more at his notes and then folded them up. "Tor was more formal than that, but that was his message."

"What did the Council members do?"

"There wasn't anything they had to do or could do. We weren't in session. The things I heard members saying pretty well justified Tor's charges. They seemed to feel Tor was just beginning another move to make us pay more for ships and men. It was cynical and thoughtless."

"What about you?"

Cabing looked at her appraisingly for a moment and then said matter-of-factly, "Tor is completely correct about what's bad in the situation, but he can't set it right by anything as simple as withdrawing from the Council. I think that's what makes the members cynical. The trouble isn't even like a wild grape vine strangling a tree. It's in the structure of the two countries. Tor knows that. He almost said as much. He also knows Islandia is in trouble. This could be a good time for him to strike for a clean solution. I think he means what he says."

"To fight Winder would be civil war," she said. "Could it come to that?"

"I think it could."

Alwina looked at me, her face worried but sharp with interest. "You are an experienced, active officer, Isla Frare. What do you think?"

I smiled and shook my head. "I know Tor is a fine seaman," I said.

NEXT MORNING in the Council chamber I felt as vulnerable as a swimmer among sharks. Woking, my Army colleague, went about the strange business of being an Isla with unobtrusive self-assurance and obviously felt none of my anxiety. To be sure, he was six or seven inches less conspicuous than I, but this didn't account for it, of course. He was a man who took pleasure in feeling unnoticed and was unnoticed. Isla Cabing had said only that, aside from the ability to vote properly when necessary, he and Admiral Lamas in concert had chosen us for our different talents, leaving me as usual to make what I could of it.

Inside as well as outside, the Council building is one of the few public structures in The City that gives me the feeling of openness and lightness. For once the builders avoided arches when they could and made the lines vertical and horizontal. The pleasing effect is strongly reinforced by tall spectators' galleries on three sides of the seating floor.

During sessions, the Council arranges itself more or less informally, in accordance with several customs. The presiding Isla, the senior member in point of service, sits at one end of the room at a raised table and wears a light surcoat of white cloth with broad bands of brilliant blue at the cuffs and blue facings at the collar. He has beside him a recording secretary in ordinary dress and an orderly in a plain, white tunic. At the far end of the hall by the entrance door, he also has a sergeant-at-arms, the most splendid figure in the place. The sergeant is not in fact armed with any edged or pointed weapon, but over a scarlet tunic he wears a ceremonial sword belt inlaid with silver and carries a long oak staff knobbed at the end.

Military Islar wear tan surcoats with the facings of their service, red for the Army and green for the Navy. The provincial Islar, distinguished only by blue at the collar, tend to sit near the table along with the most important of the plainly dressed departmental Islar, while the rest spread out toward the entrance, roughly in order of seniority. There is one member, however, who insists on standing and two others who prefer to sit where they sat the very first time. That is their privilege. Then there are special seats for Islar whose families have held unbroken membership for several generations. In spite of all this, the Council is not a large body, seldom numbering as many as thirty-five.

The afternoon before, I had walked with Isla Cabing to his home, partly as bodyguard and partly to hear the report of the pursuit party. The report told us little we hadn't expected. There were two fugitives differing considerably in weight or in burden. Nothing otherwise significant about their tracks. They went to the west shore of the point about halfway between the palace and the mainland. No marks of a boat on the stony shore, but signs of what probably was one in the brush above it. Nothing dropped and left behind, or at least nothing found.

Cabing gave me supper and actually talked for a while. "Alwina was being lackadaisical and willful this afternoon. She likes to try me from time to time. But she has a mind, as you can see. Actually she's better trained in statecraft than any new King we've ever had. Her father began teaching her the job six years ago, when he guessed she would have to do it. I admire her knowledge, but I don't mind admitting here I'm frightened at what she may do. We're in danger from inside and out. Nerve she has. Sense, I don't know."

The present troubles began, Cabing said, with Alwina's

great-grandfather, Alwin XVII. Much liked and admired as a man, he was a controversial King and in the final reckoning a poor one. "I was too young to serve under him, but wild as I was when I began to study him, even I knew he was a bad soldier. And we're still suffering from him. Alwin was the extreme case of a King who, like so many of ours, commands armies and not fleets. That's natural, but maybe not altogether good. As a country we love the amateur and hate the truly trained man. To us there is something improper about using an advanced skill for a living. It puts your sincerity in doubt. Well, I won't argue the opinion, but amateurs have weaknesses, too. Navies are likely to be more professional than armies. Even in war three quarters of their job is dealing with the sea and they do that all the time anyway. It cuts down the imaginative expectations. The training wouldn't be bad for soldier Kings."

In many ways we have been fortunate in Islandia since the time when we drove the Bants permanently beyond the mountains. Our lands are fertile and our people industrious and not over many. So far our mountains have protected us as long as we have been vigilant, as have the oceans with the help of our fleets — that is, Winder's fleets for the most part. The single greatest evil for us was the coming of the Saracens in the north and the growth of their two great cities, Mobono in the east and Sulliaba in the west. They are forever hostile and threaten us constantly by land and sea. The original Saracens have become a swarming mixed race, the Karain, but they can call on the Demiji, nomadic bands of mainly Saracen stock, and on the native Bant tribes of the deep interior.

It was at the hands of the Demiji that Alwin XVII came to grief when he undertook a badly planned war beyond the mountains. He cost the country thousands of dead, unknown wealth, and left it a legacy of bitterness and undefended borders. He was, as Cabing said, the disastrous and picturesque amateur. He was last seen among the mists of the great peaks making fierce play with his great sword, holding back the Demiji pursuit.

Four years after that heroic scene, Islandia was still in a condition of interregnum, with Alwin's son and the Council playing pull-devil-pull-baker with its unhappy body politic. With public anarchy and private ruin everywhere in evidence, the contestants finally consented to consult the victim. Out of the dim past they called up the National Assembly, that legendary gathering of all Islandians which it was believed had proclaimed the nation out of the original tribes. In any case, a new Assembly met in the plain between the Reeves River and the Aira and produced a resolution directing that until Alwin XVII returned, or until his death was reliably reported, his son was to rule in his place at the pleasure of the Assembly and to pay heed to the advice of the Council.

I asked Cabing about that great Assembly and he laughed at me, saying, "You find it hard to believe? People do in this decadent time. I never imagined there were so many people. I was a very young soldier in a company charged with responsibility for health and safety. That part was very bad. We couldn't begin to keep up with the filth. Lots of people died. Armies police themselves, but not crowds. We didn't know much about that then. Still don't. I don't know how many were there, but it was the National Assembly and no doubt. I tell you it was impressive. People came with their own votes, naturally, but also with written votes for families and villages that they were to cast. Those votes were accepted. Regional meetings chose representatives to a general committee. That appointed a drafting committee. Then the resolution was presented to the whole Assembly and ratified. The real touch of genius in the whole thing was the creation of the regency. One man must have done that. I wish I knew who he was."

When I was about to leave, Cabing poured me a cup of wine

and said, "I want to thank you again for your resourcefulness today, Frare. If we do win tomorrow, my death — or my life, for that matter — won't be so important. After tomorrow . . . No, it doesn't matter now. Pay no attention."

"There's something I can do, Isla Cabing?"

"No, thank you. Not now anyway." He smiled and shook his head. "I was merely going to insult you by pointing out the obvious. You will have seen it long ago. If we lose, there shouldn't be any more assassination attempts. If we win, then the target changes. I'll talk to you about it tomorrow. Good night."

Today it was plain the Council would have no absentees. Visitors were rapidly filling up the rear gallery, but the two side ones were being held empty. At his table up front, Isla Cabing surveyed the gathering impassively, said something inaudible to the secretary, and then rapped loudly for general silence. He called the Council into session and announced that the business of the day was first to make official declaration of the death of Alwin XIX and then to consider the succession to the throne. The Council affirmed Alwin's death by voice vote. He then explained that he would call those who wished to speak against Alwina in alphabetical order to the number who wished to be heard. By agreement among Alwina's supporters, he and Isla Mora would be the only speakers in her behalf. He would then listen to proposals and the Council would vote. He warned the gallery against demonstrations and called the first speaker, Isla Anent.

Anent began to invoke tradition. He had said that tradition was sacred and inviolable and a good thing that should be observed when there was a stirring above me, and Tor, accompanied by half a dozen companions, strode into the gallery on my left. Tor sat down at once and gave his attention to the speaker. In the swirl of motion I was only aware of a large,

brown-haired man in a russet coat and a white shirt, but as
Tor leaned forward I saw a strong, beaked nose above a wide
mouth and a long, clean-shaven jaw. The other men remained
standing behind him, opening their cloaks, looking curiously
around the hall. Four of them were wearing side arms. The reality of obvious things often allows their acceptance for a surprising length of time. If your horse is stolen from the tree you
hitched him to outside your house, your first thought is that
you must have put him in the stable. Second after second
passed us by, myself included, before we recognized the insult
done us. Then there was a joint, sibilant indrawn breath of
shock. Tor sat unconcerned, listening to Isla Anent still cir-
cumnavigating tradition.

Isla Cabing rapped on his table. "Your pardon, Isla Anent,
one moment." Then he turned to the gallery and said in a
strong but still conversational voice, "King Tor, we are always
glad to have you with us as a member or as a guest. We are
also pleased to welcome your countrymen here and invite
them to observe our proceedings. If it were explained to them
I'm sure they would understand and share our strong feeling
about carrying weapons in this place."

Tor rose and turned in one motion. He saw the long daggers
hanging from the four belts. What he said could not be heard
on the floor of the chamber, but the gestures and expressions
of his companions indicated that they didn't like it. At first
they did not stir and the silent confrontation lasted until, one
by one, the men looked down and left the gallery.

Big and solid, Tor stood waiting, his back to the Council.
Observing him, I remembered Cabing had used the word *neat*
to describe him, and it fitted. That is not something you can
say about many truly large men. Certainly not me, although I
can walk without shambling. Tor gave the impression of com-
pactness and trimness, and you felt sure his arms and legs had
been cut in exact lengths to match the proportions of his body.

You knew his joints and articulations had been fitted by a cabinetmaker and not by a journeyman carpenter. Now he straightened as his companions re-entered the room unarmed. They nodded and took their seats.

Tor turned again to Isla Cabing and the Council. With the faintest trace of a smile, he said, "The weapons are now at the outer entrance in the custody of the sergeant-at-arms. My friends brought in a vessel from Winder just this morning and have never been in The City before. They normally wear side arms. I did not notice they were doing so and did not think to tell them this chamber was a place set aside. The fault is mine, not theirs. There was no intent to break the peace of the Council. I apologize to you, Isla Cabing, and to my former colleagues."

Listening to him, I didn't doubt him. The explanation satisfied common sense. Still, a threat had been delivered as perfectly as if it had been planned. The daggers in this room would not be forgotten.

A number of speakers followed Anent. With a great deal of repetition they explained why Alwina would be a misfortune, or more likely a disaster, for the country. Some were clever, some forceful, some arrogant, and one or two were even more inept than Anent himself. The cascade of words washed over the members, eliciting some laughter and some applause and always steady attention.

Lord Dorn appeared early in the parade. Speaking with the assurance given by his name and his experience, he kept his big voice down and talked to his colleagues as though they were all in his home. He advanced two principal arguments. In the first, largely legal, he contended that the absence in Islandian law over the centuries of any mention of female succession to the throne was not accidental, that it expressed the continuing unwillingness of the people to consider such a possibility. Then, in more general terms, he maintained that now the lack of any tradition of office-holding among Islandian women would raise intolerable uncertainties between the people and a suddenly installed Queen, particularly in a time of danger. Finally, he set about mortifying Cabing for appointing me and Woking, doing it quietly, wittily, and effectively, as he had done everything else.

Before, during, and after Dorn, Cabing sat through everything scarcely moving a muscle, not even touching his mustache. At the end, having ascertained by a general question that there were no more to follow, he recognized Isla Sevin of Vantry. Sevin was a wiry, stooped man of about fifty, as nearly as I could guess, with a weather-roughened face and pale blue, almond-shaped eyes. He also had what turned out to be a cracked but pleasing baritone voice.

"Thank you, Isla Cabing," he said. "Members of the Council. I know you'll forgive an old man from the northwest hill country when he says he doesn't understand or like the new fashion of insulting women he finds here in The City. Where I come from we don't think it's polite and we don't do it. It just makes trouble for everybody for no good reason. We'd all rather stay quiet and keep on doing what we've always been doing. That works fine.

"Any sensible person knows you'll get the same amount of ability out of a batch of a hundred females as you will out of a hundred males. That's not the point. The only point is, females do things in different ways and sometimes do different things altogether. In the end you usually get to pretty much the same place, but maybe by another road or maybe by swimming instead of walking. That kind of thing can bother some people. I don't know why. If it was just a matter of having a Queen, the succession wouldn't be worth thinking twice about.

"The thing we ought to be doing something about is the succession itself. We've had a hereditary monarchy for a long time now. It wasn't good to begin with and it gets worse. It makes faction and party. It puts power in one place and keeps it there. You're a good example of what I mean, Isla Cabing. You're going to speak for all the Queen's party. The rest of us speak for our own selves and then we have to do what you say. That's not right and never was.

"This is an opportunity to get rid of the hereditary monarchy. It's providential. It's the last chance we'll get. We should elect our Kings here from among us and each Isla will give the King support in accordance with his own agreement. That's the way it was done in the beginning. It's the best way.

"So the correct vote is a vote against Alwina. This pretends no lack of quality in her. It is her fate, the good fortune of the country, that she is the obstacle in our path right now. Let us defeat Alwina and have no more of this stupid abuse of women."

Sevin sat down to solid applause, but I was not sure how much was for him and his manner and how much for what he said. When there was quiet, Cabing said, "Gentlemen, I think we've earned a short rest. I promise you that neither I nor Isla Mora will talk long. We can expect to vote within the hour." He took a cup of water from the orderly and sipped from it as people began to come up to his table and speak with him.

Lord Mora was not a young man and appeared considerably less strong than he undoubtedly was. Distinguished and tough fragility is a Mora characteristic, just as robust good health and great physical size run true in the Dorn family. Tall and very thin, his dark eyes moving from face to face, his great head of white hair catching the light, Mora stood by his chair and spoke softly and evenly. He gave a restrained, moving appreciation of the late King and described the long, conscientious training he gave his daughter. He told us Alwin believed firmly in Alwina's ability. "So do I," he said. "Men are never this well prepared. And she has the spirit to sustain herself and us now when we need it."

Isla Cabing took another cup of water from the orderly and drank it while the Council readjusted and settled. Then he began from his seat.

"We have heard a great deal about tradition, custom, and the binding force of laws that have never been enacted. I won't weary you with refutation. Such appeals do not touch our situation. Nor can they be made to unless the Council has lost its normal bearings. If so, then we are under a new and sinister star.

"I am charged with impropriety in appointing Council members on the ground that my authority ended with the King's death. I reply that the appointments were made in accordance with the King's wishes expressed to me. He has the power of appointment to the Council. And I ask, what sort of government is it in which a King's acts become invalid with his death?

"Now let us talk about the heart of our matter."

He looked around the chamber, seeming to assess the spots of hostility and support. "How many of you have given any thought to the fact that Alwina's great-grandfather is still alive? Legally, that is." There was stillness, unbroken by any motion positive or negative. "Apparently no one. Then I think I should read you the exact wording of the resolution passed by the National Assembly forty years ago. '. . . since the true King is absent, his son shall be acting King in his place, to be crowned when news of his father's death is certain, and, only so long as he is chosen to that position by the Assembly, to act in lieu of his father and in trust for his father, and to be governed in all things by the advice of the Council.'

"What this means is that the Assembly has set up a constitutional form that you cannot brush aside at your whim. You can wreck it, but you can't ignore it. It is my belief that the Assembly — or important segments of it — intended the regency to be permanent. In any case, Alwin Seventeenth still reigns

27

after the terms of two regents. Not many Islandians would say that the years of Alwin the Good were not in fact good domestically. We must stay healthy at home to make head against the troubles that swarm on us from outside, from north and south and from the sea. We have all known Isla Mora for many years. He testifies to what he is in a position to judge. Alwina's qualities are real. As Islandians we are all proud of our pragmatism. We are a sensible people. You have the authority to accept Alwina and continue the regency. So, in the name of reason, ally yourselves with her.

"The alternative is bleak, hateful, and dangerous. No responsible man mentions the possibility of civil war without a feeling of sickness and horror, but the specter is there. You can reject Alwina, but you do not have the power to declare her great-grandfather dead. You cannot choose another monarch on your own. You will have to convene the Assembly. If anyone thinks he knows what a new Assembly would do, he is far wiser and bolder than I am. Just as in the Council, other things besides wisdom reside in the people. If the Assembly reflects your division, who would care to guess the consequences? That is all I have to say." He sat back in his chair, adding, "Now I would welcome a proposal from the floor in form for a vote."

The first few votes were spoken before I started to count and by then it was too late. I never did pick up the tally, but there was no doubt about the high frequency of *nays*. Some were delivered in strong, assertive tones and some in casual, confident ones, but many sounded puzzled and unsure, as though they really were requests for an ultimate piece of guidance. I took to watching the faces of the voters as they stood and answered, and I could have sworn that the lips of the uncertain ones sometimes formed *yea* before they slacked off to *nay*.

After the last vote, the chamber fell so silent that from the far end I heard the scratching of the secretary's pen as he finished his count. Across his feet and legs at the table, cutting him dramatically into upper and lower halves, fell a beam of early afternoon sunlight, full of swirling, dancing dust motes. He stretched his arm through the sun and into the shadow, handing Cabing his work sheet.

Cabing looked at the figures and announced quietly, "The Council recognizes Queen Alwina. We have saved ourselves from a great folly by the margin of one vote and may count ourselves fortunate. That ends our business and I declare . . ."

The swelling uproar drowned him out. Men turned to each other and climbed to their feet, questioning, objecting, and waving their arms. The protests rose to shouts, and throughout the chamber there was a straining pressure toward Cabing's table. From either side of me men reached across me, shaking their fists at each other under my nose. From the entrance the sergeant-at-arms bent forward, peering at Cabing for the signal Cabing didn't give. He sat at his table with his arms folded, looking at the tumult with contempt.

Then, powerful and clear as a bugle, one voice overrode everything. "Listen to me, Islar! You know me! I am Dorn! Hold still! Do not give him the excuse to call his soldiers! He is waiting for it! He tells us not to summon the Assembly. Why? Because it will defeat him! But we shall call it! That is our answer to him and to Alwina! Alwina is not Queen! She will not be!"

The pushing around me changed direction while the shouting dropped to mutters and then whispers. Looking about me I saw Alwina herself in the gallery across from Tor. She stood alone by the railing two paces in front of her attendants. She wore a dress of some wonderful blue cloth with a gold thread in it and a plain gold fillet controlled her shining hair. Her beauty now was all of one living piece made up of her dress, her quickened breathing, the freshness of her skin, the suppleness of her figure, the color in her face, and the snap and sparkle of her eyes. And she hadn't come here to be an animated statue. She stood swaying easily under those good shoulders of hers, and her immense vitality, no longer flickering or dispersed, played over us down below as she reached out her hands for quiet.

"To those who joined me today," she said in an effortless, carrying voice, "I say welcome to a long and honorable partnership. There is work for us in our country for as long as we live and then longer. We need each other."

Then she looked over our heads at Tor directly across from her. "To King Tor, our neighbor and, I hope, our friend, I say, greetings and good health. I am told you spoke sensibly here yesterday and got fools' laughter in reply. Next time speak to me, King Tor."

"To the others of you," and she flicked her glance again back and forth along the chamber floor, "I say I do not accept what you've done. I am Queen whether or not it suits you as individuals. Good men doing bad things are worse than bad men doing bad things. I'm sure some of you are good men.

"You heard Lord Mora say my father trained me long and carefully in the craft of kingship. He did indeed. One of the things a ruler learns is when not to reveal what he has learned, but there is no reason not to tell you how much your day's work smells of the old popish League. In those days the nobles of the Council, members of the League, Catholic converts, wanted the King's power for their own. You will remember what came to them as the ripe fruit of poison. What is it you want? The anarchy of Isla Sevin? Do not suppose a vixen is easier gentled than a fox. I am as implacable as Alwin Fifteenth.

"Isla Dorn, my respected uncle, has told you that all you need to do is summon the Assembly and it will take care of all your requirements, satisfy your dearest desires. No more

Queen to worry about. All the authority of the Crown will sprinkle down like so much League holy water to the Council's faithful. Well, I say, rest assured. And, also, rest easy. You don't even have to trouble to convene the Assembly. I have already done that in my own name. My messengers rode out while you were casting votes.

"I wonder what you and Isla Dorn will say to the Assembly when you rush to greet it? That you plan to tear the land apart province by province? For my part, I am informing the Council now what my policy will be and what I will tell the Assembly. Whatever else may come about while I am Queen, I will follow three aims. To reconcile Islandia and Winder. To secure our borders. To smash the Karain by land and sea."

She turned then, walked out of the gallery, and, with her attendants, left the Council chamber.

ALWINA GAVE A DINNER for Tor two days after her appearance before the Council, the eve of his return to Winder. Beforehand, while we were all still outdoors in the garden of Alwin House, Tor came up to me and said, "You are Frare, I think. I am interested to meet you. When I talked with Isla Cabing this afternoon, he gave you high praise."

"That was generous of him," I said.

Tor touched me on the shoulder and led me a few steps aside into an empty corner from which we could see the entire company and the whole garden washed in the golden light of early evening. "Cabing told me," he said, "that you are in charge of security measures for this evening." He let his eyes move across the garden to the palace and back. "Now that I see this place, I wish there were no party, even if it is for me. So easy to get at. An open invitation. I hope your precautions are thorough."

He was perfectly right, but it was not his affair. I looked at his questioning blue eyes on their own level, feeling irritation and suspicion in equal parts. In fact, my colleague Woking was responsible for everything outside the palace, I had responsibility for things inside, and our arrangements were comprehensive. I said, "I don't expect trouble tonight."

"You reassure me," Tor said, smiling not altogether pleasantly. "Isla Cabing thought he might be late getting here. He asked me to repeat to you the matter I gave him."

"Then please do," I said flatly.

"Do you remember the men who came into the Council meeting armed? No," he said, reading my eyes, "they are not planning violence. They're merely resentful Winderese now on their way home. Officers of mine. One of them, Nyall, fell into a queer talk later that day in a wine shop on the quay. It was dim inside the place. Nyall would recognize the man again, but could describe him only as youngish, heavy-set, bearded, shaggy, and certainly Islandian. The man gave no name, but set about questioning Nyall. They were alone at a table. The man affected a rough, bantering manner and wanted to know how much Nyall really disliked Islandia and what he was ready to do about it. He was contemptuous and said all the Winderese he knew were better with their mouths than their hands.

"Now Nyall is not a hothead or a fool. The episode worried him and he told me about it. He thought he was being recruited as a killer. It worried me, too, but I am not as straightforward as Nyall, and I thought there was a strong chance he was being entrapped. So I went to Cabing, who at least doesn't deal in entrapment, and he asked me to tell you. Now I have done so."

It was true that Cabing was late and, as I could see, actually arriving at that moment. The man of the wine shop could easily be the heavier of the two dart throwers. Obviously, Cabing had not told Tor of that encounter. I said, "Thank you for your patience, sir. I'm glad to have that information. I'm sorry to have been rude."

"Not rude," Tor said, "just suspicious. Unfortunately, necessary for both of us. But not again tonight. We should go back to the party."

Alwina had arranged the dinner within hours of her speech to the Council, and echoes of that explosion were still rolling out of The City. There was nothing secret about this affair, although there was no public announcement of it. Now three tables were set in a room next to the garden, Alwina with Tor at the center one, Cabing presiding over the one to her left, and Mora over the other. My cousin, Bodwin, looking too young to be out at night, sat in Alwina's claque at her table. My place was with Mora next to Tenira, a graceful young woman I had met the day before when we were making final plans.

From the outset conversation at Alwina's table flowed fast, with eddies of laughter and repartee, Alwina's own voice clear in all of it. As beautiful as innocence itself, she started things off by kissing Tor soundly before she seated him. This drew applause from the guests and a pleased if startled smile from him. Then, although Tor was on her right hand and although she looked directly at him, she made her remarks to the rest of the table as well, tossing the morsels to her hounds to chew over and bark about. Her manner toward Tor was friendly and informal and, as my ears kept insisting, patronizing. Her sallies, too, could carry portions of private, local meaning, so that the ensuing laughter, while never directed at him, sometimes excluded him. Aware of this or not, Tor sat through it good-naturedly. In much the same way, Alwina also teased him now and then, lightly and jokingly to be sure, but occasionally with a sting, as when she said Winder was to Islandia what a tail was to a mermaid, and waited for a comment.

"Pure frustration," Bodwin said promptly.

"Perhaps," Tor said surprisingly, "but we're certainly her strongest member."

Beside me Tenira said quietly, "Good for Tor! I don't like to hear her when she's talking like this."

About twenty-five, Tenira was slender, with light brown hair, gray eyes, and a soft rose color that came and went below the surface of her cheeks. She sat with her long hands quiet and the points of her collarbones showing appealingly at the base of her throat. Her mouth, which obviously enjoyed smil-

34

ing, was serious. "I think you told me you were Alwina's teacher," I said, "for all those things besides statecraft. I've seen her three times now and on each one she's been a different person. What is she like?"

"You have seen three of her?" she said, smiling now. "There are as many more. Twice as many. I don't know how many. I lost count long ago."

"Is she a good student?"

"I don't know how to answer that. Brilliant, yes. Good, no — not from her teacher's point of view. Some things she takes and some she leaves, and she changes everything to suit herself. I suppose everyone does that in a modest way, but her scale is breathtaking. For a long time she wouldn't learn arithmetic because she said things weren't alike and she wouldn't hurt them by making them alike with numbers. Two apples, for instance. She meant it. I love her dearly, but I don't know." She looked around and laughed. "I should be quiet. Have you ever had a silence catch you in full cry?"

A moment later, as though she had commanded it, a sudden, general silence surrounded Bodwin at the top of his thin and assured voice. He looked around, shrugged, and went on in a more private tone, but Alwina stopped him. "No, Bodwin! Let us all hear! What are they saying in The City?"

Unruffled, Bodwin began once again, his voice a little breathy like a recorder. "Your opponents have devised a masterly piece of reasoning against you, Your Majesty. They claim you cannot legally summon the Assembly and the argument goes like this. If you were the Queen you could call the Assembly, but you wouldn't need to. Therefore you wouldn't call it. But you do need to call it because you are calling it. Consequently you are not the Queen and have no right to call the Assembly to determine whether you are the Queen. Hence you remain not the Queen without the right to call the Assembly. I think that returns properly to its beginning at least twice,

35

but I'm not sure. In The City they're more skillful at this than I am."

"I don't imagine Isla Dorn has wasted his time with that," Alwina said after she had been amused. "It doesn't matter which way they go around the circle. My messengers are beginning to come back. The Assembly will meet in two weeks."

Just then, in answer to a message from Woking, I excused myself to Tenira and left the dinner for a while. Woking's men, very pleased and very excited, had picked up a suspect, not far from the trail of the previous attackers. He was found where he shouldn't be, heading where he had no business going, and furthermore he was surly and unpleasant to look at. Also he was very strong. Chances were he was a killer and we couldn't take any chances. The trouble was that he was unarmed, had nothing on him but some old lengths of twine, and went to sleep every time the men took their hands off him.

Finally, on a hunch, I sent for Marbry, the Alwin forester. He took a look at our prize and said, "Yes, it's Bikat. About time he turned up. An old friend. He poaches these woods every spring. He's not pretty, but he's no harm to anyone. I'll take care of him if you want."

When I sat down again next to Tenira, she said, "I think things are about over. You haven't missed anything important. Lord Mora said some nice things about Winder and Tor. He's a good man. My family have always been Mora people."

Alwina stood up then and the room grew hushed. Whatever her manner had been, whether she had been rude or mean, these things didn't seem important now. Dressed in black, with gold at her waist and throat, she was youthful, lovely, poised, exuberant; the force and splendor of her presence turned everything else to inconsequence. Tor sat looking as if he were seeing a vision, and perhaps he was. Her words did not need to be winged, although they were startling enough.

"You all know the Assembly meets in two weeks. How long that meeting will go on I can't guess, but when it is over I mean to travel through the country. Islandians and I should be more than names to each other. A Queen, a first Queen, is different from a King, from one more King. I take nothing from our Kings, but Islandians should see with their own eyes how this is so.

"My strongest personal wish and my first policy as Queen is to reconcile Islandia and Winder with the help of King Tor. As an earnest of this intention, my purpose tonight, in informal friendliness, has been to honor Tor and, through him, all the people of Winder." She picked up her goblet from the table and turned partway to Tor, her voice warm and her eyes shining with pleasure. "I give you Tor, who first spoke the truth in the Council — and at the same time to Tor I put a question. As I journey through my own country as a living, breathing woman, I will wish for the opportunity to be also more than a name, a friend if they will let me, to our neighbors in Winder. Why not? This is a time of beginnings. So I ask you, Tor, will Winder invite Islandia to visit?"

She raised her wine and drank to him, as all the guests rose and shouted and drank with her.

Tor rose to his feet while she was still standing among the shouts and cheers. He looked immense beside her. He held his own untasted goblet half hidden in his huge hand. His smile was surprised and pleased, his voice when he spoke full of appreciation and humor, but his eyes were careful. Wherever he had been for a moment or so, he was back on earth now.

"Your kindness to me this evening will indeed be taken by my countrymen as an honor to them. I'm sure they would relish it even more if the food and talk I have had could come with it. The savor of those things I keep gladly for myself. It is good to know we have such friends in a country we admire and — it must be admitted — fear."

He turned and bent his head to speak more directly to Alwina. "Will Winder invite Islandia to visit? Winder will, and does so this instant. When the time comes and you approach our border, you will hear what sounds like wild applause. That in fact is what it will be, but you must remember that we are not quite like Islandians. We do not cheer and clap our hands. What you hear will be our mermaid tails slapping against flat rocks. We have learned to manifest great enthusiasm that way. So visit us when you can. You will become more than a name to us, and you will be much more than merely welcome." Then he disclosed the goblet in his hand and drank to Alwina and the company.

Next morning I left my rooms early to go to the shipyard near by and give instructions for the work on my vessel. There were few men around and the place had an irritating air of casualness about it. Three other small ships like mine were in for minor refitting, but as had been the case for some time no new hulls were on the ways or planned. I learned my ship was four days behind schedule. After some plain words to the effect that I would supervise the job myself with a rope's end if I had to, I left in a bad temper to keep an appointment with Cabing.

Cabing had the side door of his room open onto a narrow balcony and the sun poured in along with the sounds and morning smells of the garden just below. Sparrows and grosbeaks were stepping, bobbing, pecking, and chirping on the grass and darting in and out of the branches of the surrounding trees.

He nodded toward all this activity and said, "You see, no crows."

"Just so," I agreed, "no crows."

"Well, Frare, what did you make of last night's party?"

"She is surely astonishing," I said, with no idea where we were heading. "That's not the young girl I first saw a few days

38

ago. Or maybe that girl is as real as last night's Queen. She stunned Tor, but . . ."

"Tor might well be stunned. I was myself. Just the same, he kept his balance well enough to hold his own or a little better. But I interrupted you."

"It was along the same line," I told him. "I thought Tor gave her clear warning either to stay home or bring a real offer."

"Yes," Cabing agreed. "In his place I wouldn't want that beautiful child wandering around my country armed with winning smiles. She could take Winder from him. Maybe she will."

"Then it's decided? She's going?"

"You don't approve?"

I didn't need to answer. There was nothing in my position requiring me to, and we both knew it, but I shrugged and said, "It seems to me the plan is both bad policy and dangerous. Anything she gains that way won't last."

"I can't say you're wrong," Cabing said. "I don't know." For what seemed like a long time he looked out into the sunlit garden where now a big black and white cat washed himself in the middle of the lawn while the birds scolded him from the trees. "With that said, Frare, the Queen and I want you to go to Winder now as her ambassador. Before you say anything, let me describe things a bit."

I sat quite still while Cabing's words washed around in my head assuming a new order of their own. He told me the threat of assassination would follow Alwina to Winder without question. After she arrived my main job would be keeping her unharmed. Before that I was to get ready for it. I was also to arrange the dates of the visit, all the procedures, and the schedule of events. I was to use the time learning the ways of Winder and coming to know Tor as well as I could. Success was urgent, too, because of military danger. The naval alliance with Winder must hold up, because attacks from the north, by sea and land, were certain later in the year. I think it was then I first heard the name Kilikash, but it may have been later that morning.

I was never in any serious doubt about accepting. I never consciously asked myself whether, disapproving an aspect of policy, I should wash my hands of it and everything else. That would have seemed slovenly. I remember no surprise, or pride, or elation, or fear. Undoubtedly I was feeling some shock, but I responded at first as I would have to an unusually difficult and complicated problem in navigation.

I said, "What do I do all these things with, Isla Cabing?"

"Talk to Lamas about that when you leave here. He's expecting you."

With that a bit of perspective came to me. "You know, Isla Cabing," I said, "I'm not an ambitious man. That gives me a discretion the Queen might not want in her ambassador. Have you considered that?"

"I understand you," Cabing said. "The Queen and I decided we wanted you."

"Thank you," I replied, feeling pleasure for the first time. "I have one more point, and then I'll see Admiral Lamas. About the Queen's safety. May I take Tor into my confidence?"

"How do you feel about it?"

"He was offended last night when I didn't. That doesn't matter, but in his own country it will be different. And without his help I'll make the Queen's life miserable. Day and night."

"Then I'll add that to your discretion," Cabing said, smiling.

Admiral Lamas also had a circus of birds outside his room, but they were gulls and his garden was a sandbar in the mouth of the river. He was older than Cabing, stockier, not as spry, and his brown, bald head carried the puckered scar of an old sword wound. He was fond of me, as he was of each one of

40

his small band of ship captains, and today for once he explained matters.

"Admiral," I said, "you talk a lot about this man Kilikash. I never heard of him before today. What do we know about him?"

"Not much, Frare, but I'm sure he'll teach us a lot before long. He commands both on land and sea and the Demiji bands work better for him than they ever have for anyone else."

"You say we'll be fighting him before year's end?"

"Well, what do you make of it, son? Kilikash is collecting a big fleet in Mobono. That we do know. What's he going to do with it? Count his ships and send 'em home? We're not going to attack him and he knows it. The Karain have always wanted to drive us out. Or break us up in small bits. They've tried often enough. Now they're in good shape to do it at last. Better weapons. Better ships. An able leader. And we're divided and falling apart."

"So once again the key is Tor," I said. "What about our own ships? What is our real strength compared with Tor's?"

"You're expecting me to say it's what it should be, one third. Well, it's not. It's less than a quarter. Actually it's worse than that because Tor's own strength is low."

"Are we building anything?"

"Not much." He spread his hands and shook his head at me. "You know the answers, Frare. You don't need me to tell you. We pay Winder to have our Navy. We haven't the extra money, the yards, or the shipwrights."

"Pretty picture," I said. "Well, so that's the way it is. I guessed it was bad, but not that bad. Admiral, may I take my ship and my crew to Winder?"

"Sorry, Frare, but no. Your *Thist* is a nice boat, but she's not big enough. In our poverty we have to make some sort of showing. I'm giving you the *Earne*. Seen her? Built in Earne six months ago. Good as any ship we've ever made. Take your own fifteen men if you like and hand-pick twenty-five more. Be sure they're good. They'll be your security force, too."

"Thank you, Admiral," I said and stood up. "At least not everything's black. I'll get at it."

About midafternoon I went to the lower river bridge to meet Tenira and in a few moments saw her walking toward me along the coast road from the west. Unaware of me at first, she was looking ahead into some private distance, her oval face with its high-bridged nose pensive and grave. Then she turned her head, smiled with a quick flash of teeth, and came running up the bridge with her hands outstretched.

"I've been hoping I'd see a large, calm sailorman," she said. "Her Majesty is very much Her Majesty this afternoon."

We climbed out of The City to the upland of grass and trees where I had come to Alwin's funeral. The last of our path led through cherry trees on the edge of blooming and past plowed fields, some with green sprouts showing, some still wholly brown. The brilliance of the morning was fading now as a high, thin overcast moved in from the southwest. It would rain tonight. We walked side by side on the springy turf and sat now and then on outcroppings of gray granite still warm from the diminishing sun. When I asked, Tenira told me she came from Reeves, where her family held land above the river and not far from the town, a valley said to be the richest in all the province. She'd always been interested in the school there and she was starting as a teacher when King Alwin needed a tutor and companion for his daughter.

"I seemed to please them both," she said, "although I don't remember trying to. Things went very well for a long time, really until the King's last illness. Now I can see trouble ahead. It's natural. Alwina loves me, but she won't need me very much longer. I'm becoming a hindrance. She doesn't mind opposition from outside and she handles it well. You've seen her. But she doesn't care for disapproval from her dear friends. From her father she had to accept it and heed it. She doesn't have to from me."

"Does it happen often? Your disapproval."

"No, and then I usually keep it to myself. But she knows perfectly well when I should disapprove, so it amounts to the same thing. But it isn't how often I disapprove that causes the trouble, it's the fact that I will inevitably sometime. She doesn't like living with that. I sound like a dragon. I'm not. Alwina thinks quite a lot about Om, which is to say she thinks about herself. The alliance is unintentional, but it's hard to compete with."

I told her what had happened to me since the dinner — as much as I could just then. She listened with her lips slightly parted, her gray eyes watching me, interested, amused, concerned, and once or twice alarmed. When I had done, she said, "Are you pleased, Frare? Are you proud?"

"It's hard to say what I feel," I replied. "Everything Cabing and Lamas told me made things worse. Worse and bigger. Each possibility seems to lead to others. Worse and smaller. They all narrow down to Winder. And then, although he didn't say anything about it today, I know Cabing is afraid of the Assembly. Everything could drop down that hole. I haven't thought about being pleased or proud or even frightened."

"I don't mind if you're not proud," she said, smiling. "That's a measure of what you think of yourself. But it would be all right to be pleased, wouldn't it? To be chosen. Just a little bit pleased?"

"All right, if you say so I'll be pleased. It's not hard and it surely won't hurt. I'll tell you what I was thinking while old Lamas was itemizing disasters this morning. There aren't going to be many people to trust in Winder. I thought how lucky I would be if you were in the Queen's party."

"I am going to be," she said. "Now you see why you have to be pleased. I am so glad it's you, Frare."

We had climbed to the small ridge at the southern edge of the upland. Everything before us now was one or another shade of gray, the motionless water of the bay, the unwrinkled sky, the squares and rectangles of The City at our feet. Tenira's arm and shoulder touched me as we stood quietly together. My body sent me stirrings of desire. *Apia* or *ania*? Lust or love? Who could credibly tell them apart — or want to at the moment? From a slight lift in her breathing I guessed that she felt those stirrings with me, or recognized them. But the signals were still peaceful and benign, promises and not commands.

"Things aren't so bleak now," I said. "Knowing you'll be there lifts my heart. This morning I didn't see much light in Winder. As I said, no one to trust. I feel better."

"So do I," she said with a catch in her voice. "Maybe now I'll keep on having the sense and the nerve not to tell Alwina that people are trying to kill her."

"What do you mean?"

"I talked to the duty officer that afternoon you and Isla Cabing were here. You ordered him not to tell Alwina, and he didn't, but he told me. I'm not stupid, Frare. It's not Cabing anymore. It's Alwina, isn't it?"

"We think so."

"How serious is it?"

"We have to think it's very serious."

"I don't suppose . . ."

"No, we have no one to suspect. That happens to be true."

She sighed then and said, "To be a suicide or murdered are honorable fates for women in our history. Poor Alwina! She's been having a bad day on all counts. From what she overhears she's beginning to think she may not have won that encounter with Tor last night. That gravels her."

"Does she draw the lesson?"

"What lesson?"

"That she can't have Winder for nothing."

"I don't think so. I told you she changes things to suit herself. She's making this entirely personal. She may pay the wrong price for Winder, but I'm afraid it won't be a small one." She shrugged her shoulders to collect herself and to dispel a shiver in the growing chill. "I must go back to my lovely and willful Queen. This has been a relief and a joy, Frare."

I took her hand and we walked quickly down the path toward the darkening city.

I KEPT the *Earne* at sea for a week and then brought her in through the northern reach of Winder Sound to Winder town. A fair breeze from the northwest blew warm across the rocky, fissured headland to the left under a sky swirling with round, white clouds. On the right a mile or so away, the long, low bulk of Sea Island, covered with pines and dune grass, showed in profile like a slightly bent bow against the cord of the waterline. The *Earne* seemed to flow across the wave fronts, leaving behind a smooth, undulating track. Ahead, at the end of the sound, the town lay at the bottom of a semicircle of crags and canyons broken by one broad pass to the east.

As we crossed into the crowded inner harbor I put the ship into the wind, while part of my crew downed and furled sails and the rest had out the sweeps. We eased into a berth and tied up after as smart an operation as even I could wish. I was proud to have Winder see it.

The extra days at sea had done us good. The *Earne,* like most of our newer and bigger ships, carried two wishbone masts. I liked the addition, but it took some getting used to. I had followed Lamas's advice to hand-pick my men and even improved on it by asking my original fifteen to suggest candidates. The result was a crew not only physically tough and capable, but one that already had the beginnings of internal coherence. Big and complex as the *Earne* was, she did not need forty men to sail her. That number was her full fighting complement. During our cruise into the southwest, I put into effect two new ideas, one of which I'd had in the back of my head for a long time. The other came to me while Cabing and Lamas were describing my job.

It was customary on Navy ships to assign one part of the ship's company permanently to ship handling and the other to fighting, and to train them almost exclusively for those duties. This made for a good front line everywhere and no reserves. I formed my men into two groups of twenty and trained each in both seamanship and combat, alternating the ship handling between them on a twenty-four-hour basis. I noted a marked improvement in the level of seamanship, a sharpening of combat readiness, and the rise of a spirit that was simultaneously competitive and mutually supporting. Some of this would have taken place no matter what scheme of organization I chose, but by no means all of it.

Then, anticipating the special work that would be waiting for us in Winder, I further divided my forty men into ten groups of four, my intention being to achieve flexibility as well as power. My fours would be able to operate as units, combine upward into larger groups, or subdivide into pairs and singles. The men would learn to have confidence in themselves and to depend on each other. I ran the risk Alwina had seen in her childhood objection to arithmetic — that the power of numbers to efface identity did not really make two men interchangeable any more than it did two apples — but I believed the plan was sound within limits. I talked to Nicking, my lieutenant, about it, and we agreed to start it at sea and develop it ashore.

Now, leaving Nicking in command and the *Earne* still fully manned and ready for sea, I stepped onto the Winder quay into a small crowd of interested and not too friendly onlookers. One man told me where I could go with my Islandian ship and it was not back to The City. But as they listened to me inquiring for Tor's house they grew less hostile and finally a towheaded boy stepped forward and agreeably offered to guide me. He took me up a narrow street of steps cut into a gap in an abutment of cliff. Through turns and switchbacks this route led eventually to a benchlike meadow more than a hundred feet above the harbor. To the south and east the ground fell away to the town in gentler fashion, but here was Tor's house.

The building was sizable and designed along plain, pleasing lines, but it was merely a lodge beside the Alwin establishment and even very modest compared with the houses of great nonroyal Islandian families, like the Dorns and the Moras. I understood Tor lived here with his mother and an uncle, his father having drowned at sea. I understood, too, that he had a sister with a family of her own living elsewhere.

Tor received me civilly, even with a kind of disgusted cordiality, looking at my credentials and saying, "So Her Majesty decided to come in spite of what I said. I can't say I won't enjoy seeing her, but I wish I could. Well, Isla Ambassador, you and I will do our best and I won't treat you as shabbily as you did me. Let's go down and get you straightened out."

On the quay Tor looked carefully at the *Earne* and then followed me aboard, where Nicking had fallen the men in for review. I presented Tor to the crew and them to him and then took him on a tour of the ship. At the end he looked at me thoughtfully and said, "Lamas actually did tell me you were a sailor. My compliments on your ship and crew." Then he cupped his hands and called for a boat. "We'll give you a place of your own."

With the help of our sweeps a six-oared boat towed us yard by yard along the waterfront until we came to a completely unused jetty. At Tor's instructions we made fast there. On the landward end stood a row of barracks that would take care of me and the off-duty portion of the crew. I accepted this somewhat restricted mooring rather than one out in the harbor because I had already decided it was better to have my men immediately available than my ship. At the same time I politely declined a suggestion from Tor that I take up residence with him.

So began our period of waiting and preparation, a time we expected to be tedious, but knew we needed. I at once named leaders of the teams of four and appointed commanders for the sections of twenty. We began hard training right away, starting with long conditioning marches and hand-to-hand fighting, armed and unarmed.

We held our combat sessions just out of town in a secluded hollow guarded by rocks and trees. I kept Tor informed of what we were doing, but he couldn't resist coming down to see for himself. When he arrived, I was demonstrating a throw-hold I wanted the men to practice. Tor watched for a moment and then walked forward, waving my student away.

"Show it to me," he said.

I looked at him and had no doubt what he meant to do. No one — superior officer, King, or ordinary spectator — interrupts in that way unless he wants to prove he is better than you are. I stepped toward him and applied the hold. Tor broke it, as I expected, and then caught me sharply in a hold of his own. Before he could clamp it tight, I spun loose, staggering him sideways. While he was still unsure of his feet, I again clapped on my original hold and committed myself to it. Rolling backward over my hip, he fell hard. He gathered himself smoothly to his feet, but he was shaken and surprised.

He studied me and I waited, totally unsure what was coming next. Then his face cleared and he said, "I asked you to show me and you did. Go on with your class. I'll watch."

When I had the men back at work throwing each other around, I walked over to Tor and Nyall in answer to a signal from Tor. "I've just asked Nyall to pick a group like yours," he

49

told me. "They can train with your men, if you'll let them. I like your idea for this kind of force. I think we'll both feel easier later on."

Of course I agreed with him, without saying that's what I had hoped he'd do, and next day Nyall reported with a selection of Winderese sailors that matched mine fairly closely, seeming on average merely a little younger and a litle smaller. Tor and I each spoke a word of welcome to the combined force, giving them a real but imprecise notion of their importance. Then something strange and fortunate took place. Tor and I finished our talks standing side by side. Quite naturally and without prearrangement, we began to demonstrate on each other the new holds and maneuvers scheduled for the day. The men liked our show and talked about it at intervals all day. Tor and I took the hint and made a pattern of the performance, keeping it up through armed as well as unarmed training. There was no doubt this contributed to a solid sense of unity, something we wanted greatly, but the other part of the truth was that Tor and I had stumbled on something we ourselves thoroughly enjoyed. We began to have private exercises and contests with a variety of weapons beyond the needs of the troops.

To describe Tor as very good is unfortunately boasting because there was little to choose between us overall. It's fair to say we were both better than merely competent. But, granting a certain level of skill, and having nothing to do with our rank, one thing that clearly intrigued the troops was the fact that we were both big men. This set us apart in a fashion that is easier to sense than to analyze. There is a way in which a genuinely big man is different in kind from a medium-sized or small one. The distinction has to do with weight, height, and strength, of course, but the key to it is scale. A truly big man needs a setting of his own, and the consequences of his actions in the ordinary world are often out of drawing. His casual domestic mistake turns him into a force of nature. Tor's muscles were more visible than mine, and his movements of hand, foot, and body were quicker. My reach was longer, giving me more resilience and depth, and I could move faster over the ground. Although we ran even in performance, our differences in style left the possibility of catastrophe very much alive. The men sensed this and responded to it without naming it or necessarily liking it. We also knew it and might have stopped, but we didn't. It seemed somehow as though this element of risk helped define the relationship growing between us. It was a way of reminding ourselves who we were.

One afternoon after an extended bout with long swords in which I pressed Tor closely for a while, he said, "That may be your best weapon, Frare. Do you like it?"

"Yes. It suits me."

"But you don't teach it to your men."

"The long sword's no use in close-order work."

"How about aboard ship?"

"Not much better there."

"Why not? I let my men use what they want. Short swords, long swords, dirks, axes, maces. They like it that way. They do well enough."

"I'm sure they do well," I said, "but, with proper deference, not well enough. A long sword takes too much room. A man needs several clear feet around him. You can't get that on a ship. No. The best way is close-order there — shields, short swords and posted companies of bowmen. But sea fighting makes no sense anyway. Ships should never get close enough to board."

"Is that what you've been telling Lamas?" Tor asked, amused. "What's the matter with sea fighting?"

"It's land fighting on water. Men against men, hand-to-hand. We only use the sea a little. Look at Kilikash. He's building a fleet of galleys in Mobono. They're just platforms for men. With luck they can ram something. The only good thing about them is that they'll move in a dead calm. They haven't much range, they won't handle in a breeze, they won't go to windward, and they can't stand up to weather. Our ships will do all those things. We're almost where we ought to be, but we still have to board and do land fighting. And with smaller crews. It's stupid."

"You want movable castles to attack each other," Tor said. "What are they to use? Catapults?"

I joined him in laughing. All such engines were synonymous with clumsiness and inaccuracy. "Well, something one twelfth as big and twelve times as good. The idea's right."

Aside from instructing the men, I was much in Tor's company at this time, certainly as much as Cabing could have wished, but the effects on me may not have been exactly what he counted on. I like to think he would have responded similarly in my place. Tor was an attractive and admirable figure, as he pursued ways to come to terms with his inclinations and his problems. It was easy enough to like him, and I did, but I also found myself giving him respect and sympathy. He didn't disguise his worry about what Alwina's mission would bring to his country and himself. He could see no good in it, but he was still expectant. I didn't think he was in love with her then, and I may have been right, but he couldn't get her out of his mind.

Tor gave me a brown and white pony named Lon, a charming animal with both spirit and patience, and took me on rides through his kingdom, samples of what he might show Alwina. I remember occasional pasturelands, tiny gardens on the warm side of houses, and deep, quiet forests where the wind in the upper branches seemed no more than the memory of a wind. But mostly I recall stone, stone in all shapes, cliffs dropping into gorges, crags and jagged peaks against the skyline, and literally hundreds of twisting, rocky sea inlets. On one ride we stood on a land's end in southwest Winder while the huge, gray waves, more than sixty feet from crest to crest, rolled in from across an utterly unknown distance of empty ocean. They rose and broke passionlessly on the rocks with a roar and a boom like a bass drum, throwing thick sheets of spray up to pause deliberately, fall, and hiss back. It was a hard, beautiful land, much poorer than Islandia.

The men and women we encountered were for the most part spare and agile, with long faces and boldly cut profiles. They were courteous, but spoke little and pondered before doing that. Their speech had an almost singsong rise and fall to it, along with a lengthening and flattening of the vowel sounds which I now realized I had heard attenuated in the town and in Tor's and Nyall's talk. Here, in its pure form, I found it difficult and mildly unpleasant.

Near the head of the larger inlets there was usually a small cluster of cottages with boats moored in protected pools or drawn up above tide level. There were always nets drying on the rocks. Often, on the edge of deep water, there were stocks holding ship hulls in different stages of construction. From the look of things, no work had been done on any of them for many months. For some time we stood looking down at one vessel on which a cunning piece of mortising had been left unfinished. At last Tor turned away, saying, "I hate to see rotting ships. Islandia hasn't paid any ship money in a year. There's something for Alwina to see if she wants. Let her be more than a name to that."

We rode home through an afternoon of dark wind-clouds through which the slanting sun turned the gray crags amber and laid sword strokes of gold across the forests and the hill pastures. The ponies pricked up their ears and began to canter without urging. At the edge of Winder town we dismounted and led our horses through the narrow streets, Tor responding to the greetings that came to him. As we climbed toward the

53

house, we paused on a level stretch and looked back on the town and the compact, crowded harbor. Tor's eyes lighted up and an affectionate, reflective smile crossed his face.

"Funny place to be fond of, isn't it, Frare? Not like The City. To us in Winder The City is something like Rome to the barbarians. A place of impressive mumbling and intangible wonders in fine buildings. Every time I go there I am instructed in the revealed truth and have my errors corrected. Oh, yes, two of my ancestors were Catholics in the days of the League. I know some of the language. Enough to see that the Church never left The City. Prelates like Cabing explain to me that in Winder we pay no Islandian taxes. We have all the benefits and privileges of Islandian citizens and we pay no taxes. On the contrary, we even get paid for our ships and men. We should be very grateful and we should show it. Well, I've looked for all those benefits, and if exclusion and discrimination are benefits, then we're as fortunate as Cabing says. We get no food from Islandia. We get no . . . There are a great many things we don't get and I won't bother you with them. The only thing I know we get from Islandia is Islandia itself. I mean," and he pointed north, "those are Islandians down there and not Saracens. I don't undervalue that fact, but sometimes I wonder. I've heard it said the northern Islar get on not too badly with some of the Saracens. Even get iron from them. No matter." He shook his head, put his hand on my shoulder, turned me around, and started us off again up the hill. "When you write home, Frare, tell Cabing I'll keep my agreements even if he doesn't keep his. Just the same, in his own interest he'd better send the money he owes. If this Kilikash goes to war, I'll fight with what I have. I won't use my fleet to bargain with. I'm a fool that way. But he can be sure I'll find something else."

I stabled Lon, went back to my room and heard a good report on the day from Nicking. What Tor said about iron was interesting, if it referred to anything new. Islandia has no iron, or very little. We don't use iron nails or bolts, for example. All our wood joining is done with mortises, lashing, fish glue, and trunnels. North of the mountains, however, iron is plentiful, and the Saracens improve their use of it year by year. They are making comparatively light, strong armor of steel, while ours is still all leather. We have enough iron for a number of tools and a selected range of weapons, but even here the scarcity leads to rationalizations, such as the one concerning the cross-bow. We don't use it, we say, because it's slow, cumbersome, and inaccurate. The charge is probably true on all counts, but we have never made our own version to find out, because the bow itself and its fittings require steel. There has always been some sporadic, more or less surreptitious, iron trading down along the northern borders, but raw iron, by its nature, is not a good contraband. It's too heavy and bulky. It would need a lot of organization and a visible effort to make iron smuggling amount to anything. I thought Tor's vague remark was merely thrown in to support his general complaint, but it certainly was worth reporting back to The City.

Just before dark that evening the first courier boat came in, a small cutter with a crew of four including the captain. He was a freckle-faced youngster named Rann, who told me Lamas was assigning two boats to courier duty and that they would crisscross back and forth. Rann would sail again in the morning and pass the outcoming boat somewhere at sea.

In the dispatches, Lamas told me small squadrons of Kili-kash's galleys had been reported on maneuvers outside Mo-bono. He didn't say who reported them. Up farther south, Islandian fishermen had seen a galley skulking in and out from behind islands, presumably coast watching and mapping.

Cabing wrote me that the Assembly was then in session and that the first meeting had been touch-and-go. There was a substantial representation of skeptical, middle-aged men who didn't succumb at first sight. They didn't seem to care particularly whether Alwina was a woman or a griffin, but they had their doubts about a child. Only Alwina's courage and her trained, tough Alwin good sense in policy matters prevented a disaster. Then the opposition from the Council overplayed its hand, and that helped. Now Alwina had the Assembly eating out of her hand and they would give her a strong mandate. She had requested, actually ordered, Cabing and Mora to join her on her tour of the country. Cabing said they agreed under protest, but would turn back at the border of Winder. Things were just too dangerous for them to be away any longer. Someone had to see to the country and mobilization. He asked for a dated schedule of Alwina's Winder visit.

Then he concluded, "The assassination nightmare grows worse. Every success the Queen has increases her danger until we have this thing scotched. Woking moves closer, but he is justifiably cautious and does not speak openly. This is too grave a matter to chance implicating the innocent. He says he hopes to have something for you in the next dispatches."

And then there was a letter from Tenira. After some warm but unsentimental reflections on our afternoon together, she said, "The pressures, crises, and triumphs of recent days — as only an anxiously preoccupied man like Cabing would not observe — are having a powerful effect on Alwina. If she were older and had previously shared this cruel kind of responsibility, she would be able to sort things out differently, now that she is carrying the burden alone. But of course she hasn't, and I can see her developing an unshakable confidence in the Queen which does not extend to the young woman. I know this because of little private things she says to me and then later brushes aside or won't admit. She has a disconcerting tendency now to speak to individuals as though they were large crowds, and I'm sure she doesn't know it. Bodwin, whom I don't much like although I welcome him at present, is at the palace daily, and his sallies do not spare the Queen. Alwina, however — as Alwina — appears to enjoy them, as though she were watching the futile attacks of unreason on an impervious institution. The girl I taught so long and have grown so defensively attached to, I'm afraid is becoming a collection of unmeeting wishes all by herself — unmeeting wishes in the sense that I think she really does not permit either part of herself to tell the other what it hopes for. It is absolutely pointless, as well as impertinent in the social sense, to worry about her, but I can't help it."

In a personal way I found it much easier not to worry than Tenira did, but I trusted her perceptions and they forced me to think all over again about the meeting I was arranging here. I felt Tor was in earnest about his duties as King, that is his obligations to Winder, but if I understood him at all he put little reliance on his office to help him discharge them. For that, he counted on his abilities as a man and of those he had no doubt. The Queen of Islandia irritated him and sometimes amused him, but Alwina herself was a different matter. The uncertain girl Tenira talked about had somehow suggested herself to Tor and the possibility of her upset him. That was as close as I could come to describing what I saw. He was finding his double awareness very hard to handle. How was he to regard her and how was he to proceed? It seemed to me his position was humanly sounder than Alwina's, but very likely more vulnerable.

Over the next two days Tor and I worked out a schedule good enough for me to send to Cabing. It had enough detail to let the party know what to expect and it was loose enough to allow for additions, weather, and temperament. We decided that Tor would not go to the border to meet Alwina, but would leave that job to Nyall and me. "My regal dignity will stand anything," Tor said. "It's Alwina's I'm thinking about. She won't be too happy in body or spirit when she reaches that debatable spot. And why have a ceremony for an audience of rockwood bushes? No. My mother will set up a guest camp a mile outside the main gate here. Alwina can rest and dress there. Then she can enter, fresh and clean, and become more than a name to all the grateful citizens of Winder town."

"You aren't going to let her forget that phrase, are you?" I said.

He thought for a moment and then shook his head. "I'm sorry, Frare. Of course you're the one I'm not allowing to forget it. I won't use it again."

I left his house, with its ample, sparely furnished rooms, and climbed down the short way to the barracks to finish my dispatch. An hour later, I was exchanging cases with Perin, the captain of the second courier boat, when Tor appeared in the doorway. I pointed to the only other chair, wished Perin a good voyage, and put the dispatch case on the table beside me.

"You should have stayed with me when I invited you," Tor said. "Then we wouldn't have to go chasing after each other. More important, we'd have a place that would hold us both." He raised his hand. "I know. A good officer doesn't do that. I agree. I came because I have a proposal for you."

"So?"

"Our ship on western coastal patrol just came in. We keep one out regularly. Another ship will sail tomorrow. Ordinarily Nyall would be in command. He's next on the rotation. But I haven't taken the patrol for some time and it's something I don't like to lose touch with. So this patrol is mine. Would you like to come along?"

"How long will it take?"

"A week to ten days — depending."

I had already made my calculation and knew the answer. Three days or three weeks, it didn't matter. "Yes," I said. "I would like to. Very much." And then another idea occurred to me. "But would you consider this? The *Earne* is a first-class ship. Her crew is first-class. They both need work. Why not take us as your ship?"

"I hadn't thought of that," he said. "Everything you say is true." Then he shook his head. "Just the same, I'll have to thank you for the offer and the compliment and say no. I don't think your men would object, but I shouldn't command Islandian sailors. Certainly not now. I could command through you, but that would be awkward and still questionable. I don't want to slide back into being an Islandian Isla. Anyway, on this trip I want to be in direct control. However — and you've given me an idea — I could easily use a contingent of your trained men to come along under your orders."

I saw his point and agreed and he stood up to go. "Good, then. If the wind stays reasonable, we'll sail with the ebb in the morning."

It was some time after Tor left before I opened the dispatch case. What went through my head was not coherent enough to be reported as thought, but it had something to do with the position in which I found myself here in Winder and the position I had agreed with Cabing and Lamas that I would try to create for myself. They were identical. The trouble was I had not deliberately laid myself alongside Tor. I had not practiced principled hypocrisy. In short, I hadn't followed instructions. What had happened had come about somehow as the result of a proffer of friendship unintentionally made and unwittingly accepted on both sides. There it was. What I had was Tor's gift, not my acquisition. I could even feel the preliminary stirrings of dislocated loyalties, but they were not in conflict quite yet.

I finally reached for the dispatch case and opened it. There was only one message this time. Cabing wrote:

"Woking was stabbed to death early this morning. The watch found his body just after dawn in the street outside his house. The murderer took the weapon with him. The house was not broken into. We don't know whether anything was taken from the body.

"The house yields no information and Woking left no notes anywhere else. Unfortunately, as you know, he told me nothing that points anywhere. It is possible he knew less than I thought, but that in itself shows the murderer will kill on suspicion to protect his plot. All our plans stand because it is at least as dangerous to change them as to go ahead. And some, like Winder, cannot be changed. I need not tell you that Winder is now the most natural and likely place for an attempt. So look to your arrangements. I call your attention to the boldly defensive nature of Woking's murder. So look to yourself, too. The Queen needs you alive.

"The news of Woking's death is closely held here and will stay that way. It will not do to have public rumors of an assassination plot. The Queen does not know of the conspiracy on her life. Tenira and I agree she should not. Not that it would frighten her, but it could tempt her to something foolish. Do not inform Tor of Woking's death. He would have to tell some of his own people.

"Woking thought highly of you. He would have wanted me to tell you."

I read the message again, and a third time, and then held the corner to the candle flame. I carried the paper torch to the hearth and, when it burned out, stirred the warm ashes into the cold ones already there. I had thought well of Woking, too, but I had never told him so.

As Tor hoped, we did sail with the ebb in the morning, but in a chilly rain that came down intermittently out of broken clouds. The wind from the south-southwest, however, gave us no difficulty in leaving Winder Sound. In spite of the news from The City the night before, I came on board in high good humor, a kind of perverse bad-weather cheer that frequently affects me and that others as often find distasteful. Tor's ship, *Aspara,* the gull, was single-masted and smaller by some tons than the *Earne,* so that my sixteen men added to Tor's two dozen drew from him the comment that he understood better now the objection I had to long swords. By afternoon the wind backed into the west, the weather brightened, and we came around on the long eastward slant toward the mainland. The *Aspara* showed herself both fast and handy.

I was interested to learn how Winder handled routine cruises like this one. In the case of islands, for example, Tor did not sail around them nor did he go close inshore, but he made sure of certain places on each one. "We run a patrol," he said, "not a search. We can't do that. We don't search unless we think there's something to find. If we catch anything, we're likely to catch it on the wing."

I asked him if the patrols were good prevention and he said, "Well, when we stop patrolling for any reason, there are more raids. Patrolling isn't a good answer, but it's something. As it is, we catch one or two galleys a year and hear of twelve or fifteen others. As far as I know, the raiders are on their own. It's plain piracy. Sulliaba smiles on it, but doesn't run it. Mostly the galleys are medium-sized or small. They raid the whole length of the coast, but they stay away from big rivers and towns. They like open country and isolated places. There they take what they can and burn what they can't. They kill more often than not, and they always steal children. Youngsters bring high prices in Sulliaba. So do young women."

"I didn't know there was a regular trade."

"There isn't," Tor said, "but it sounds that way when you talk about it. You can see why raiders don't live to get home if they're caught."

In the days immediately following, in accordance with Tor's description of the tactics of raiders, we swung out to sea around the river mouths and deltas of Earne and Doring and later of Thane and Dole, and stayed close to shore everywhere else. In talking about the coast and his patrols, Tor opened a part of himself I hadn't seen before. I was accustomed to him as a Winderese Prince, and admired him as one, but now for the moment he was none of that. When he spoke of the people he was protecting I heard no overtones of his patriotic suspicions of his big Islandian neighbor. He seemed to lose political identity and become a personal guardian concerned about his responsibility and the inadequacy of his strength. One afternoon, off an empty stretch of Farrant shore, he came back to the subject, saying, "Raiders aren't easy game. We lose ships to them. Too often. And they don't always stick to pattern. Every once in a while they'll put together a pack of three or four galleys. Then they'll hit in the estuary country. But it's early in the season for that now. No new crops. No fattened animals."

As we moved down the coast the weather grew warmer as expected, but less from actual geographical change than from a steady circling of the wind into the northwest. Gulls followed us now and then, doubtless as their namesake, but they got little from us and showed their disapproval with harsh shrieks and accurate droppings. By this time the ship was noticeably less crowded, for the men found ways to consolidate their gear and even themselves. You no longer risked breaking your neck by stumbling over a vagrant shield or a sleeping and unstowed sailor. At last we crossed the line of the Sevin River and saw the great peaks of the barrier range, still deep in spring snow, rise up in the northeast. As we turned progressively westward to weather the huge promontory that almost encloses Sulliaba all of my men were leaving Islandian waters for the first time in their lives. They were aware of this and made jokes about it, but they were uneasy.

We rounded the headland by night and first light found us in the middle of the broadest stretch of Sulliaba Bay, with what might be haze, or perhaps even the smoke from the cooking fires of the city, low above the southern horizon. Buildings were beyond the edge of sight. "This is as far as we go," Tor said. "This is the limit for regular patrols. We stay here for a while to make sure they see us."

"Doesn't that make things too predictable?"

"No. It doesn't say we won't wait for a few days south of the cape. Or keep on north for a while and then come back. We do those things."

The sun, just now clear of the heavy green hills to the east, hadn't yet turned the smooth, dark surface of the water to glaring steel. The bay, narrowing as it approached Sulliaba, lay empty and still except for the lapping of water against our hull. It was hard to suppose there was anything conscious within the horizon to make the observation Tor counted on, but he assured me there were eyes, many of them. A land breeze began to slide down the eastern hills and reach out toward us in cat's-paws and riffles. The air was still cool as it reached us, but it felt and tasted stewed and carried in it the moist suggestion of stagnant water and compressed layers of rotting vegetation. The sensation came as a shock in contrast to the resinous sharpness of land winds south of the mountains. The Karain was not far away from here.

"I wonder what's really in there," I said. "Beyond the hills. Do we know?"

"Jungle," Tor said. "So I've been told. Very hot. Very thick. Lots of rain, but no wind. Steaming. Crocodiles, snakes, monkeys, birds, savages — Bants and their relatives, not Arabs. Panthers in the east where it's not so wet. There's supposed to be one big river running all the way north."

I nodded. "Lamas has an account — an old one by one of your sailors. He took a ship north along this coast. Many days — no, several weeks beyond here. It kept getting hotter and the winds grew lighter and fitful. At last he came to the end of land and turned east and some south. Then he came to a place where a great river had pushed mud flats miles out to sea. The water was brackish that far out. He thought the river must drain the continent from the mountains north. He tried to find a channel through the mud and kept going aground. He said he almost reached the line of the coast when he had to turn back. His crew had scurvy."

"Was there a chart with it?"

"No chart," I said, "but there is a hint he made one and kept it for himself. You said there are no winds in the jungle here. I suppose you know there are months on end each year when there aren't any reliable winds off our east coat."

"Yes, I know it," Tor said. "My people call it the dead ocean."

"Is that why Kilikash is building his fleet in Mobono and not here?"

"I don't know, but it's a good guess. It gives his galleys an advantage. But Miltain is the best place to invade anyway." He looked at the sun, now well above the hills. "We've been here long enough. Let's go. We'll becalm ourselves just talking about it."

For a long time I thought we were effectively becalmed. From our seemingly fixed place on the motionless water I could not see any shift in bearing between us and any point on land, but the bearing did change when I wasn't watching. Helped by the tide and the expiring land breeze, without actual steerageway, more drifting than sailing, we eventually drew level with the headland. There we picked up sporadic puffs of what we could see was a brisk northerly wind a mile or so ahead. Once in open water, Tor gave up reference to the coast and set a course that would take us to the barrier range at Islandia's northern border. He turned the *Aspara* over to Durr, his sailing master, and joined me at the rail.

"This is the part of the voyage I really wanted to make," he said. "It's why I took over from Nyall. It's also why I invited you, although you may not want to join me."

"Join you?" I said. "I have. I'm here. What do you mean?"

"I'm going looking for iron."

So there it was again. The notion had real power for Tor, and yet it filled me with the kind of resignation you feel when someone insists on pursuing a discredited case. The truth was, I suppose, that I was even more the victim of my unreasoned wish to forget the subject than he was of his to explore it. He was certainly right in the sense that iron was vital to Islandia. I said merely, "Go on."

"Suppose someone is getting iron from Sulliaba. For a price."

"He'd want to keep on getting iron. The price would have to be political. Subversion. Treason. What makes you think anyone is doing that?"

"What makes us think anyone is plotting regicide? Just suppose it's so."

"All right," I said.

"The place could be any of the provinces on the west coast, including Winder, but let's take the simple case. Let's say it's Vantry. Vantry is inaccessible and bone-poor. Its name means just what it says, *far place*. No one knows or cares what goes on there."

"You mean, if it had iron, it could make commonplace goods, nothing different or noticeable, and feed them into the high-priced Islandian trade. It could do very well for itself."

"Something like that. Say it is that. Vantry has two passes into the iron country, the Sevin and the Omoa. It brings in a trickle through them. It always has, just like the other border provinces. The stuff travels in pack saddles and the country is brutal. You know how little gets in that way." He raised his head for a moment to watch a school of porpoises splashing and making rainbows off our starboard bow. "Well, our last patrol stayed close inshore north of the barrier range. Patrols regularly turn west right at the mountains the way we did. This one found something we didn't know existed. Because of the light and the turn of the coast you can't see it unless you're very close in. A river through the northern foothills has its mouth there. It must run through some of the western iron country behind the Sobo Steppes. I want to take a look at it."

For the sake of good relations I knew I had to accept the hazards of an investigation of this unknown river in hostile country. In the abstract, the idea of organized, seaborne smuggling was plausible enough and I was surprised at the strength of my skepticism. No doubt my feeling that the risk was both large and unjustified had something to do with it — that and the fact that my men were indicated as crew for the boat we would use. I picked two teams, eight men, and told them what the job was. They listened, with some complacency I thought, as though they expected something of the kind and assumed

66

that's why they were there. Reflecting on what I might have expected and had not, I swallowed the lesson in silence. Plans called for the *Aspara* to stand on and off the river mouth for a day and a half if necessary, but not to enter. At the end of that time, if we had not come back, she was to sail for home.

I asked Tor politely if he weren't being irresponsible, when so much depended on him, in going upriver himself and leaving Durr in command. He used his kindly and kingly manner to reassure me he was only doing what the situation called for. We were merely going up a river. The danger wasn't that great. "You have to give those instructions," he said, "even if you're only going fishing."

In a false dawn prolonged by the eastern foothills, we put the boat over the side and climbed down into it, six rowers, two relief rowers, Tor and I. The hill crests now glowed on either side of a thin crimson slice of the sun. We and everything ahead of us were still in dark shadow, but well out to sea the water shone blue and white in the fresh sun. Our nameless river had only a small bar at its mouth and a patch of troubled water defined that for us. Tor chose the north channel and we went in fast on the rising tide.

The stream led us almost due east with a slight southward shift as it edged past the flanks and butts of forested slopes. On our right the hills piled up into range after range of great mountains in the distance, and on our left a denser woods rolled away over small elevations and rounded domes. As nearly as I could, I relieved two of the oarsmen at regular intervals. As the stream narrowed above its mouth I posted the two resting men, bow and stern, with strung bows. For the most part we were out of reach of hand-thrown weapons, but I had always dismissed Saracen archery too lightly. A few of the Demiji made short, double-curved, laminated bows. These were not as powerful as ours, but they were serious weapons.

If there were any in the woods today, we were in trouble.

For several miles we felt some lifting effect from the tide, but the water grew slowly less brackish, then fresh, and the stream's own natural current ran against us. Nowhwere along either bank was there a sign of what we were looking for, no landing stage, no used spots on the shore, no suggestion of a trail. For all we could see or hear then, the river might have been untouched since the beginning of the world. High overhead a hawk seemed to be keeping us at the center of his huge circle.

Three hours or so on, we came to an island and took the narrower, deeper southern fork past it. Here Tor and I also picked up bows. And here we first heard the drum. The rowers, straining against the faster current in the narrowed channel, didn't break their stroke, but snapped their heads around like the rest of us. The sound seemed to come from the woods on the north bank just ahead. We passed the island, the river became whole again, the current moderated, and the drum was still just ahead of us and to the north. It stayed exactly there, barking, coughing, whining, and sometimes threatening. It never settled to a rhythm, but sometimes it almost did, and there would be moments when you felt you were used to it at last. Then it would change its voice once more and the anxiety would leap up again. Over the hours we grew very well acquainted with that drum, and every time the channel forced us out of midriver I knew from myself that the men had gooseflesh on their backs underneath the sweat.

Then the drum left us as abruptly as it had come. The river now was smaller, but there was still ample depth. We had come more than fifteen miles, climbing some, and the country was changing character. On the right the landscape was bigger and more open, with occasional glimpses now of tableland between us and the far peaks. On the left, the forest was still as thick as ever, but the trees were different, mixed hardwoods and conifers. In place of the drum we began to hear, or rather feel, something else. It was not a sound at first, but a pressure on the senses.

I looked at Tor and he nodded. "Yes, this is the fall line. This has to be what we're looking for."

The sight and the full sound came upon us together as we rounded a long, easy bend to the left. There the hills jutted out, the forest rose in a single leap, and between them the river fell toward us in a thirty-foot column of black water and white spray. Suddenly we had to shout to be heard.

"Here's where they make the shift," Tor roared in my ear. "A galley comes upstream this far. Rafts and small boats bring the iron to the top of the falls. Then they slide it down. We'll find the track."

But there was no track. To the right of the falls the cliff rose in a sheer, wet face that couldn't even be climbed. On the left, Tor and I and two men hauled ourselves up the untouched slope, tangled with deadwood from above, root by root and trunk by trunk. At the top, beyond the sluice where it gathered itself for its plunge, the river wound its way east once more, here somewhat wider and shallower. There was no boat landing, no cargo dump, no evidence that a boat had ever been here, but high overhead there was still a hawk.

We plunged down the wooded cliff, scrambled into the boat, and turned back. The drum picked us up where it had left us. There was no doubt about what it was saying now. It was commiserating with us, telling us how sad we were and how unfortunate, how hard we had worked for nothing. There was little talk among us on the long, fast trip downriver.

Later, with the *Aspara* plowing south again, I asked Tor once more what made him believe there was important iron-smuggling going on. At first he thought I was mocking him and turned angry, until I said, "I'm not laughing about today. We were wrong and that's too bad, but it doesn't amount to much. I'm interested in how it all started."

"All right," Tor said shortly, "you remember I told you Nyall talked with some kind of conspirator or provocateur in The City. Well, one of the things he said was that there was iron to be had — presumably for Islandia's enemies. That I was inclined to believe. It made a direct sort of sense and didn't sound like the kind of trap Cabing would set for me, if he were setting one."

"Did you tell him about it? The iron, I mean."

"No. I'll leave that to you." Then he reverted to his preoccupation and humiliation. "What do you make of that drum today? Doesn't it show they were expecting us and knew what we were looking for?"

"No," I said, "not to me. I think you're letting it get under your skin. It shows that they — whoever they are — were watching us and wanted to let us know it and had a good time making us look foolish."

The subject stayed touchy and we didn't come back to it soon again. Unfortunately, I saw the drumming — after it was over — as comic and tried to ease matters by treating it as a joke on all of us. This was a mistake. The episode rankled with Tor and for a time made him unapproachable on other matters. When I saw what I'd done, I began to ask myself what I would have made of Nyall's story if I'd been in Tor's place. I turned the circumstances around in as many ways as I could, and each time came to the conclusion that I would have taken the information seriously and would have investigated the river if I'd had the wits to think of it. It was too bad the exploit turned out to be ridiculous — and even worse that something in me had persisted in finding it funny — because Tor had behaved sensibly and with extraordinary loyalty to Islandia, considering his position. I found an occasion to tell him a good deal of this and the weather between us brightened noticeably.

We made good time up the coast and I worked my men steadily and hard in special exercises. They were rounding into fine, resourceful troops, and Tor was generous in his praise of them. Because you can't recover practice arrows at sea, I wasn't able to do as much with archery as I wanted, but I did do something. Accuracy wasn't what I was interested in anyway, because they were good marksmen. The Islandian bow is a formidable weapon, which has been neglected in recent times in favor of the throw-dart and the spear. Developed for foot soldiers, it has range, power, and penetration, and can be handled fast by good men. Better for its purpose than the good though rare double-curved bow, it is much superior to the general run of Saracen equipment, which is short and light on the draw and was originally meant for horsemen. The Islandian bow is not something to discard. From my men I wanted volleys in unison. Without arrows I gave them the formation and the count to pick, nock, set, draw, and release. We made progress.

On this southward passage we sailed inside the big islands of Boultsea and up into the deep indentation that almost cuts Winder peninsula at its base. It was seldom visited by raiders, Tor said, and added that if I wanted to get off and walk at the farthest beach, I could be in Winder town in half a day. When I told him I thought I would stay on board, thank you, he laughed and pointed to a small island ahead of us and to port. Stretching back from it in our general direction, creamlike in the midday sun, ran a curved line of foam that might mark the passage of some endless sea serpent.

Tor said, "That reef . . ."

"Oars! Oars!" the lookout called. "Oars in sight! Off the port bow! Beyond the point!"

Tor and I jumped together into the lower rigging. I saw the point, but nothing more. It was farther beyond the island than the island was from us. There was a flash of light and then again nothing. Then another flash. Sunlight on wet oar blades. The distant ship changed attitude from bow- or stern-on to silhouette. It was now a long, low shape against the water. Tor held the rigging with one hand and shaded his eyes with the other. "She's seen us. That's why she turned. A small-to-medium galley. Maybe eight oars to a side. Two men to an oar right now. Fifty to sixty men." He was silent for several moments watching. "Has she been ashore? Did we interrupt her first? Ah, yes, she's heading for the island."

He swung down onto the deck and I followed him. "That captain will try to put the island between us. If he can, then he can play with us all afternoon and get away after dark. He's counting the reef as part of the island. That's smart of him. He thinks he has the game won now. Maybe he has. We'll let him keep on thinking so."

The relative position of the island made Tor's point clear. Our present course, a broad reach east of south, would intercept the galley before it reached the island on its own shortest course if it weren't for the reef. We would strike that almost in the middle. If we turned to circle the reef or went on around the island, we would put the galley in control of events. The enemy captain knew it was one or the other. We saw the beat of his stroke go down.

We kept on at an angle toward the line of foam and then eased off to hold a parallel. The galley, seeing us commit ourselves, altered course for the reef, to be in a position to keep the island and its tail between us. Now we were running within fifty yards of the breaking water and the invisible rocks. Tor said, "There is a gut through this. My father knew it and told me, but I never ran it with him. We're coming near the place, I think. We'll have to do this at full speed."

First he sent men to loosen the lines and hold them ready in the cleats. Then he took the helm himself and beckoned me to stand with him. Even closer now, the broken water sounded very loud and so, suddenly, did the creaking and straining of the ship's gear. We weren't looking for a break in the foam and spray. The passage would be too narrow for that. What we wanted was a place on the surface where the water swirled but stayed smooth. In the same instant we both saw it — what seemed like it.

Tor forced the rudder over. The bow began to swing and he called "Brace up the yard!"

Now we shot straight for the reef. Together on the helm Tor and I held the bow up against the crosswind and the sea. We must not slide to leeward. Water fell across the bow from both sides and then drenched the entire deck. The ship squirmed and twisted in the grip of the current and we waited — all of us — frozen. There was no shock of collision. We heard no tearing from underneath. The spray blinded us and water pulled at our legs. Then, all at once, we were through the reef. We stood between the island and the galley, now only half a mile away.

I called my men together and gave them instructions. Taking position on the bow and stern decks in open ranks of eight, they opened their skin pouches and strung their bows. There were no wet strings. Tor's men armed themselves and put weapons within reach of those doing the ship handling. Durr had the helm now and Tor stood beside him, watching the enemy, glancing up at the draw of our sail in the steady breeze.

We were now back on our original course, and the galley, as though she were going to pass us a short distance to port, rowed toward us almost straight into the wind, her clumsy single square sail furled. Her oarsmanship was magnificent, the blades entering and lifting as one, the beat quick, the stroke short and powerful. As the distance narrowed fast, the galley held her position to our left. Then her six forward port oars rose from the water and stayed lifted. The stern oars dug in at right angles and held. The helm went down and the starboard oars kept rowing. Then, seemingly within her own length, the long galley pivoted toward us through ninety degrees. The helm went back to center, all oars rowed, and she came back up to speed. Her ram would strike us amidships. I had heard of such a maneuver but never believed in it. I watched with my mouth open.

Tor watched, too, but to more purpose. When the galley picked up the stroke again after the turn, he signaled to Durr and called to his sail handlers. Our own helm went down, the yard swung with the ship and we were once more running parallel and opposite to the galley, but this time to windward and only an arm's length away. I called to my archers, and those on the bow drew and loosed and drew again. Our bow scraped the galley, snapping off the forward oars before sliding away. My stern bowmen loosed a volley, and then another, and then a last.

By now the *Aspara* had run beyond the galley, and Durr brought us about to come back on the other side. This would be a slower passing because we were now overtaking. There was bloody disarray on the galley. The captain, nimble and cool, was everywhere on his ship, exhorting here, giving directions somewhere else, sorting out the shambles at the rowers' benches. My men had done what I told them. Shooting together but picking their targets, they aimed over the near bulwarks down at the rowers on the far side. Men were slumped over the benches, lying on the deck, and standing coughing with arrows in their chests. Their captain came back on deck and stood, fists on his hips, watching us come down on him from astern.

With a slower approach our impact was less and we broke only two or three oars. The enemy was taking cover, so I signaled my men to shoot at will. Arrows were coming our way now, and I heard a crossbow bolt thwack into the railing beside me. I saw my men open out and change position as the *Aspara* moved. They looked out their targets and then released crisply. They were not getting easy shots. They weren't refusing hard ones, but there were more misses. The slaughter was over for the moment and we were beginning to be hit. A man-at-arms went down with a bolt in his thigh, and one of my men took a wound in his bow arm. We had reduced our numerical disadvantage, but how much I couldn't guess.

As we pulled ahead to make another turn and another run, a man sprang alone onto the galley's narrow foredeck, swinging around his head a small, metal claw tied to a light line. Beside me two bows hummed. The man fell with one arrow in his throat and another in his armpit, but he had made his throw. The hook arched up and over the high end of our yardarm. Before anyone could cut the line, the galley crew hauled it taut and the hook grabbed the swinging yard, fouling it in its own halyards and jamming it into the standing rigging. The great sail flapped and slatted, and the ship lost way in the middle of its turn, rolling side-on to the galley. Her remaining oars rose and fell and rose again. The ram moved toward us.

Tor jumped down into the waist, but had no time to form his men. The ram hit us a glancing blow, knocking us all down, sliding and grating along the hull. Hurled grapnels hooked themselves onto the bulwarks, binding the vessels together at an ungainly angle, and the enemy swarmed across into the accessible waist. From the heights of the stern and bow, we poured arrows into their mass, hurting them badly, clogging their way, but we couldn't stop them. With the dead and wounded falling between the ships, they came until there were no more to come.

From below us, amidships, the din and stink and flash of weapons rose in a composite wave against the senses. Tor, with a dozen men, held a space at the foot of the mast. The others, alone, back to back, fought where they found themselves. I saw Durr go down with a sword cut across the face. The Sulliabans, with their round shields and curved swords, were everywhere and around them all, shifting, moving, striking, lunging. We could do no shooting into that cockpit.

Before the enemy could come up to us, we left our bows and dropped onto the flanks of the fight, one section to port and one to starboard. Extending our lines the depth of the waist, we turned inward and pressed ahead. The enemy had to whirl to meet us, not sure of their backs. Across the top of the battle, I yelled to Tor, "We have them on the flanks! Cut them in two!"

Then it was shields and short swords, hacking and stabbing, unremitting, parched, timeless work, the peril as great from either side as from the man in front. I saw faces, eyes, teeth, shoulders, arms, blades, cuts, and blood all at once and separately. I couldn't smell anymore and heard only a whining roar. I guessed how the fight went by the pressures around me. Once I looked up and saw that Tor had moved out from the mast, recovering some of his separated men. They now made a line across the middle, and the enemy was caught in two pockets between us. The slashing and stabbing went on, the enemy fewer now and slower.

Suddenly the sounds stopped. At a word from Tor our lines opened out to leave the Sulliaban captain standing alone, a great wound in his right side, his normally brown face gray. Holding his side to keep himself together, he looked around the frightful deck and said faintly and clearly, "Are there any still alive to join me?"

Slowly, seven men staggered or crawled from where they lay, and the captain, gripping his wound with both hands, led them in procession across the ship. They slipped silently over the edge into the sea and the captain followed them.

By the time we boarded the galley a minute or two later, there were only dead men there. Tor looked at me and said, "They're pirates. It's drown or hang. They always go overboard if you let them. I let them."

The sense of time began to come back into an afternoon that was still only half gone. Our losses were heavy. Eight dead and twelve wounded, of which two of the dead were mine and three of the wounded, but none of those badly. In addition I had a cut across one cheekbone and Tor a gash in his thigh. There was a great deal to be done.

As routine we salvaged all metal fittings, weapons, and tools from the galley. Next we loaded her with the rest of her dead, cut her loose, and set her well afire. Tor sent a party in the boat to explore the shore near where the galley had been sighted. He sent a carpenter to test the hull where the ram struck, a team to free the sail and mend the rigging, another to clean the ship, and still another to wash our dead. Durr was one of them. We would bury them overside at sunset. Tor and I tended to the wounded.

When the boat came back it brought a puzzling story. Holder, the man in command, said there were only two houses anywhere near the place of the sighting. Both families had seen the galley that morning and fled inland. When the galley pulled out, they went back to their homes and found nothing touched or taken. No Sulliaban had been in either place. Holder and his men found nothing to show that the galley had landed anywhere. About a mile down the beach they did see some faint, confused footprints — no keel marks — in the damp sand just below high water mark. The dry, loose sand higher up showed nothing. Whether these signs were made by a landing party coming and going, by native observers, or in the course of a rendezvous it was impossible to know. All they proved was that men had been there since the last high tide.

Tor thanked Holder, told him to get the *Aspara* under way and then asked me, "What do you make of it?"

"I wish they weren't all dead."

"Yes," he admitted, "there's that. But they are. And it wouldn't make any difference. Only the captain knew and he wouldn't have told us. He couldn't even be still alive."

"Maybe," I said. "Anyone who was in the boat could have told as much as we need. Ah, well. I think you told me it took about half a day to get from here to Winder town overland. Is that right?"

"Yes. Half a day to a day. I don't know exactly. I've never walked it myself. Why?"

"Do you suppose they landed an assassination party?"

"I hadn't thought of that," he said, and straightened up abruptly. "Yes, I think that's just what they did."

"So do I," I told him. "They weren't raiders. And what better place than Winder? If they kill Alwina or fail, maybe they can implicate you."

"They'll kill nobody! They'll never get to Winder. I'll catch them. Holder!"

For several moments he was the Tor I'd first met in the garden before Alwina's dinner, angry, headstrong, arrogant, but in the end he didn't turn back and he did see reason. "Look," I said, "you won't catch them. All you'll do is give your hand away. They haven't got anybody to assassinate yet."

"All right," Tor said. "We'll sail back."

"Tell me," I said. "These people remind me of your iron. Whoever wants that iron, why would he have to use that empty river? Couldn't he get it just as easily straight from Sulliaba?"

"More easily. But not secretly. And not without risk."

"Why not? He knows your patrols. The stuff could be put ashore almost anywhere on the coast. Even Winder. You made

78

that point yourself. Our catching this ship today was pure luck."

"Yes, it was," he agreed. "I see. Our friend could perfectly well carry iron and assassins on the same ship but to different places. Why not? Well, not again for a while."

O N T H E   D A Y of Alwina's arrival, Nyall and I rode out of town toward Inerria at the head of thirty-two men. Until we left, no one but Tor and I knew we were going. The breeze dropped as we moved inland, and the early morning sun began to draw out layers of pungent smells from the ground, the bushes and the evergreens with their new, light-green tips. Nyall sniffed the air, as if savoring the difference from the salt smell of the coast.

Nyall had puzzled me ever since I saw him first, when he came into the Council chamber armed. In Winder I got along with him well. He was a good officer and the men more than respected him, mine as well as his own. He put his heart into our venture, and thanks to his ingenuity and ability — and something more — our small combined force turned out better than even I had hoped. Nyall had what I can understand only as generosity of spirit. That is what transformed us from two groups of men identically trained into one organization, held together by its particularities. The men were firmly and casually confident of the skills they knew each one had; their critical appreciation was of a high order, their overt emotional level low, and no one ever used the word loyalty. This kind of result is not achieved just by being a nice man, or a tough one, or by having any namable combination of qualities. Nyall had done it by what I have called generosity of spirit, but of an austere kind. It was directed toward our eighty men only, not the world at large, and yet he had not made them his personal troops in any sense. They knew he highly admired something in them that they sometimes showed, and they felt this recognition as a sign of a great if undeterminable value. They experienced it themselves. No one wears this kind of thing on his sleeve.

My pony Lon felt very good in the fresh and fragrant morning, sidling back and forth across the trail, putting his feet down twice where once would do. Nyall turned his lanky, bony frame in the saddle to follow Lon's doings. "Tor found you a good one," he said. "That's a nice horse."

"We like each other," I said, and rubbed Lon's neck. He snorted and blew and lifted his head. "Better save all that strength, friend," I told him. "I don't get lighter with the miles." I had the feeling the day might be the first really hot one I'd known in Winder.

Nyall looked back at the long double column of horsemen behind us. "Well," he said, "the next week or so may tell us how well we've done our work. I wish we knew more, but I suppose that's too much to expect with this kind of job."

"Nothing new?"

"Nothing more than you know. We found their tracks in several places. Enough to think they're near town or in it. Probably six and maybe eight of them. At a guess they're a mixed party — some Islandians or perhaps Winderese and some Saracens."

"You never guess without a reason," I said. "Why do you think that?"

"Why a mixed party? Basically a pledge of mutual commitment. And they need to have people who can appear in public without giving them away. That's important."

"Even if they have confederates here?"

"Even then. Some things they have to see with their own eyes." He looked askance at the sun, pulled off his wool parka, and folded it into a saddlebag. "Frare, what is this new Queen of yours like?"

"Young. Very beautiful," I said. "But you saw her at the Council meeting. She's very much aware she's both a monarch and a woman. She doesn't merely know this, she's conscious of it every moment. A King can take it for granted he's a man. I wouldn't want to be Alwina."

"Nor I," said Nyall without levity. "What does she want?"

"You heard what she said. To come to friendly terms with Winder. To defeat Kilikash and secure the frontier. I think she wants those things. I hope so."

"Yes, but if what you say is true, I wonder if she can. There's enough fire inside her to hurt all the time. I sympathize with her. It's a lot easier for me to like Islandians than to stomach Islandia."

Near midmorning we entered a small valley with a quiet brook running more or less down its middle. The valley floor was reasonably level and open, and the immediately containing hills rose steeply but not more than two or three hundred feet. On the same side as the trail, in a clearing in the low bushes and short jack pines, a House of Quiet stood above the rocks and sand along the stream bed. We dismounted here to water the horses, and we stretched our own legs in the aromatic warmth, loosening up under the somewhat wider sky that covered us now. I asked Nyall about the House of Quiet, saying there didn't seem to be as many here as I remembered at home.

"Everything's scarcer in Winder," he said, "including Om. There's a story about this place. There was another House of Quiet here once, a smaller one. In those days the field gods liked this spot. Cam and Bos kept fine trees and rich grass here. The tale goes that a Winderese member of the Catholic League stopped here on his way to The City to talk to the bishop about becoming a priest. He went into the House to see whether Om would make his existence known to a Catholic. While he was inside a thunderstorm passed over and lightning set fire to the valley, burning up everything in it, trees, grass, House of Quiet, and the Leaguer. Cam and Bos were offended and have never permitted grass or trees to grow here again."

"I see," I said. "Why were Cam and Bos offended?"

"I don't know," Nyall said, and mounted his horse. "That's all the story tells."

We went on as before but more quietly, neither men nor horses as exuberant as at the beginning. Nyall and I continued to look carefully at the land on either side of the trail, which would be important to us when we returned with the Queen. As we went on, the country grew more and more cross-grained, the ranges of southwestern Islandia shouldering against those of the Winder peninsula. Not long after noon we came to a flat, hot, open stretch covered with sweet fern and dotted with scrub pine no taller than a man's shoulder. The plain here spread a considerable distance to ridges on the left and right, but about two hundred yards straight ahead it ended at the foot of a low hill, down whose face came a zigzag track. Nyall raised his hand to signal the halt and dismounted.

"Is this the border?"

Nyall smiled and shook his head. "Nobody knows where the border is. That may not be Inerria," raising his right hand, "or Doring," raising his left, "but everyone agrees," and he nodded at a large, sandy mound a few yards ahead, "that anthill is in Islandia. Make yourself comfortable."

That was impossible. There was no shade, and the sun seemed to concentrate upon this place all the energy it drew into itself from the wide heavens. So I walked among the troopers, asking about them, about their horses, making jokes about Tor's good sense in staying home, comparing observations with the unit leaders.

I am no student of assassinations, although I have read accounts of some in other lands, and know my country is not the only one to practice the rite. Doubtless there are many ways of classifying political murders, but for my purposes it seemed most useful to divide them into public and private varieties. I couldn't disregard either, but I thought it comparatively unlikely that the Queen's household would produce or be penetrated by a killer and that there would be a knife in the back, a strangling, or a poison cup. To be sure, such a thing could happen any time and anywhere — but elsewhere more easily than in Winder. For such a private deed circumstances were better at home. Events so far pointed another way. That left, or rather emphasized, every minute of every day and night the Queen was in public. To be successful an attempt required advance knowledge, careful planning, zealots ready to die — and luck. Today was less likely than other occasions, because the conspirators could have no advance knowledge, and consequently nothing better than a makeshift plan. Just the same, the flanks of our column would be vulnerable. My men, leapfrogging, would scout on foot, eight men to a side, all the way back. Every three miles the foot scouts on the flanks would change places with the other sixteen men, who had gone ahead with all the horses. Now the heat began to worry me.

When I thought, as I inevitably and often did, of the kind of person I might expect to be one of the killers, or the instigator, I had a total failure of the imagination. I couldn't picture or characterize a person who could live among us unnoticed and have such an alien spiritual shape. I couldn't get over the conviction that his intention must somehow show. I had been no help at all to Cabing about this. The nearest I could get was the thought that such a person either must live at an astonishing pitch of abstraction in which people become the attributes of essences, or be so narrowed by an emotion that all his sensibility was squeezed out. I didn't believe I knew any people like that.

Wiping my face with the back of my arm I walked toward Nyall and, distorted through the sweat I had just pushed into my eyes, saw two riders come over the crest of the hill and start down the switchback trail. On the plain in front of us the heat wavered above the rocks and sand, and the descending horses, shifting from haunch to haunch, stirred up bursts of yellow dust that rolled into a cloud behind them. Nyall and I mounted and rode out to meet the Queen's party. Almost everyone in it looked as dirty and hot as we were. I presented Nyall at once to Alwina, so he could offer Tor's greetings. Excusing myself, I turned aside to speak to the officer commanding the escort, an interview I looked forward to with apprehension and wished to have over. In this case I had no idea what sort of officer court protocol might have produced.

The man's name was Trant, and in looks he somewhat resembled the sound of it, being both spare and squared-off at the corners, with glinting blue eyes and a sharp chin. He was also my senior by some ten years. We greeted each other formally and he handed me an official letter. I broke the seal and found Cabing's affirmation of my authority short and adequate. I asked Trant, "Are you familiar with this order?"

"I haven't read it, but Isla Cabing read it to me. I should tell you, Frare, I protest it. I don't agree with it and don't like it."

"How would you have it, Trant?"

"Your position here is ministerial. My command is military. I should be independent, not subject to civilian orders. Your policy, yes, but my action when it comes to that."

"Did you say this to Cabing?"

"I did."

"I see he didn't relieve you. What *did* he do?"

"He said he would take note of my protest if I would accept his order."

I couldn't see the faintest trace of a smile anywhere about him, and so I didn't dare laugh. I said, "I'll be glad to do the same thing. I recognize and will report that you are accepting orders under general protest. Is that satisfactory, Trant?"

"That is satisfactory."

"Good. Then let's get to work. I don't intend to meddle with your men, Trant, but there is so little difference here between policy and action there is no place for two voices. Your fifty men are the only regular Islandian troops here. They're a diplomatic courtesy and a bodyguard. They're not military. They are official guests in a friendly, foreign country and they're not to forget it. The state of affairs here is delicate for us. There is also serious danger, but it doesn't come from Winder."

As I described my own men and my arrangements for the trip back, he listened carefully. "Your scheme is good," he said, "if your men don't wilt in the heat."

"That's a possibility, but it won't be so hot when we're out of these pockets."

"Are you actually expecting an attack this afternoon? Or is this precautionary?"

"Both," I said. "The attacker chooses the time and place. I'm certain there will be an attempt sometime, but that's about all I know."

"Small or in force?"

"Almost surely small. I think it will be fast, hard, well planned, and based on some better deception than just surprise."

Trant smiled. "That's the way the best ones are done. They're hard to handle. The important thing is to keep your men from being pulled out of position. Only one more question. Does the Queen know this?"

"Not from me. Cabing told her there was danger — general danger — particularly in these early days and that there might always be some. I don't plan to be more definite than that if I can help it. What would you do?"

"I wouldn't say more than that," Trant replied. "Especially — if I am to believe you — since you don't seem to know anything more that would help her." He pulled at his long chin and looked around at the fragmented column. "I'd better pull all this together. Look, Frare, here's how we'll supplement your dispositions." Ticking off his fingers, he gave me a new arrangement for his advance and rear guards, his center party, and the number and locations of his flank guards and outriders. He knew his business and my respect for Cabing went up another notch.

As the column formed and started off, I dismissed my men from guard duty and sent them away on their proper jobs. Nyall then told me the Queen would like to see me and I reined in beside her. The weather was not sparing her. She looked as hot and sweaty as anyone else, and there were wet streaks of grit on her cheeks, but there was no droop in her shoulders and her eyes were sharp and alert.

"Good day, Frare," she said. "That is, in a manner of speaking. I didn't know our part of the world was able to produce anything like this."

"Nyall tells me this heat is common in these inland boxes, Your Majesty."

"I'm adding rapidly to my education," she said. "You've managed all this very nicely. And I see you've tamed Trant. I expected to have to settle a dispute between you. How did you accomplish it?"

"Tame him, Your Majesty? I did nothing like that. I told him that since Isla Cabing accepted his service under protest, of course I'd be glad to do the same."

She gave me a speculative look and partly repressed a smile. "You're more perceptive than I thought, Isla Frare. Now Trant will work like a dog for you. He likes to think his men are of the Household and he makes a point of honor of protesting any order that doesn't come directly from me. That may cause trouble someday, but now it's touching." She drew a handkerchief from her saddlebag and mopped her face. "Not queenly, but necessary. Can we reach the town today?"

"Yes, but not until after dark. It is still a long, hard trip."

"Let's do it anyway, Frare. I don't want to spend another night on the road. Nyall told me about the guest house. That was a nice thought. It will make the meeting easier. He also told me about a trip to some shipyards and a boar hunt. That sounds exciting. It never occurred to me to ask, but I didn't realize there were wild boar hereabout."

"I didn't either," I said. "There is a large colony in one of the seaward mountain valleys. Tor thinks their ancestors came ashore from a shipwreck in the days of the League."

"That's the first good thing I've ever heard about the League," she said. Turning in the saddle, she surveyed the reformed column from back to front. "Trant has fifty men here. How many have you, Frare?"

"Not quite three dozen."

"More than eighty men to protect the Queen on a peaceful journey. What a sad thing! My father used to go where he pleased with no escort at all."

"This is a state visit to a foreign country, Your Majesty. Your father never made one. Besides he ruled in quiet times. There was no threat from Kilikash. Your father didn't have to ask hard choices of the people."

She laughed shortly, saying, "You put things too gently, Frare. I give the people hard choices merely by being Queen. And Kilikash threatens because my father is dead. Because I am Queen. That's what they say in the Council." She slapped her hand against her thigh. "Please go and send Tenira to me. I know you want to see her, but you can wait a little while."

I did as I was told and found Tenira some distance back, grimy but somehow neat, encouraging three weary ladies of the Queen's household. She smiled when she saw me and said, "Hello, Frare. I wondered if you'd come out with the welcoming party. I'm glad to see you."

I said, "I was afraid you might not come at all. But you didn't fail me. I'm forbidden to talk to you until you've been to see the Queen. That is, you're summoned."

"She's in a summoning mood today," Tenira said, and smiled again as she rode forward.

I then dropped back even farther to speak to Bodwin, whom I was startled to see on this expedition. "Why so surprised, Cousin?" he asked me. "Do you think I turn up my toes outside The City? You should know better. And the heat doesn't bother me. You can see I'm not suffering the way you are, Frare."

Indeed he looked as fresh as I had felt many hours ago. "No, you're durable," I said, "but I didn't think Cabing would risk letting you bring your tongue along."

"He didn't want to, you're quite right. But he relented when I gave him a promise of silent behavior. Keeping it so far has been the least of my troubles. There's nothing to talk about and nobody to talk to if there were."

"I'm sorry for you," I said. "Still, I didn't suppose you would go through such a hardship merely to observe human behavior. Only animals could be worth it."

"You have a point," he admitted, "and I'll never disappoint you again. But I really was very curious and it's been worth it. You cannot conceive the astonishment and relief with which many of our intelligent fellow citizens discover that a Queen is actually a human being like any other woman they've ever seen. I believe they expected a two-headed calf or a hippogriff."

"Does Alwina tell them she wants to be more than a Queen to them?"

"Yes," Bodwin said smiling, "at every hamlet. It is a dreadful thing to keep saying, isn't it? I confess I find it very moving. She so clearly means it and in the best possible way. It gets an excellent reception."

"If she uses some form of it tomorrow," I said, "be sure to watch Tor's face."

I joined Tenira as soon as I saw her leave the Queen. She plainly did feel the weather, but less so than anyone I'd seen except Bodwin. We smiled at each other and rode on quietly side by side in the blazing afternoon. Our horses accommodated themselves to each other without bothering to exchange any identification signals. Lon was not showing distress or even complaining, but for all his strength and spirit I was worried about him. I must seem intolerably heavy to him.

After quite some time, as though we were resuming a talk in progress, Tenira said quietly, "There's been a lot of success recently. The Assembly. Even the Council. This tour of the country. She's feeling sure of herself — as Queen. I wrote you about it. It's still growing. She expects the people here to rally round her the way ours have."

"And that will make everything all right?"

"It's supposed to go a long way."

"Does she mean to give anything for it? Equal rights with Islandians? Citizenship?"

"She hasn't spoken of that to me. I don't think she sees the trouble that way. Not now. To her it's a matter of broken promises and personal dishonesties. She thinks those are the things that have built up the hostility. If she can bring the people of Winder to trust her and like her, then there can be a new day. It's going to be like the Assembly all over again."

"What part does Tor play in all this?"

Tenira shook her head. "I don't know. I'm even more uneasy than when I wrote you. This new confidence of hers changes things. It's as if she'd forgotten she had a private self. She always speaks of Tor now as a political opponent. I'm sure she's more than half in love with him, but she doesn't admit any personal feeling for him at all. At the same time she's certain he's strongly attracted to her. She counts on it."

"I see," I said. "She will win the people with sweetness and sympathy. Tor will be weakened by infatuation. So she will get a reconciliation on whatever terms she wants."

Tenira made a gesture of distaste. "I didn't say just that and I wasn't thinking of anything so deliberate. I'm sure Alwina doesn't mean it that way."

"I'm sure she doesn't. There are nicer ways to put it. Particularly for a woman who wants to keep herself from interfering with her queenly duty."

"Yes, Frare, perhaps. You don't need to be nasty. Be fair. You've no idea how much she has to give up to be Queen. You're Tor's friend, I think. You know something about Winder now. How do they feel about us here?"

"Watchful and suspicious," I said. "I was annoyed just now and I showed it. I'm sorry. But I'm the Queen's friend, too, and I'm her minister here. Still, if she doesn't listen to Cabing, there's no reason she should come to me. Her plan may work for all I know, but there's one thing badly wrong with it. It takes the other side for granted. These people are tough and they're not just Islandians at heart. I don't think they're going to be touched by gracious condescension and girlish charm. As for Tor, he may be smitten — I don't know — but he's tough, too, and he doesn't impress me as a man who gets infatuated. If Alwina gets anything here, I think she'll have to pay for it."

Tenira smiled. "I suggested that to her, but she doesn't want to understand me. She tells me I'm her friend now and not her teacher any longer and, what's more, I never was her teacher in politics anyway."

"Well," I said, smiling back, "that may be, but I'll bet this maneuver she's up to now is not one her father ever taught her."

When Lon raised his head and twitched his ears, I suddenly realized the temperature had been slowly going down and I had been comfortable for some time without being aware of it.

For a moment I was almost resentful — at being taken by surprise and at the waste of not being conscious of the pleasure of the change — but I sniffed the new air and said to Tenira, "Better have a wool jacket ready. It'll be cool soon. Excuse me for a while."

I rode forward to where the relay waited with all the horses. The men there said the first full shift on foot had been exhausting and they were done for after it, good for nothing. Now, with the drop in temperature and a rest, they felt all right again and knew they could last through. Nyall came up at this point after a stretch with the men in the field and confirmed the estimate. We agreed to speed up the column.

During the long afternoon the temperature kept sliding gradually down through the range of unawareness and finally beyond. By the time we reached the House of Quiet we were all wearing parkas again. Here, while the horses fed and drank and we did the same, we considered once more whether or not to camp for the night. If so, this was the place to do it. There was perhaps an hour before full dark and then another three hours before moonrise. No other place had this combination of water, space, and natural protection. The consultation didn't last long. Alwina called on us in turn and heard one different reason after another for pressing on. At the end she broke out into youthful, silvery laughter and then said in a voice that was not so young, "One purpose and three arguments. It sounds like those unanimous agreements we have about fighting Kilikash, except here it does no harm. For myself, gentlemen, I'll give you a fourth argument. I wouldn't camp here under any circumstances, for I can feel the place is already occupied. Lead on!"

The oncoming darkness slowed our pace again and changed the terms in the equation of defense and attack. During daylight, my durable men had searched the flanks to the distance of a long bowshot, working up and along the steep sides of hills when necessary. They saw nothing and heard nothing except animals and birds, from whose behavior they could guess little because of the disturbance they themselves were making. Nyall and I and they knew perfectly well we hadn't proved that no one was out there, only that whoever might be there had been kept down. Now, with no lights showing, danger moved from the range of arrows and throw-darts, closing in around us with the night. I thought of a shout and a sudden, shadowy struggle on one side, while from the other came a swift glide with a dagger from behind a tree, a bush, or a rock. I drew my scouts close to the column and changed their formation from line abreast to line ahead. Trant pulled his outriders in to the very edge of the trail and formed his flank guards into an envelope around Alwina.

There was little talk and the faint forest sounds were taken up in the low, complex mutter of the column, the placing of hoofs, the snuffle of horses, the creaking of saddle leather. Time moved, but we did not seem to. The dark forest was changeless and after a while one could even confuse the angle of climbing with that of descending. The trees and our path kept pace with us, rolling along like a reverse treadmill, the same turn to the left always just ahead, the same cluster of rocks forever on the right. Moonrise silvered the trance and blackened its edges, and the forest kept on moving past, repeating itself.

Then there were shouts ahead! Shouts, torches, and firelight! Warmth and walls and faces! There was Tor's mother, tall and gaunt and friendly, welcoming Alwina. There were the sounds of unsaddling and taking down and spreading out. Nyall and I went to the men and congratulated them, telling them no less than the truth — that this was a day's work few could match. I said to Nyall, "We won't have anything quite like this again. We'll be working with plans. It may be as hard, but it won't be like this." Then I lay down to sleep.

I dreamed I was walking beside Alwina down a hallway I had never seen before. It was wide and lofty and straight to the eye, but it felt narrow, and I knew there were twists and turns in it. There were no windows or lamps, but the place was brightly lit. Alwina said, "Where are the ships? They should be here." The hallway grew airless and we were both very hot. We talked about how hot it was. I felt sweat on my own face and saw it on hers. Her hand came up with a large handkerchief. She wiped her cheeks and forehead with the white cloth and then held it out in front of her dripping wet with blood. Waking up, I saw the moon straight overhead. I was thinking about the dream when I went back to sleep.

In the morning the dream was still on my mind. I do not believe in the direct significance of dreams, but this one reminded me of something. I found Nyall and said, "That house in town Tor is turning over to the Queen. I know Tor has chosen the staff himself. I know we will be in control of the inside and the grounds, and Trant will keep the gates. But I don't know who's in charge of it now. Do you?"

"I know the staff is there waiting."

I shook my head and said, "That's what just occurred to me. We've made all kinds of plans to protect the Queen. They're all based on keeping between her and danger. We haven't forgotten the private side, but we haven't pictured it much. There are places we can't go with her. Those we should clean out before she gets to them. What's to have prevented someone from slipping into that house these last few days and being in hiding there now?"

Nyall looked at me as though I had turned into a snake in front of his eyes. "So very easy," he said softly. "I'm going into town now with the men for the meeting ceremony. I'll take two extra fours and ream that place out."

When Trant formed up his troop and Alwina came out of the guest house, I saw how small her party really was. In addition to Tenira, there were five women. I recognized their faces from Alwin House as attendants of the Queen, but I knew only one by name, Sissona, the oldest of the lot. Of the men, in addition to Trant and Bodwin, one was Decker, the major-domo with whom Woking and I had worked the night of the banquet; another was Birket, whom I knew as an assistant of Cabing's; the third I remembered having seen with Mora; but the fourth was a complete stranger to me.

Alwina appeared in one of her best and favorite colors, dark green, with a polished buff belt at her waist and a dusty-red scarf at her throat. We clattered the short distance into town and drew up on one edge of the main square, which was formed around a fountain by the intersection of three principal streets. We saw Tor leave the far side of the square and walk toward the fountain. He was all alone. On our left, its front ranks only a few yards from the fountain, clustered a crowd of several hundred. Here and there in it I could pick out the faces of our men. Those of us in the Queen's party dismounted and gathered in front of Trant's horsemen. Then Tenira and I walked with Alwina part way across the square. There we stopped and she went on across the cobbles toward the fountain, the crowd, and her towering host.

She moved well as she always did, her head up, her body suspended from her shoulders, and her legs swinging full length from her hips. A swirl of chilly wind from the harbor tugged at her shining hair, lifting it off her neck. Tor waited, ready to take her hand and bow. But Alwina would not have it that way. Reverting to her banquet toast, she ran the last few steps, put her hands on his shoulders, and lifted her face. She reached only to his chin. When Tor saw what she wanted, he lowered his head, and she kissed him on each cheek. He smiled, but did not return the salute. There was laughter in the crowd, not mocking, but amused at the awkwardness. Tor then spoke simply and briefly, introducing the Queen and welcoming her to Winder. He held out his hand and she used it as she jumped up to the rim of the fountain.

There she stood quiet for a moment, the wind rippling her clothes, beautiful as a leaping deer, radiating youth and strength and purpose. What she said that morning was not taken down and is mostly gone, but her words are only a portion of what is lost. To say her performance was spontaneous would be true. To say it was polished and calculated would be equally true. She put into it everything she had acquired from her father and all she had felt, learned, and observed by herself. It was the perfect expression of her passion and success, of her new sense of completeness as Queen.

She told the audience how she felt about being Queen, that the job was not foreign to a woman's nature, no more foreign than being human, than being able to think and love, than being born and dying. She described the fight against her in the Council and told how she had refused a contrived victory and how she had supported Tor. She told of the great meeting of the Assembly and of her triumph and vindication. She disclosed the danger in the north, the threat of Kilikash to Islandia and Winder together. She said she became Queen with a firm and public policy of breaking the Saracen menace and achieving reconciliation and friendship with Winder. And, last of all, she told them why she had gone on her long journey to visit among her people.

"My people and I," she said, "we both needed the same things, knowledge of the other and mutual confidence. I was that unheard-of thing — a Queen. No real woman could be such a thing, and if she could then a Queen must be bad — surely unnatural. They heard me speak and answer, saw me walk, ride, eat, and wince in pain from the sunburn on my nose. We tested each other and we were both real. We believed in each other.

"I have told my people, on roads, in villages and towns, that

I would like to be more than a Queen to them, more than just a monarch who looks down at them like markings on a map. I am also one of them, a woman and a citizen as well as Queen. As a friend and companion I would like to share their problems with their country, their fears of the outside world. They and I will be better for it.

"Here I would like to make the same plea to you, with the difference, of course, that I am not your Queen. But I would like to be more than just a neighboring Queen to you. Your friend and companion, if you will let me, who knows your troubles and feels them with you. Winder and Islandia share a language, a country, and an enemy. We are ancestral cousins if not in fact brothers. History has joined us inescapably. Friendship lies no farther away than our outstretched hands. And whatever destiny may send, it will be the same for both of us. My people are beginning to know this, and I think you've known it for a long time. I have come to you as a messenger of good will from my people. I hope you will send me back as a bearer of good will from you."

With a wave and a nod, she jumped down to the street. For a few moments there was polite applause, and then the back edges of the crowd began to thin. Tor thanked Alwina and then walked back with her in our direction. She had been flushed and happy when she waved to the crowd, but now her face was white and her lips made a hard line. Tor's face was impassive, but I saw pain and compassion in his eyes.

FEW OF THE Queen's party were close enough to experience the full impact of her rebuff. In any case its effect was softened for them by the bustle and confusion of settling in Islandia House, as the handsome building was temporarily called. The place was large and not far from Tor's home on the cliff above the harbor. Tor had been at pains to staff and furnish it well. I did not intend to move in there myself and I was not pleased to have Sissona inform me that a set of rooms was prepared which the Queen expected me to occupy. Sissona told me this with the kind of placid, moral conviction women can acquire along with domestic authority, and I realized suddenly I was confronted with the Household itself. Her graying hair and round, smooth face let me know I could make no working alliance with her as I had with Trant.

"Thank you, Sissona," I said. "That's most kind and thoughtful. Please tell the Queen how grateful I am. It will be a pleasure to be here and use the rooms as much as I can. Unfortunately, I must stay in direct touch with the men and that means living at the barracks. They are a joint force and I owe responsibility to Tor as well as the Queen."

"I will tell her Majesty, Isla Frare. She will be disappointed."

Sissona's tone left no doubt that disappointment was a familiar euphemism for her disapproval and Alwina's displeasure. Still, I had told her the truth, if not all of it. To do my job I had to hold onto my freedom of movement, to keep access to myself open, and above all else to avoid being blinkered and directed by the deceptive clarity prevailing inside Alwina's intramural hierarchy. That morning I stayed at Islandia House only long enough to make sure that everyone was accounted for and then put my lieutenant, Nicking, in charge of our duty sections. Nyall joined me as I departed, and we were checked and cleared by Trant's men at the outer gate. This aspect of things seemed to be going well.

Because we were mounted, Nyall and I took the long way around down the back of the hill. He was looking grim and, I finally realized, shaken. At last he said, "That was a fortunate thought of yours this morning, Frare."

"What do you mean? You didn't . . . ?"

"Yes, we did. We came within five minutes of catching a killer." He shrugged and shivered as though he felt footsteps on his grave. "Your Queen charmed me yesterday and I like her, but I wish she hadn't taken it into her pretty head to come here. She is irresponsible. She cannot know what she is doing. It's not just her life she's playing with. If you and I can't keep her from being murdered here in Winder . . . it will save Kilikash a great deal of trouble."

"I've thought of that," I said. "I've thought about it ever since I left home. What did you find?"

"A room. More like a closet. In the back of the house a corridor runs between the kitchen and the pantry and then drops down some steps and divides. One branch goes past a stairwell and out into the stables. The other goes by the root cellar and the milk cooler out to the wood shelter. The milk cooler is in use now, but the root cellar isn't. Across one end of the root cellar is a deep closet with empty bins racked up against it and old coils of rope on pegs up above. The closet may have been used to store tools or seed or both. Nobody knows. Anyhow, that's where our man was. He planned to wait us out. He didn't move until he had to."

"How do you know?"

"We found a candle in a dish on the floor beside some blankets. The wax was still wet and hot. He went out through the wood shelter. One end of the shelter is only a few paces from the property wall and in a place that's pretty well out of sight. The wall is rough enough to climb if you've studied it for holds. There were scuff marks on it. And then the woods begin just the other side."

I reined in and stopped. "Who knows about this?"

"Me, you, and the eight men with me. I don't believe they'll say anything, but I didn't order them not to."

"Maybe they won't," I said, knowing they would, at least to their comrades, "but it makes a problem anyway. Can you send them to see me?"

"Yes. Whenever you want."

"Make it right now. I'll see them on the *Earne,* not in barracks. Then you go straight to Tor and tell him the whole story. Also tell him I'd like to talk to him about it as soon as he can."

The eight men gathered around me on the empty afterdeck of the ship where it thrust out into the harbor beyond the end of the jetty. From each man I heard an account, with comments, of what had happened and the accumulation of details made a sensuous reality out of Nyall's bare-bones outline. I smelled the snuffed-out candle and the urine and the dirty blankets, and I saw the boot scrapings on the wall. As the last man stopped talking, one of the section leaders caught the eye of the other and then said, "Isla Frare, you haven't said anything about secrecy yet, but we know you're going to. We've been talking it over. Is it all right for me to say something for all of us?"

"Certainly."

"There's no sense telling you we're mixed units. You made us that way. The point is that doesn't matter to us. We know our job and what we're for. We like the Queen and don't want her to get hurt. We know what could happen between Winder and Islandia if something happened to her here. And there's another thing. After this morning we know these people are real and we don't want to get beaten. We're not going to do anything to make us lose. So don't worry about telling us not to talk. If you say keep quiet, we'll keep quiet."

"Thank you, Crask," I said. "Thank you all. I don't like keeping secrets for the sake of keeping secrets. I don't like keeping secrets at all. Partly because it's very hard to do. So if we decide to keep this one, we have to be serious about it. Let me ask you how you will feel about not talking to your comrades about what you found this morning. How easy will it be?"

From their expressions, some of them hadn't thought of this. "Most secrets aren't betrayed," I said. "They dribble out. Ten men — that's you and me and Nyall — may possibly keep a secret, but not eighty — not in the nature of things. A secret loses its urgency once it is repeated and it becomes gossip at the second remove. You will talk of this among yourselves — you can't help it. Your comrades will overhear you. Then all eighty will be referring to it and be overheard outside. Someone will tell a relative or a good friend in confidence. And so it will go. One thing worse than losing a secret is to think you have one when you don't. That mustn't happen to us. We mustn't fool ourselves. I hope we don't have to make a secret of this, but I'm going to ask this of you now. Give me twenty-four hours to find out. For that long don't say anything to anybody, not even to each other. I'll let you know tomorrow morning."

No messenger from Tor came until midafternoon. I found all the lower part of his house taken over by preparations for the dinner for Alwina that evening. He saw me upstairs in a back room overlooking the stables and the long descent to Winder town. "Hello, Frare," he said. "You haven't moved into Islandia House?"

"Not yet."

"I see." He studied my face then before he said, "You know it's a great convenience to me to have you where you are?"

"Would you be willing to mention that to Her Majesty?"

"Gladly. Let's hope it doesn't get you imprisoned." He rose from his table, crossed the room, and shut the door on the sounds of activity downstairs. "I'm very sorry about the stingy reception Alwina got this morning. I know it wounded her and I hate to see that. It's too bad it has to happen. She puts the best of the Islandian message with real love, but unfortunately she doesn't change it. She doesn't see she can't say those things to my people anymore. It won't work. They don't like it. I can't endorse it. I feel sick about it for her — and for us. Do you follow me?"

I said very quietly, "I can't properly comment to you on her policy, Tor."

"No, but you can understand me."

"I can and do."

"Good. That's all I wanted." He returned to his table and straddled his chair. "Now what do you want to do about this other business?"

"Talk about it first. Should we keep it secret?"

"Why not? Whose business is it to know?"

"Cabing would agree with that. But . . . All the usual arguments one way or the other come out about even and they don't amount to much anyway. But there are two others that do."

"And they are?"

"The first one says the story is certain to come out in any case — distorted — as rumor and gossip. Some member of the staff of Islandia House saw or heard something. One of my men says something careless. Something of that sort will happen. That's not good if we're committed to a secret."

"I understand. What's the second?"

"The second," I said carefully, "assumes the worst. Suppose we fail. Suppose the killers get to Alwina. It has to be part of their plan to involve you. It would be much better for both our countries if you had already shown clearly in public that you knew of the existence of a plot and had taken strong joint measures with us against it. That fact would be very important, because my word, or Nyall's, on the matter would not be worth anything. I would already have been hanged anyway."

Tor sat looking past me at the sequence of evil possibilities. Then he said, "What do you want to do?"

"I don't," I told him. "I want you to do it. That's the effective way. You should tell Alwina first and then make the story as public as possible."

"You can be a difficult man, Frare. My inclination is to keep it secret. You leave out of your assessment the fact that news of assassination plots is a great stimulant — when you haven't any assassins to hang. One band of murderers is enough. Let me think about it for a while. I'll let you know this evening." He stood up. "After Alwina's experience this morning, I'm afraid my dinner of welcome is going to be constrained. Till then."

Before Tor's dinner the company gathered for a while on the terrace overlooking the harbor, as a quite different group had previously done in Alwina's garden, and it occurred to me how nice it would be if garden parties led only to garden parties and not to the events leading to garden parties. Moving among the guests, Tor's mother, Attana, paused for a moment where Tenira and I were standing and said, "How good to see people as pleased with each other as you two! It suits you."

We both laughed and Tenira replied, "It's hard not to be pleased with Frare."

"My son agrees with you," Attana told her. "For different reasons, I'm sure. I think I like yours better."

As she moved on, we walked to the edge of the cliff and

stood by the low parapet where we could look straight down at the quay past the backs of sea swallows perched on the narrow ledges. Behind us the number of guests grew and the buzz of conversation rose even though we were outdoors. Alwina's dinner for Tor had been small for political reasons. This was very large for identical reasons. Alwina was to have a big and influential audience to offend or to please. I asked Tenira about the effects of the morning's fiasco and the change in her face would have startled Attana if she had happened our way again.

"She called me in after she'd seen everyone else," Tenira said. "That's usual in any crisis. Bodwin is spared this exercise. Sissona and the others anoint her until she's about to be sick and then she calls for the vinegar bottle. That's me. This morning she was pacing around like a wild woman. I knew she was offended and angry, but she looked the way she used to when she couldn't make up her mind whether to sulk or have a tantrum.

" 'They're all lying to me,' she said. 'They don't dare tell me the truth. They don't know what it is. At least I can depend on you to tell me what I don't want to hear. Tenira, what went wrong?'

"I said, 'I'm not a good person to ask, Your Majesty. May I remind you of what you've told me so many times? I don't know anything about politics.'

" 'Don't evade me, Tenira! What happened? I've never meant anything more in my life.'

"Of course that was so and made it very difficult to tell her anything. I said, 'Maybe you didn't allow enough for the fact that these people aren't Islandian.'

" 'But I did. I kept telling then I knew they weren't Islandian and I wasn't their Queen. You heard me. I don't know what you mean.'

"I said, 'Yes, you admitted they weren't Islandian, but you offered them just the same things you offer Islandians. Nothing different. These people have no quarrel with their own King. They don't care about your enemies in the Council or your victory in the Assembly. They don't feel threatened by Kilikash the way we do. Maybe they should, but they don't. Their grievance is with us, with Islandia. You didn't talk about redress, only sweet friendship. On our terms.'

"She thought that over and said, 'That's silly! A public square isn't the place and, besides, I'm not at all convinced about those grievances. You'll have to do better than that, Tenira. What else?'

"I said, 'Until now you've been talking to your own people. You've been wonderfully successful. You can always start a current running between you. You tried to do that today.'

" 'Yes, I did and I failed. I know that. But people are people, with all their differences. They respond to honesty and friendship. I gave both today. I gave with all my heart, but they were deaf to me. You haven't explained that. Why?'

"I said, 'I'm not sure I can make you see this, but if I had been a Winderese woman this morning I would have been angry and I would have thought you were a hypocrite. You would be a young woman, a foreigner, who insulted my King by ignoring him and insulted me through him. You tried to come between us and, in doing that, you were contemptuous of us both. You were full of new love for us, but it was self-serving. You wanted to buy our ships and our men, and when the ships were sunk and the men were dead nothing would have changed. And you were worse than the Islandian kings before you who wanted the same things because you were a beautiful woman and you traded on that.' "

Tenira finished with her face averted, looking down at the water far below, her hands locked tight on the stones in front of her. I drew a breath and said, "Poor, dear Tenira. What got into you?"

"I don't know. She goaded me and I had to. I started speaking and that's what I said. I love her and I'm afraid for her. And of her."

"How did she take it?"

"I thought she was going to strike me. She did once or twice when she was a girl. But of course she didn't. She said, 'You know me and you don't believe that of me. They don't know me and so they may.' The trouble is that since this morning I do believe that of her, but not that she believes it of herself."

"Perhaps now she does."

Tenira shook her head. "The Queen still overrides everything and can do anything. The Queen may admit a tactical mistake to herself, but Alwina hasn't done anything bad."

Tor's dinner was not a long one and it did not suffer from constraint as he was afraid it would. Alwina was astonishing. She had had no mortifying morning. She had not talked to Tenira in shock and disarray. She was gay, unforced, attentive, and appreciative. Toward Tor she was respectfully friendly, and casually deferential toward Attana. There was no shadow of reserve or flicker of second thought. When called on, she made a graceful little talk brimming with curiosity and humor and without any theme of mission. She ended looking forward eagerly to whatever Tor had planned for tomorrow.

In his turn, and against my safety advice, Tor outlined possible programs for the next day and several others. In doing so he gave me the answer he had promised for this evening. Diverging for a bit on the subject of Islandia House, he said the building had once been a headquarters for noble Catholic converts and had escheated to the Crown after the collapse of the League. In recent years it had stood vacant for the most part, or presumably so.

"From the Queen and her party I have had good reports of the staff we provided to make the house livable and them comfortable, but those excellent staff members did fail to discover that the place already had a tenant. Early this morning a party of our joint special force, led by Nyall on instructions from Isla Frare, inspected the house before the Queen's arrival and found a modest home inside a large closet down in the disused root cellar. I understand the searchers were guided through the last few yards solely by their well-trained noses. The resident, probably not overly alert in the circumstances, carelessly left his smell behind and he may miss it. No doubt the quantities of soap and hot water since have discouraged him from returning for it. We would like him to know, however, that we will gladly give him back his blankets — now immoderately clean — if he will call on Isla Frare at the joint force barracks." There was my release for my eight men. Tor's invention did not strike me as hilariously funny, but he told it well enough for laughter and he completely robbed the incident of shock. I was pleased with it.

After that chancy first day, things settled down and, at least on the surface, the visit began to follow the pattern Tor and I had worked out for it — water and land trips, inspections, sightseeing, and a few special ceremonies. Alwina entirely gave up the effort to win the people by direct appeal and she did this without saying anything or consulting anyone. She merely turned around quietly in her tracks. Wherever she went she was interested and friendly, she always subordinated herself to Tor and accepted his statements. She rarely spoke directly to a Winderese in public until after Tor had opened a conversation. Nyall, who observed her closely and grew to like her a lot, said to me, "What you see mostly is a charming, natural, controlled person. You have to look sharp to see anything else, but there is another person there, too. When nothing is happening, when people are letting their attention wander all over the landscape, then she looks at Tor in a different way, as if she were trying to find something in him or force something into him." I saw the intensity, too, and also an uncertainty that reminded me of the girl Cabing had first taken me to see.

Just as Alwina had predicted, I had no more trouble with Trant. He kept his bargain loyally and cheerfully and we got along well. His troops were good, and Nyall and I depended on them for the things he and they could do. Sissona was another matter. There was no bargain I could make with her and, if there had been, she wouldn't have kept it. In her world, where one domestic order of things constituted rightness, the terms of external agreements had no standing. An outside, semi-independent power with influence in the Household was not to be tolerated. It must be brought inside and housebroken. She did her best to have my invitation to Islandia House changed into orders to take up residence. Failing in this, she did succeed in preventing me from seeing much of the Queen except in the strict line of duty. I couldn't resent all this as much as I would have liked because Tenira kept me aware that my opinion of Sissona's henyard tyranny was not exactly unbiased.

For all my freedom, however, and valuable as it was, Nyall and I came no nearer to the assassins perhaps because we stayed too close to Winder town and looked too intensely there. I don't believe I ever really expected to find them, but there was a time before Alwina's arrival when Nyall thought he could. If anything positive was to be done about the killers, he was the one to do it, as he frequently declared, but they vanished into a realm of social and geographical emptiness where his probes heard nothing and touched nothing. To disappear in this way, he finally admitted, was not too difficult provided they had at least one native accomplice in a position to keep them informed. After the Queen reached Winder, of course, all our strength and ingenuity were needed for defense.

That is not to say we did not gather a quantity of facts and rumors. Those came in all shapes and sizes and from all directions, from Tor's court, from Alwina's establishment, from the town, the waterfront, the ships in harbor, from our own men on duty and off, not to mention the courier vessels from Cabing, which now resumed service. One of the most popular morsels in a gaudy way was an apparently true story to the effect that Kilikash had declared his intention to put Alwina in his harem as his fruit of victory and personal spoil of war. As Bodwin said, that lurid fantasy stimulated "many dour minds to delighted heights of vengeful jealousy."

As a rule, Nyall and I did not both go along with Tor and Alwina on the almost daily expeditions. One of us went in charge of the security detachment and the other stayed behind to make sure nobody set up a trap or an ambush behind our backs. After our close brush with both success and disaster on the first morning, we were sharply conscious of the need to look in every direction at once. Even so, there were times between formal occasions, or around their edges, when Nyall or I could leave things in the hands of the other and take a few private hours without feeling uneasy about it. Alwina herself did not take her entire entourage on all her outings and sometimes, for reasons she did not disclose, left them all at home.

Early on the morning after Tor's dinner, Tenira and I took a small boat and sailed up the south arm of the bay on the Sea Island side. Before long we saw a small cove with a protecting point hooked part way around it. It looked attractive and self-contained, so we turned in and found a narrow, white sand beach with a stand of naturally spaced pine trees beginning at its back edge. Here, in some shelter, the trees grew taller and straighter than on the windward shores. We beached the boat and waded for a while in the cold, clear water and then walked into the woods over the needle-covered ground. Well inland from the beach, in the barred and scattered sunlight at the base of a long rock, we saw a damp spot and a tiny film of water against the stone. We began to dig there with our bare hands, laughing as we got dirtier, piling the soft soil and the small stones in a rough semicircle. When we had a deep, brown mud puddle between us, we stood up and smiled at each other and then looked back down at our excavation. We didn't have much time left before joining Alwina's ride to the grazing country, but we told each other this was a spring we had discovered, and promised to come back. A few days later we did and found the water settled, sweet and rising up from the bottom between the ground and the rock. We didn't tell anyone about the place and went there whenever we could.

Few of the Queen's party ever came to the barracks except Bodwin, but he found it the first day and came back often. I came to enjoy him more than I expected and was glad to see him whenever he turned up. Somewhat surprisingly the men liked him, even though he made no attempt to speak their language. Some qualities in his airy manner, his startling ambiguity, and his habitual irreverence combined to appeal to them.

About halfway through the Queen's stay, on a day of rest for all contestants, Bodwin ambled into my cramped quarters, turned in the doorway, and stood looking at the jetty where the *Earne* lay. "Cousin," he asked, "is that the only ship in the Islandian Navy?"

"No," I said, "not quite."

"I've never been on her, or anything like her. Is it permitted for me to board her?"

I led him down the jetty and across the gangway. Once aboard he inspected the ship and asked questions with a sharp, quizzical interest. Then he walked to the afterdeck and stood leaning back against the stern rail, where he could see the whole vessel and anyone on deck at a glance. "Tied up in Winder," he said. "Would you like to have her at sea?"

"Yes," I said, "but that's only a professionally sentimental answer because you raised the subject. I haven't been dreaming of keen winds and salt spray. The ship will be just as good at sea another time."

"I take it this is a good ship."

"Yes. Very good."

"Better than anything Winder has?"

"Somewhat."

"A pity there aren't more like her."

"Well, Cousin," I said, "she's better in the sense that my sword, which I had made for myself, is more nicely balanced to my hand than that sentry's sword, which the Navy gave him, is to his. Mine may kill a little easier, but no deader."

"You mean if we built as many ships as Winder, ours would be no better than theirs?"

"No. Ours wouldn't be as good. Nowhere near as good. Winderese ships are excellent. All of them. We'd have to spread our skilled shipwrights so thin we'd be lucky if our boats didn't capsize in harbor."

Bodwin nodded as though I had confirmed something for him, not as though I had told him something. "Then that part of things is solid. I wasn't quite certain. Cousin, have you heard of any talks between Alwina and Tor? Anything about an agreement to alleviate the intolerable grievances of this long-suffering and oppressed people?"

"No," I said, "but then I wouldn't necessarily. I'm not on the direct route for that stuff. Not anymore."

"Don't feel sorry for yourself, Cousin. Neither is anybody else. Besides, there haven't been any talks. But there is one thing for which you're in a splendid position. Is Alwina winning the people?"

"She's given up the appearance of trying," I said, "and she's better off for it. But winning them? Not from what I hear. Now they think she's pretty and nice and silly. She does foolish things, but she's only a girl and she does have sense enough to be courteous when she thinks about it. But her advisers are bad."

"How about Tor?"

I turned around to look back over the harbor and to see his face without having to keep swinging my head. "You mean how are the new tactics working on him? I don't know. As a man I suspect he's becoming increasingly cut up and tender. I imagine the King disapproves of that."

He glanced at my face and then turned his gaze back to the masts and the bare rigging. With his round, blue eyes, smooth face, and fine, light hair waving in the wind, he looked simultaneously very young and very old, as newborn babies often do. "Tor the man is going to be attacked from the rear," he said. "This afternoon — in fact just about now — Sissona is paying an informal call on Tor's mother. It's all her own idea. She so much admires Attana and wants to take the opportunity to know her better. She's been thinking about it and they do have so much in common. It would be a pity. After the ice has been broken and the proper things have been talked about and put back in their proper places and the cakes have been eaten and the lips have been dabbed for crumbs the right number of times — after all that Sissona will begin to reminisce about Alwina. Such a dear, sweet child always. So good-natured and loving, but a handful at times of course. Never for long though. So responsive and always came right out of her tempers and moods. Hard to believe she's Queen now. Things so different and, yes, so difficult. Not easy to find one's new place. But one thing mercifully didn't change. Alwina couldn't close her heart to Sissona. Not after all these years. Still the girl under the Queen. Some things didn't change. There was tenderness and love in Alwina, Sissona knew, even if Alwina wasn't sure of it. This was springing up in the child touched to life by Attana's son. Sissona knew this because she could read Alwina's feelings so well, so much better than she could. She so hoped for the child's happiness. She had no way of guessing, of course, and it was just her hope, her own hope. Wonderful things did happen. Treaties and clauses were so sad to think about in connection with young people. They surely deserved that much of their own. But of course one never knew and it was such a temptation to run on like this."

I stood staring at Bodwin after he finished his grisly parody. "Does the Queen know about this?" He shook his head and shrugged, indicating either that he didn't know or wouldn't say. "How do you know?" Another shake of the head, advising me not to ask foolish questions.

"Why are you telling me?"

"That's more sensible. To keep you from being taken by surprise," he said. "I'm not representing anyone, you should be relieved to know. Just my own sense of fitness. I respect it more than I do Sissona's. I'm a courtier, an observer, perhaps an interpreter, and I'm lucky enough to know I have the reign of a great Queen to observe. I live by my political senses, which are far better developed than yours, Cousin, although I admit yours are more than rudimentary. I'm just as horrified at Sissona as you are. I don't share the fashionable notion about Winder that it's cruelly abused and full of loving folk who only want a little consideration. They're a surly lot. They have the best of the arrangement. If they're poor, it's because they're feckless. I admit that doesn't help matters and I agree the only solution is to bring them all the way into the nation, obligations, privileges, and all, and then sort things out. Poor malicious Sissona. She would have one family with two inheritances ruling two adjacent kingdoms with no common citizenship and different laws. She doesn't care about Tor, but she thinks that way Alwina won't have to yield anything. Well, that's a very large, nasty cat Sissona has just stuffed in the bag along with the others there. Who knows? It might just stay there and do nothing. But if it comes out, it's likely to be in a bad temper." He smiled and spread his hands. "I know I'm out of character. Being a busybody. And such moral indignation! Still, to leave you in ignorance . . . A serious mistake."

"Yes, it could have been," I said mildly, not sure exactly how his warning to me would help matters and more than a little startled by his elaborate defensiveness. It occurred to me that he might be in love with Alwina himself and the thought gave me a quick, warm sympathy for him. "I see I've underestimated Sissona," I said. "I thought her capacities for unpleasantness were much more passive."

Bodwin declined to be drawn in that direction. He started walking toward the dock and changed the subject. "The Queen talks of nothing but the boar hunt Tor has arranged. Are there really such animals here? I hoped they were mythological."

Bodwin of course knew perfectly well there were boars in Winder, but most of the Queen's party did not. In fact many didn't know what boars looked like or even what kind of animal they were. As Bodwin wished, they might as well have been mythological. At Islandia House, where few people had the initiative to incur Sissona's displeasure by going among the Winderese and learning things for themselves, enthusiasm for hunting boars was high among those who thought the sport was conducted on horseback, and low among those who feared they might have to walk. A few who thought boars flew kept talking about hawks and falcons. The hunt was planned for two days before the Queen's departure, and speculation about it grew more imaginative as the last inspections, trips, and ceremonies were ticked off the list. The only event after the hunt was a return dinner Alwina planned for Tor.

With time to ourselves on the day before the hunt, Tenira and I sailed out to the cove, our private refuge, with a hamper of food and a skin of wine. Walking back into the woods we found animal tracks around the spring and a few brown pine needles floating on its clear surface, but nothing had fouled it or harmed it in our absence. Holding her hair away from her face, Tenira knelt by the rock and drank from the pool.

As we walked from the shade of the woods to the sparkling beach once more, I told her Bodwin's tale of Sissona's call on Attana. She listened with a mixture of amusement and regret, but not of shock. "That may have happened," she said. "It's quite possible. I don't know that it did — and I wouldn't because my advice is never asked beforehand. She knows what I would say. I'm there to chasten and forgive her afterward."

"You're referring to Alwina?"

"Of course. Sissona did it — and probably with pleasure. And I'm sure she thought of the way to do it. But she didn't act on her own. And it wasn't her idea. She would like it when she heard it, but she doesn't think that far beyond her own spider's web."

"Bodwin laid it all to Sissona."

"That was the only way he could tell you, Frare. You must have seen that. He's not as cynical as he lets on, and it embarrasses him to show how intense his loyalty is. He idolizes Alwina. He can't bear to have her tarnish herself. Or what he thinks is tarnishing herself. It's better to make her be misled or hoodwinked or taken advantage of. Anyway, you didn't believe him about that?"

"No," I admitted. "I couldn't. But what about you? You didn't know this, but you're not surprised or upset."

She sighed and sat on the side of the boat, looking down at her bare feet in the sand. "It's too late for that. I don't like it. I wish it weren't so. A scheme like that is unworthy of either side of her — the Queen or the woman. It's petty. And I agree with Bodwin that it may be very dangerous. But I'm not surprised. It's too natural after all the pressure she's been under. I've seen it coming. Or something like it." She left the boat, came toward me, and took my hand. "I think you're feeling I should go and face her with it. Aren't you?"

"No," I said, "I'm not," and took her in my arms and kissed her.

115

"Thank you," she said. "That was nice. But I think you were, because I was wondering about it myself." Side by side, each with an arm around the other's waist, we walked slowly down the beach, following the edge of the water, our toes digging into the wet sand. "Have you thought about confronting her yourself? Or about Bodwin doing it?"

"Yes, I have. Everything else aside, Bodwin couldn't do it. As I guessed and you made clear, it's emotionally impossible for him. And me? Well, in the first place it wouldn't work. As a person or an officer I don't matter enough to Alwina. My opinion doesn't count for anything. Well, then, should I do it anyway? Does it affect my loyalty? Am I unable to go on serving? Do I have a larger responsibility I have to demonstrate? I don't think so. What she's doing isn't heinous. I think it's wrong. Like you, I don't like it. I don't respect her for it. But it stays within limits. I can still feel it's on her conscience, not mine. I don't have to make myself a public prig about it."

"Do you suppose my situation is any different?"

We swung around and headed back for the boat with her on the down side. "I don't know," I said. "Tell me."

"Then, yes, my situation is different. There can't be any question of loyalty for me because I love her and that changes everything. Everything except self-respect. I'll have to talk to her sometime. She'll talk to me if I don't and maybe this time she'll send me away. I've told you she consults her conscience — that's me — afterward. And this is already afterward. Maybe Attana will keep Bodwin's tiger in the bag, but I can hardly believe that."

As we opened the hamper and poured wine, we talked about going back to Islandia within a few days and what was likely to happen then. I said I thought I would probably sail the *Earne* straight back to The City, but I hadn't any orders yet and didn't know whether Alwina expected to go with me. Tenira said she thought Alwina probably wouldn't, that she would stick with her party and go back as she had come, seeing more villages on the way.

We weren't in a solemn mood. This was holiday, the food was good, and the weather enough to make anyone joyous, but we kept drifting away from light and casual things back to serious ones. The vague but imminent campaign against Kilikash — no one at Islandia House was calling it war — concerned us too much to ignore. Also the matter of our own relationship to each other — not explored or defined and about which there might have been no urgency in other circumstances — stood now ambivalently in front of us, part promise and part threat. The letters we had exchanged by courier, and our mostly public meetings since, had established a kind of intimacy between us that was genuine but unpredictably limited. More simply, I thought I was falling in love with her — and when you realize that much you are already there — but I kept stumbling over the evidence that I presumed to know her better than I did.

"We won't finish Kilikash in one try," I said. "Or two. Or three. We haven't anything to do it with. If Kilikash is serious, he has a good chance of finishing us. Cabing says this himself, but I'm not sure he feels it in his bones. Tor does know it. Do you think the Queen does?"

"She doesn't say so to me. Nor to any of the rest of us. She doesn't talk in terms of fighting. Just about making the borders safe. And clearing the coasts. I think she knows, but she hasn't any reality to measure by." She looked up at me over her wine cup. "What will you be doing, Frare? Living on your ship for years and years?"

I smiled and shook my head. "It may not be my ship. I only have it as a loan. Tor and Lamas will find plenty for me to do, but to tell the truth there aren't any plans. Just Tor's and

Alwina's unmeeting wishes and boar hunts. You've said two or three times that you might be leaving Alwina. Or that she might send you away. Do you mean that?"

"Yes. All that is coming to an end, one way or another. It's no longer good for Alwina or for me. I've said this. She uses me as a kind of confessional device for her conscience. My disapproval was a guide once, but not anymore. And it shouldn't be. She tells me I'm not her teacher any longer. And yet she comes to me for criticism so she can have the illusion of both penance and absolution. I don't like that. She'd be better off alone with Om." She smiled and tossed a crust of bread toward a gull off the beach. "She doesn't really care for that, but it's beginning to be more attractive than the pretense that I'm her better self. What she hears as my constant moralizing I know is furiously irritating."

"So what will you do?"

"I'd like to go back to Reeves while there's time. I haven't seen my father and mother since I was a girl myself. They aren't young anymore. I think they may have had doubts when I accepted the King's offer. I don't regret it now, but I'd like to see them again, and all the others, and the country. It was nice being a girl there. You could talk to your friends about what came into your head. You didn't have to think out your words ahead of time. And there were dogs and cats and cows who had important things to say. I don't mean I could get any of it back — just that it would be nice to see where it all was once."

As she spoke, I watched the play of feeling on her long, lovely face, the passage of memories and their connected emotions from inside to outside as they first showed themselves in her eyes and then took on expression around her mouth. This was a story of herself without defenses. "I understand very well," I said. "Do you want to stay there?"

She was silent a long moment and then answered, "No."

I knew how difficult it was for her to say that. She had just renounced the court. Now she was cutting herself off from home and family, from the powerful, growing cult of customary virtues. These were her two anchors in life and she was admitting she belonged nowhere. Few men would willingly put themselves in that position. For a woman to do it required the courage of an extraordinary sense of identity. It also ensured that what I now meant to do must come without ease or grace.

"I've never told the Queen," I said, "but I don't want to go home to live either. Not that there's anything wrong with the province of Niven. It's me." I filled my cup and sat down on dry sand. "Well, all this leaves you no reasonable excuse, except one, not to accept me. I've been thinking about asking you for a week now. You can't be surprised. It must be showing all over me. What do you say?"

"Say? What is the reasonable excuse?"

"That you don't love me."

"Did you just ask me to marry you?"

"I thought so."

"Oh. Then ask me again. Clearly this time."

"Will you marry me?"

She knelt down beside me and put her hands on my shoulders. "Before I agree to this, I want to ask you some questions. I need to be sure of some things. You are offering me a virtuous marriage?"

"Whatever that is," I said, puzzled. There was an odd light in her eyes.

"You are a staid and placid man, I've observed."

"Is that what I seem?"

"Of course," she said. "What else? I know I don't arouse *apia* in men. I try not to, but one can never be sure. We would have a life of pure *ania*, wouldn't we?"

"That isn't my idea," I said. "You do us both an injustice.

119

You don't recognize what you see. I don't know what pure *ania* is, but there's been a lot of not so pure lust staring at you since Alwina's dinner. Is that what you wanted to know?"

"Hold out your hand," she told me. I did and she took it in both of hers. "Steady as a rock," she said. "Not a tremor. There's no passion in you."

"You're looking for it in the wrong place," I said.

She stood up, ran her hand back over her hair, walked slowly along the beach, and then turned into the woods. Feeling very unsure of what was happening to us, I got up myself and finished my cup of wine deliberately. I saw only two things clearly — that I must not run after her and that we must not stay physically separated in this emotional labyrinth. Following her into the woods I found her by the spring as I expected, staring down into it. I put my arm around her shoulder and she moved closer to me.

"I offended you, didn't I," she said. "I had to find out if you asked me out of kindness because you thought I was a derelict."

"I see," I said. "That was silly. There's no way of finding that out by asking. You have to make a judgment of me."

"I know."

"You didn't offend me," I said. "You confused me. And you frightened me."

"It's not that important now. I'd really already judged." And then at a tangent. "Alwina frightens *me*. I'm afraid of that farewell dinner for Tor." She stooped down, dipped her forefinger in the sweet water, and then stood up. "We may never come here again."

"That's a long time."

"Maybe not so long." She shook her head, looked around through the grove and then back down at the spring. "This is nicer than Reeves or Niven. And we did make this place. It would be hard to do any better."

120

Without saying anything I picked her up and carried her a few paces aside to a spot where the ground was firm and dry and where a light breeze eddied in from the bay. As I set her down and then lay down beside her, she placed her hands on either side of my face and kissed me. Leaving the words *apia* and *ania* on the threshold along with our temporal belongings, we found our way by degrees into the timeless room of self-transcendence. When we emerged, shaken and disoriented, we resumed our clothes and walked down to the beach hand in hand without once touching the ground.

On the sail back to Winder across a freshening breeze that often splashed us with spray, I asked how many of the Queen's party were actually going on the hunt in the morning. "Everyone but Sissona and Derek," she said. "They think they have to get things ready for Tor's dinner. That wretched idea of Alwina's!"

"Why does it worry you so much?" I asked. "Is it just one too many dinners? Or is there something particular about it?"

"I don't really know," she said. "I suspect Alwina may use it for another of her dramatic tricks. But that doesn't explain it."

WHEN I ARRIVED at the barracks in midafternoon, I found the place swirling with activity and Nyall relieved to see me. Outside, a courier boat from The City was just tying up at the wharf while, inside, an excited messenger from Trant was talking excitedly about help for Islandia House.

After Nyall and I had calmed the messenger enough to speak, he remembered that he knew nothing at all himself but that he did have a note from Trant. This informed me circumspectly that there had been trouble within the kitchen staff, that Trant had everything in hand but that he would appreciate advice on what to do next because the people involved were Winderese. At the same time, I welcomed the courier officer and received dispatches from him for the Queen and for me. Then I summoned Nicking, gave him the dispatches for the Queen, and told him to deliver them, consult with Trant about his crisis, and report back. "Go on foot up the cliff stairs," I told him. "It's quicker."

It took me most of an hour to read Cabing's sobering budget of news, and only when I finished it did I realize Nicking hadn't come back yet. I was still locking the papers away when he hurried in and said, "I'm sorry to be so long, Isla Frare. I was kept waiting while arrangements were made. There is to be a meeting at Tor's house right away. You and Nyall are expected to be there. I was to tell you it will deal with the new dispatches and Trant's trouble."

"What is Trant's trouble?"

"I'm not sure. As I said, I spent my time waiting. Someone in the kitchen seems to have knifed someone else. Sissona told the Queen and the thing was out of Trant's hands before I got there."

Nyall and I climbed the hundreds of steps quickly, not wasting our breath in talk, and arrived at the same time as a sizable group from Islandia House. This included several of Trant's men shepherding two prisoners, a woman and a man with a bandaged shoulder. The soldiers took their charges on to the stables in the back. The rest of us — Alwina, Sissona, Trant, Nyall, and I — went in and took places around the large table at which Tor was already sitting. I had the feeling he was angry, but I may have misread him for his face was calm and so was his voice when he said, "Let's start with the episode in the kitchen. Trant, will you tell us briefly what happened? Just the facts."

Trant was admirably concise. "Conyer is a cook. He was alone in the kitchen starting the preparation of a special dish for the banquet day after tomorrow. Kirila — also a cook — came into the kitchen just then and saw him take out of his pocket a small pouch, which he began to untie. She asked him what he was doing. He didn't answer. She came to him and seized his arm. He struck her and pushed her away. She screamed, picked up a meat knife, and stabbed him. Her scream brought others into the kitchen at once."

"The dish he was making is complicated," Sissona said. "It must be done in several stages and it takes at least two full days. Her Majesty requested it, and it was intended only for her and King Tor."

"Conyer," Tor said, looking at his own lieutenant. "Nyall, you should know something about him."

"I do," Nyall said. "I chose him and gave him a strong recommendation. He has cooked in this house, Tor, for you and your mother. He is about fifty, not married, and has never been strong. His father is dead. He lives with his mother on a farm belonging to his father's family a mile or so outside town. In ordinary times he cooks for the family clan. It is a close-knit group, even in our terms, and is intensely loyal to Winder, but is known for its approval of Islandia. The other men are farmers when they're not shipwrights or sailors. When I talked to Conyer I found him proud of his cooking skill, but as though he was grateful for it. In other respects he seemed to me an unworldly and innocent man. The relatives I talked with had the same opinion of him."

"We don't *know* he was poisoning the food," Alwina said.

Sissona sniffed. "Of course he was. That dish requires nothing from a secret pouch. Not at any point."

"Trant," Nyall said, "did you manage to save that pouch? May I see it, please?"

Trant shifted his square shoulders and from an inner pocket produced a small cloth bag secured by a knotted drawstring. "I don't know what this is. There hasn't been time to try it on an animal." He pushed the bag carefully across the table.

"Thank you." Nyall undid the knot gently with his long, bony fingers, loosened the top of the bag, and held it to his nose. Then he placed it back on the table and spread it wide, exposing a mound of dark, brownish powder. With the point of his dagger — the same one he wore in to the Council meeting — he delicately isolated a number of individual grains and studied them. Finally, he reclosed the sack and pulled the drawstring.

"More than half of that," he said, "is the dried, powdered inside bark of the Dakob tree. That gives it its smell. By itself the bark is good for some fevers and increases the heartbeat. The rest I think is a mixture of dried and ground-up insects and beetles. I've seen one or two other concoctions like this, and I believe what Conyer had is a love philter."

124

Sissona sniffed again, but Trant exclaimed, "That's what the cook said it was!"

The Queen leaned forward with her elbows on the table and her chin cupped in her hands, looking at the pouch. "What do love philters do?" she asked. "I used to hear of them when I was a child. Not from Sissona. I thought they were old wives' tales. Or rather old wives' magic, for I never doubted they existed."

"They do not create love, Your Majesty," Nyall said dryly. "Often they do nothing at all. When they do work, they produce bodily manifestations of the grossest kind of *apia*. They irritate and stimulate the body far beyond its capacity. They bring about a state of physical excitement that can last for a long time and become exceedingly painful. Philters are not poisons in the sense Sissona means, but people can die from them."

Silence followed this explanation until Tor broke it, saying, "Let us see the woman."

Kirila was thin and not at all pretty. About thirty-five, she had straight, brown hair and large, frightened black eyes always moving. She was one of those people who have never had a complexion, only a soiled, tan monochrome. She sat at the table with her shoulders gathered around her as though she were cold, but in reality just to keep from trembling. She told us, in more detail but taking much longer to do it, exactly what we had already heard from Trant. But what did come through in addition was her hysterical compulsion to protect Alwina, more accurately Alwina's food, at whatever cost to herself.

At the end, Tor thanked her with gentle kindness and told her she might go. As Kirila rose and paused uncertainly, Alwina hurried around the table and threw her arm around the older woman's shoulders. "I hope you will stay and cook for

125

me," she said. "What you did was brave and quick. I think you saved my life. I am very grateful." Slowly, in return, Kirila gave her a smile that made up for all the prettiness she didn't have.

"Now," Tor said, "there is Conyer. Trant, will you get him?"

While Trant was away, I felt a vague uneasiness fluttering around the edges of consciousness, as though things were happening in the wrong order or growing out of proportion. I remembered having the same sensation when Tenira was talking about Alwina's dinner for Tor, the subject of all this disturbance now. The feeling did not define itself or persist, however, and I forgot about it when Conyer entered the room. He was a medium-sized man with thin brown hair and a pleasant, rather melancholy looking face dominated by a large nose. Standing between two of Trant's well set-up men, he looked shabby and frail. There was blood showing through the bandage on his shoulder and, although he didn't seem to be in pain, his face was pale and drained. With an abrupt gesture of his hand, Tor turned the questioning over to Nyall.

"Tell us, Conyer, why did you try to do this? What did you want to do?"

"I meant no harm," Conyer said in a quiet, light voice. "I wanted only good to happen. Good would have happened. Maybe it will happen yet."

"Explain that to us, Conyer."

"I have always loved Winder, my country," Conyer said, "but I haven't hated Islandia. It is a good place. I like it. It is necessary to us. Whenever I used to cook in this house, I admired King Tor and his mother very much and I still do. How handsome they are! How good they are! Then I went to cook for the Queen and I saw how beautiful she is! How good she is! Right away I knew what needed to happen. King Tor and the Queen must fall in love and marry. Then all of us and all the Islandians will be the same. We will be each other and all our troubles will be over. So when I found I was to make something nice just for King Tor and the Queen, then I knew I must do this."

Nyall touched the bag on the table and asked, "This is a love philter?"

"Yes, that is what it is. I've said so."

"How did you learn how to make it?"

"I don't know how to make it."

"You don't? Then how did you get it?"

"I asked my mother. I thought maybe she could make it. She agreed with me, but she didn't know how either. She said she would get it from a friend and she did."

"Who is the friend?"

"My aunt. My father's sister."

"Who else did you talk to about this plan?"

"No one at all. There was no need."

"Who suggested it to you in the first place?"

"Suggested it to me? It is my thought. It came to me because of what I know and what I do. It comes from my work and my heart. No one else could think of it."

Nyall leaned back in his chair at that and Tor said, "I think that's as far as we're going to get. I'm afraid I believe his story, but that is not proof and, in any case, it doesn't tell us whether what is in that sack is poison, philter — or nothing. We could use an animal, as Trant suggested, but if I were the animal, I would object. There is, however, one sensible thing to do." He walked the full length of the room to a sideboard and poured water from a pottery pitcher into a silver goblet. Returning, he placed the goblet in front of Nyall and said, "Use this."

Nyall undid the pouch once more and poured approximately half the powder into the goblet where it floated on the water. He stirred it in with his dagger, the steel blade scraping and scratching against the silver. Then he stood and turned toward Conyer with the cup in his hand. Conyer did not appear frightened, but neither did he seem to understand the situation, looking ready to weep from disappointment. "But that is not for me!" he cried out. When Nyall assured him it was, he tried to raise his good arm to take the goblet, but Nyall shook his head at the soldier on that side and himself pressed the rim to Conyer's mouth, tilting upward. Conyer swallowed and swallowed, dribbling from the corners of his mouth, his Adam's apple dancing erratically to accommodate the flow he did not control. Then Nyall set down the empty cup and we all stared at the wispy, wounded man as though we expected something dreadful or astonishing to happen to him on the spot. When nothing did, Tor nodded and the soldiers took him out.

As the footsteps faded away, Alwina looked right and left at her two chiefs of Household and said, "Sissona, I don't need to keep you any longer. Thank you for your help. Trant, I'd be grateful if you would go and watch over Conyer. I'd like to know what happens."

Trant marched briskly toward the door and then we waited while Sissona gathered herself together and followed him. Tor rose to escort her and close the door behind her. "Poor Sissona," Alwina said. "She would so much have liked to stay. Tor, everyone here, myself included, has behaved as though I were the only target of Conyer's dangerous affections. I apologize for that."

"No need," Tor said. "I wasn't aware of it. And anyway it's understandable. What is the rest of your business?"

"The dispatches that just came in," she told him. "You saw the boat arrive. The news is bad. Frare, I assume you've read Cabing's report. Will you set out the situation for all of us?"

"I'll try, Your Majesty," I said. "All the things — almost everything — Cabing writes about could be seen coming before you and I left The City, Tor. They didn't look good then. They look a lot worse now, partly because they're on top of us and not in the future and also because they're more severe than anyone expected. The first problem is recruiting. That's not going well. Cabing knew it would be slow during the spring, the months of planting and cultivating. But that's over now, or nearly over, in most places, and the men still aren't coming out, except in Lorria province. I think I know what the trouble is, but perhaps you should put a name to it, Your Majesty."

"All right," she said. "It's the provincial Islar, some of the bellwethers. They're sulky and skeptical. They're sitting down and waiting and doing nothing. Lorria is the proof. That Isla is working. I can't do anything about the rest of them until I get back to The City. Then I will. Go on, Frare."

"Then there's Kilikash in Mobono. At a conservative count he has between four hundred and four hundred-fifty galleys ready now. That's a third again as many as we anticipated. Cabing says he can invade the east coast any time he chooses and will almost certainly pick Miltain." I paused and looked from Alwina to Tor. "Cabing isn't a seaman. I don't doubt Kilikash has the ships Cabing says he has, and probably the troops, but I suspect he may not be too well off for crews. He doesn't use slaves. It takes time to train oarsmen and the ones we've seen set a high standard."

"Yes," Tor agreed, "they're good. Does Cabing's estimate say anything about what types of ships Kilikash has?"

"No, nothing at all. From what I knew at the time I left, my guess is that his regular ships are biremes. He'll use a lot of singles for scouting and he'll have triremes as squadron leaders. That means three men to one vertical set of oars on a bireme and six on a trireme. A lot of oarsmen. I think he has more difficulty than Cabing allows and I'm inclined to modify Cabing on timing. Right now, I think Kilikash could raid anywhere in great strength, but I don't believe he'll be ready for invasion, or a major sea battle, for a while yet. Say the end of summer or early fall."

"Very likely," Tor said, "but that's not so far away now. Anything else troubling us?"

I felt the sardonic edge of his question, but I didn't honor it, saying plainly, "Yes, the Mora Pass is open now and the tribes are coming through, setting up camps in the upper Frays. From there they're raiding south into the valleys, hitting closer to Reeves each time. They're Demiji, of course, but this time they're working for Kilikash and they're staying on our side of the mountains. They won't cross back before snow comes and maybe not then."

"What's the matter with the Isla of Islandia province?" Tor asked. "Is he one of the sulky ones?"

"That's Strang," Alwina said. "He's one of the worst. Fat and lazy and likes to sit in Reeves and call for help."

"When winter sets in," Tor said, "and you can trust the snow, it shouldn't be impossible for a picked party to fortify the pass and hold it."

"I suggested just that to Strang," Alwina said. "He told me it was unheard of and wondered why I laughed at him. That's for next year — if we're still here next year. Now I've got to put some kind of force there and get patrols into the Frays."

Tor walked slowly to the sideboard once more, poured wine into three goblets, and brought them back to the table. Leaving his own untouched for the time being, he began to pace from spot to spot in a seemingly random way while he spoke. "So now," he said, "you have given me the latest information. You've had Frare present it so I won't think it's overstated. Good enough. I accept the facts much as given. In general, and to a certain extent in particular, I know, of course, what you want. But on what basis? I think you cannot blame me too much if I insist I am at a total loss about everything. Your promise to the Council and the Assembly, your dinner at Alwin House, the reasons you announced for coming here — all these led me to expect a more serious and generous approach to our countries' troubles with each other than anything I've heard. Your opening remarks to my people were not happy. Since then you've been a charming guest, but I've gained nothing but confusion from you directly or indirectly. So what groundwork are we on now? The old one? A new one? A limited one? One that settles nothing? Or one that is general and just? I hope you will be clear about this."

Alwina set her wine to one side and leaned back in her chair, her eyes following Tor as he walked. "I came to Winder determined to make a settlement. I still am and I will be until it is done. My ideas are more generous and just than you allow now and we may well be able to agree before I leave. I hope so, but that is a chance neither of us can take. In the horrible weeks when the throne was at stake, I admit I didn't see clearly enough how brutally sharp the Karain danger is. I wasn't alone in that." She raised her hands from her lap, her fists clenched. "Now I don't dare leave here without a military agreement with you! And you don't dare let me go without one! If we fall, you know what terms you'll get from the panther. So what I'm proposing is not the old arrangement nor a new general one. It's special and specific, to serve us both only as long as it has to. Is that clear enough?"

Tor stopped walking and stood in back of his chair. "Perhaps it is," he said. "This then will be an alliance in which I appear only as King of Winder, not as an Isla of Islandia. Under my command, Winder will undertake the naval defense of both countries in return for the funds to make up all the difference between Winder's own contribution and what is necessary. I will have at my disposal all Islandian ships and crews."

"Yes to the funds and the ships," she said. "As to command, you will be Cabing's equal."

"No," Tor said, "that won't do. I'll be Cabing's equal as between him and me, but I'm your ally and not your subject. I'll consult with you, listen to advice, and plan according to our joint strategy, but I won't take orders from you. These are Winder's ships and men. They'll fight for both of us, but you won't control them."

Alwina shaded her angry eyes with her hand as he was speaking and sat on in silence after he had finished. Finally, she looked up and said flatly, "Very well. Let it be that way."

Tor swung his chair out and sat down alongside the table, saying, "Then that takes care of principle. Now what do you have in mind to *do*?"

She bent forward, hands palm down on the table. "For now we can get along with the Demiji in the Frays. For a while we can even make a virtue out of poor recruiting by doing a better job of training. We can put up with these things provided — only provided — we can handle Kilikash at sea. We must face him there. That is the only course we have. Or do you see another?"

"Yes," he said matter-of-factly. "Yes, we might threaten Sulliaba here in the west and hold it hostage for Miltain. We could do that more quickly than anything else. I've thought about it often. I'd much prefer it if I thought Sulliaba was as important to Kilikash as Miltain is to us, but I'm afraid it isn't. He doesn't depend that much on Sulliaba and, if he crushes us by way of Miltain, Sulliaba will come promptly back to him. So I have to agree with you — reluctantly."

"I hadn't considered that," she said politely. "At any rate, we do agree. And this is where we stand. We have reason to think — or hope — that Kilikash isn't as ready in some respects as he would like. But we can't count on that. We must put a fleet in the east to fight him or make him think twice — intimidate him. I suggest a rendezvous with you at Shores in six weeks. I will turn over to you then as many Islandian vessels as Lamas can find and all the latest intelligence I have."

"That can be done," Tor said.

"I expect you to come with at least three hundred ships,"

she said, and Tor shrugged his shoulders. "I said three hundred ships!"

"There will be as many ships as there are," he said.

Alwina stood up then. "Speak in riddles if you like. We all know what hangs on the answer."

I walked with her to the door, through the hall, and out into the blazing sunset where the clouds hung in ranks from angry crimson to fragile pink and the great ball of the sun stood a few minutes above the edge of the sea. She touched my arm and we turned aside toward the stables accompanied by the bodyguard of five men waiting by Tor's steps. Trant himself, still on duty, stepped out of the stables at the sound of boots on the paving stones.

"How is Conyer?" Alwina asked him.

"Demented," Trant said. "Undone. Seized. I've seen nothing like it. I wouldn't go in, Your Majesty. He's . . . severely affected."

She shook her head and moved past him. I went with her until she shook her head again and I followed her no farther. The place was warm and full of the smells and quiet sounds of Tor's horses. A few yards away Alwina stopped at a box stall with six bars across the entrance and stood looking in, her head forward, her shoulders bent. From inside, from where I stood, and distinct from other noises, I could hear discontinuous rustling and a scratchy, panting kind of breathing. Through a west window a powerful, level shaft of light painted the wood and stone it touched reddish and turned the back sides of beams and stanchions into columns of pure black.

At last, in a clear, carrying voice, Alwina said, "You would have done that to me?"

The panting kept on, but through it something reminiscent of Conyer answered, "No . . . Oohh, no! Not to you. I didn't know!"

After another moment, Alwina turned and left the stables. In

133

the fading light I could not be sure, but I thought she had lost color. "Come along, Trant," she said. "Enough is enough. Keep a guard on duty. I don't know what he can do, but at least he can be here and give water."

By the time we walked the quarter mile to Islandia House, everything was gray or black in the twilight except for a thinning line of plum red on the horizon. Trant stopped at the gatehouse and I went on to the main door with the Queen.

"Thank you, Frare," she said. "Strange duties to come together on one afternoon. I hope no one of us has to say he didn't know. Good night."

TOR HAD THE DAY begin with a bugle. I heard the unfamiliar sound as I woke up. Light, clear, sharp, the call rippled down the cliff face and drifted along the quay through the shreds of predawn mist. There were a few notes only, stated, repeated, reordered, inverted, and then said once more. It was an invitation to some inconceivable adventure so compelling I felt the blood swell in my fingers and shivers crawl along my arms. I had no notion that Tor understood or that I was susceptible to the power of such a signal. I went up the long staircases with unexpectedly light feet.

Tor's courtyard was a high-spirited, bustling place in the dark grayness. Torches flared and smoked in brackets beside the house and stable doors. Horses tossed their heads, jingling and clinking their bridle chains, and their steaming breath rose to mix with the mist in the chilly air. A strong detachment of my men under Nyall, afoot now and holding their mounts, waited outside the gate. Along the wide path from Islandia House, the Queen's party rode at a walk, with details of Trant's troopers before and behind. Tor himself came out of the stables leading his own horse and also Lon, saddled and ready for me with a boar spear lashed beside the throw-dart at the saddlebow. When Tor mounted, so did all his friends in the courtyard along with my men outside. Greetings and jests flew to and from the Queen's party and, when the two groups swung alongside, riders cheerfully jostled and contended for position along the narrow way. At a word from Tor, Nyall and I gently put a stop to this impromptu contest, lengthening the column, finding a place for everyone on the track into town.

Beyond the town we bore southwest toward the long, central spine of Winder that thrusts far out into the ocean. Here we were on moorland broken only by occasional outcroppings of rock, and we could ride as we pleased, visiting one another in the saddle. Behind us the sun cleared the eastern peaks and sucked up the ground fog that still looked like snow in the hollows. As the sun grew warm it pulled a wild, slightly bitter scent from the green and dun turf.

Trant was breathing great drafts of the air as I pulled alongside him. "Sometimes I get tired of forests," he said. "And of plowed land, too. All this space makes it a pleasure to breathe."

"You should have been a sailor," I said. "Is there any word on Conyer?"

"Early this morning Tor had him sent home. So the guard told me."

"How was he?"

"As I said, I only know what I've heard. The philter was wearing off. He seems to have been as limp as you'd expect, but likely all right. A queer business. I feel sorry for the man. That was a terrible thing he did, but I didn't get the idea he knew he was doing it. He was surprised by what happened to him. I did see that. I'm not thinking of a match between the Queen and Tor necessarily, but I guess a lot of people would like what Conyer said he wanted."

"I guess they would," I agreed. "It's a dilemma."

"Well, no harm done. Too bad the Queen doesn't like that fellow. Seems like a good man. Friend of yours, too. The old King — her father — had no use for him. Maybe that has something to do with it. But the Queen knows what she's doing. No doubt about it. I wouldn't want to argue with her. About the troops maybe, but not about that. I've lived long enough to know better than to argue with a woman about a man." He laughed and breathed deep again and slapped his chest. "I like this air and so does my pony. Just the same, it'll be good to head for home when the time comes."

I agreed with him again and moved off to say hello to Bodwin, ambling by himself on the far flank of the procession. "Greetings, Cousin," he said. "What a wonderful piece of country! We don't have anything like it at home. All these birds and small animals. I wish I'd known of it sooner."

"Trant likes it, too," I said. "So does his pony. Trant says it's the air."

"Don't try to discourage me, Cousin. I am proof even against agreement with that man. And I have to say it happens more often than you might think. He didn't happen to say anything about the serenade we had this morning, did he?"

"No, never mentioned it. But then I didn't ask him."

"Astonishingly lovely thing. We never hear a horn in Islandia now. Not even in the Army. And not often here, either. It adds another interesting dimension to King Tor. I wonder how he came on the thing. Maybe boars insist on being hunted with horns. Incidentally, where are the boars?"

"I've no idea," I said. "That's Tor's secret. Except for guards, I've no hand in this."

"No matter. I'm in no hurry. This is more enjoyable than chasing pigs. I imagine you'll be very happy when we all go home."

"What do you expect me to say to that?" I asked. "I think I'd be happier if none of us had ever come. No, I don't quite mean that. But I didn't mind commanding the *Thist*. A nice little boat to fight Kilikash with."

"You mean you don't like responsibility, but that isn't what I had in mind. I don't quite trust the Queen when she gives dinners. I was thinking about tomorrow."

"That again," I said. "More vague mumbling. I'm tired of it. Everyone has a bad word for that dinner. What do you want

137

the Queen to do? Vanish at midnight? No word of thanks? Why shouldn't she give a dinner?"

"No reason. She should, of course. It may be even harder to forget than the last. You're right, Cousin."

"Me — right? Now you really trouble me."

After one of summer's long hours of riding, broken hills encroached on the moor and, farther ahead, higher, wooded slopes defined a pass or narrow valley. Close at hand, beyond a dunelike hillock, we came suddenly upon a large, flat rock set with baskets and jars of drink. Empty carts stood nearby and some yards away a pack of a dozen hounds milled and yapped around the legs of an elderly man who stood quietly by the head of his horse.

To cheers and applause Tor dismounted directly onto the rock among the food baskets. "This is light fare," he called out, "intended to deceive you into thinking you have eaten. Come and have breakfast. None will be sated, but all will be stayed."

"A wise and merciful King!" Alwina cried. "As they say in the Karain, we hear and obey. I'm starved."

People began dismounting, moving toward the rock, their reins hooked over their arms. Everyone was in high spirits, Winderese and Islandians mingling and talking on familiar terms as they never had before. In the fresh morning and the wild surroundings, under the wide, high sky, the scene was brightly colored and yet strikingly intimate and small. From even a short distance away it seemed one could have covered the whole gathering with a pocket handkerchief, ponies, hounds, and all.

Alwina moved and talked exuberantly for the first time in days, splendid in her youth and comeliness and presence. Her lips were parted, her eyes sparkling and observant, and her tongue lively. As people came away from the baskets munching and carrying their portions of breakfast, they gathered

138

around Alwina and Tor in an irregular circle, horses on the outside, like wheel spokes without a rim.

When people began licking and wiping their fingers and going back for drinks of water, Tor called for attention. "It's time to move on. The hunting ground isn't far now. A word to our guests and anyone else who hasn't done this before. Don't spread out beyond the line of the hunt. The country is rough and it's easy to get lost. Don't ride too close behind the dogs. When the boar stops and turns, he's dangerous. That's important. And drink your fill here. I can't promise springs or streams where we're going."

Trailing the dogs and their master, we started out on the more constricted going toward the pass. The dogs up ahead were quieter now and so were the riders as they fell into column. Tor left Alwina's side and rode ahead to speak to the master of hounds. After a moment, Alwina turned in her saddle and beckoned me to join her and Tenira.

"Frare, do you know the meaning of that horn call we heard this morning? I haven't asked Tor. I was mean enough not to give him the satisfaction."

"No, Your Majesty, I don't. Even Bodwin doesn't know."

"He admitted that?" She started to smile and then laughed. "Then it must be — unknowable."

"Not this time," Tenira said. "I know. I asked the right person. Nyall. It seems that long ago horn music was popular in Winder, but she followed the Islandian taste for plucked strings and pipes, and horn music died out here. The call we heard is supposed to be used at the beginning of important things — expeditions, campaigns, reigns of kings, occasions like that. It was always sounded at the launching of ships. Nyall says it still is if there is anyone around who can play it. There were actually two performances this morning, at Tor's and at Islandia House, one right after the other. I think Tor and Nyall were the buglers."

"How very appropriate," Alwina said. "Thank you, Tenira."

As we came out of the pass we stopped and gathered together to see the hunting ground. We were at the entrance to a wide valley enclosed to right and left by high, timbered mountains with bare rock showing here and there along their crests. They were not great mountains, but far more substantial than anything we had seen that morning. The far end of the valley was out of sight. A hundred feet or so below us, the valley floor began at the bottom of a gullied, gravelly slope. From there, waves of hardwoods stretched away farther than we could see, the waves interrupted at intervals by wide patches of brush and jumbles of rock. It was also possible to distinguish low ridges within the valley itself, perhaps thirty to fifty feet high, running lengthwise like fingers, rising and then subsiding. Tor had called it rough country and that was no exaggeration. Long though our morning shadows still were, the sun was a noticeable presence across our backs now that we were away from the moving air of the moor.

Slowly and cautiously, leading our ponies, we made our way down the treacherous pitch. Judging from the occasional yelps and whines, the dogs didn't like the sharp stones any better than we did. Once among the trees, the dogs spread out, not with any purpose at this point but querulously and anxiously, and there was much casting about and sniffing back and forth and starting off and coming back again.

We ourselves came off the slope without any formation, and the trees, through which there was no track and as yet no indicated direction, made it pointless to think of one. We were a very loose assembly and riders were continually being separated from one companion in order to negotiate a tree, only to find themselves trotting beside another rider several trunks farther on. In the circumstances my men held their positions with remarkable skill and tenacity, but the same could not be said for Trant's bewildered people. In addition we found, and were found by, insects, colonies of mosquitoes and biting flies who loved us increasingly as we began to sweat.

We proceeded raggedly in this way for what seemed like a long time, accomplishing perhaps a half mile. Now and then we could hear a light breeze moving the topmost leaves, but on the ground the air was still and hot. The forest was by no means parched — there were many signs of recent rainfall — but there was no water for us. Tor's words on the subject had been plain enough. I had a skin of water in one saddlebag, but I didn't think there were many others. It is very easy to anticipate the sensation of thirst. The conditions of this outing were by no means as severe yet as those of the trip from the border, but these unexpected discomforts came in the name of sport and not necessity, and contained the threat of worse to come. The spirit of the company, measured by talk and laughter, was flagging and I could not see the Queen to guess at hers.

Tenira, thrown beside me for a few paces by some whim of the forest, thought she saw reason in the situation and the discovery amused her. "Frare," she said, "taking one thing with another, I'm beginning to suspect Tor is teaching a lesson today."

"What kind of lesson?"

"Something to do with efforts and rewards. Boar hunting and kingdom hunting. Words and deeds."

"And bugles and beginnings, no doubt. Will it have any effect?"

"Who knows? A lesson always has to survive a counterattack from resentment."

The unpredictable trees intervened then, and Lon and I ranged on as before. I followed the sounds of the dogs as well as I could, but since they came from both sides as well as from ahead they weren't too easy to interpret. The bugs were now a constant minor torment for horses as well as riders, and it did little good to think of the places where these pests were actually far worse.

Then, at last, a long distance away, one of the dogs spoke in a new voice — full, eager, urgent. There was no doubt what he meant. The ponies understood and pricked their ears. I understood and forgot the sweat and the insects. We all turned toward the steady baying and found we had to go up and over one of the finger ridges. The height was not great — perhaps forty feet here — but the ground was atrocious, encumbered with boulders and laced with fallen trees and vines. By the time we straggled down to the valley floor on the far side the whole pack was giving tongue far ahead.

Now the pace picked up and the hunt spread out in a long line, with few people attempting to ride abreast anymore. My men under Nyall, what little I could see of them, kept stubbornly to their jobs, trying to ride parallel courses on either flank. It was hard to know where I was in the line, but I felt too far back and began to move up, swinging around one rider after another.

After some minutes it was my impression that the baying of the pack sounded nearer. To substitute for what I couldn't see, I had a sharp mental picture of what was going on up there. The big boar was rocking along as fast as he could, which wasn't very fast. He was built neither for speed nor for distance. Dogs surrounded him, mostly at his shoulders and flanks, snarling, snapping, slashing, and biting. They were enraging, frightening, and hurting him. Sooner or later, he would stop and turn on them. When and where would that be? The answer was the same for him as it would be for me, or another animal caught without refuge. When he came to an obstacle — one he could not go over, one he was too tired to go around, one that would protect his back. That was when he would turn.

By now I had the front riders in view. As I looked I saw

Alwina wave her hand and point as though she'd made a sighting. Leaning forward over her pony, she lifted him to a full gallop. Tor cried a warning after her, but she paid no attention. He urged his horse in pursuit, but didn't gain. Then Tenira in turn, several places in front of me, turned her horse out of line and gave him his head. As for me, fourth on the string, I had the sudden conviction that events were taking control of us, that something was preparing to happen and I had better be there. I swung Lon wide and told him to run with everything he had. For a moment I was afraid the entire hunt would surge forward in a stampede, but no one took his attention away from the dangerous tree trunks long enough to notice.

I could no longer guide Lon over the root-snagged ground or through the onrushing trees. I had to put both our necks in his care and hope he could see better than I thought he could. Astonishingly, in spite of my size and for quite some time, he pulled up steadily on the others. At last his burst came to an end, but he still held on, stride for stride, through what was now a changing forest. First I realized that there was more light around me and next that beyond the most distant trees I could see there was something other than more trees, something very bright. We were coming to the end of this wave of woodland. Beyond the boundary of shade and dappled light lay blinding sun where details vanished.

A moment or so more and Alwina and her horse appeared to me as a black silhouette against the light, but I was close enough now to make out brush and bushes beyond the trees, together with rock and stone. Tor shouted again to Alwina, "Stop! Stop now!" and she seemed to pull back on the reins. The steady crying of the pack stopped and there was thrashing and crackling in the brush. Pulling his horse violently back on its haunches until it slid and stumbled, Tor jumped to the ground holding a heavy boar spear. Tenira now was close to Tor and I was pounding down on all of them.

Out of the thicket a dog bounded all the way back into the woods again. Trailing a dark stream of blood, his insides bulging through a great rent in his flank, he made a succession of convulsive leaps and fell at the feet of Alwina's horse. In a single, complex spasm of his own the horse stopped and reared straight up, striking the air with his forefeet and staggering backward. Wrenched forward and then back, Alwina left the saddle as if ejected and fell heavily to the ground, striking on her shoulder and the back of her neck. She lay insensible and Tor running now, hurdled her body and planted himself between her and the thicket.

Tenira, past Tor, halted her frightened horse long enough to slip to the ground before the animal bolted. She stood between the dying hound and the thicket looking back at Alwina's motionless body. "Run! Run away from there!" I shouted at her. "Quick! Get behind me!" Tor cried.

Tenira merely turned around to face the thicket. The commotion there died down as another dog emerged, not leaping and not eviscerated but dragging his right hind leg, almost torn off at the haunch. Then there came the mask of the boar — the long snout, the small red eyes, the bloody, slobbered tusks curving up. Trotting with short, stiff steps, he came out of the brush alone, dirty sides heaving and torn, the spiky bristles standing along the ridge of his spine. Tenira stood in front of him looking at him and didn't move.

The boar trotted on toward her watching her. Tor cried out to her again and I shouted, "Run! Run! Run!" I could not tell whether she was transfixed or determined to distract the boar with her own body. She gave no sign of hearing either of us. With a powerful scooping motion the boar raked one tusk up her leg and into her side. Then his shoulder struck her, driving her reeling to one side until she fell. I saw her start to drag herself farther away.

Lon stopped just where I asked him to and he trembled all

over, but he didn't break and run as I jumped down and freed the spear. He stood still and I stepped toward the circus of dogs now whirling around the boar. They pressed in on him, but they got in each other's way. He was bitten and slashed up one side and down the other, but the dogs hadn't hurt him seriously. He stood there fierce and strong where Tenira had delayed him. The dogs weren't going to bring him down by themselves and both he and they were beginning to know that. I wasn't trained in the proper way of dispatching a boar, but I knew how to kill him if I could get to him.

I moved nearer to the dogs. Then I went in among them. They were tiring. I made one false move, a second, and then a third, the spear glancing off the boar's bones and hide. He kept his head low and moved with surprising speed when he did move. At last he turned his head and thrust up at the belly of a dog bounding in from off his shoulder. He gutted the dog, but for an instant he opened himself. I dropped to one knee and drove the spear blade horizontally at his throat. It entered, passed down his neck and back into his chest. The twisting of his body whipped the spear shaft in my hands and I let go before it broke. The boar lowered his head and spread his front legs for support while the blood bubbled a little from his jaws and snout and poured out along the spear handle. Then he settled to the ground and I left the spear in him.

Spinning around, I started to run in the direction I had seen Tenira crawling, but I stopped in midstep. All around, everywhere, suddenly, in one instant there was pandemonium. The huntsmen were on top of us, careening into each other, their mounts rearing, neighing, screaming. On the ground, shadows flitted among the horses, striking at their sides and legs with knives. Here were the assassins at last, performing as I had told Trant they would. I saw Tor, spear in one hand and sword in the other, bestriding the still unconscious Queen, twisting his head from side to side trying to identify the nearest danger. Paces behind him a brown figure slid forward, knife raised, eyes on Alwina.

I sprang to Lon, still standing with desperate patience where he was supposed to be, and broke loose the throw-dart from the saddle. I could not call to Tor. He would block me in turning and be off guard himself. I was right-handed and might have enough angle to throw past him. I drove the dart hard, scarcely aiming. It whistled below Tor's upraised arm and grazed his tunic. The point took the man between the collar points of his chest and shoved out again beside the top joint of his spine. As he fell, the dart handle struck the ground, throwing him toward Alwina, and he buried his knife a foot from her head. Tor finished him.

Out of the corner of my eye I saw Nyall go down a step or so away. With his own arm raised to strike, he took a dreadful blow in the side from a knife driven by a white hand. Nyall's sword fell from his fingers, but in falling he grappled with his man just long enough for me to take a step forward and thrust out my leg. The attacker, his eyes also fixed on Alwina, brushed my knee and broke stride. Seizing him by the chin and the hair, I forced his head back over his shoulders and his neck snapped.

Then I ran to Tor and joined him, and we stood back to back over Alwina. He cried, "Welcome, Frare!" and I felt him move behind me and heard him strike. The frantic horses surged and reared around us as a center point. Their dismounted riders, mostly shocked, dismayed, and uncomprehending, either stood witless where they were or edged their way out of the vortex. A few hung onto their reins and spoke to their ponies, trying to control the frenzy.

All of that came to me as a flicker of shifting, incidental impressions while I was trying to single out the purposeful, murderous shadows coming toward us from among the horses and the trees. They seemed able to materialize from the air itself.

146

First I glanced and then I scanned and for some moments saw no shadows at all. Then I saw three in quick succession, but at second look recognized them as my own men. That frightened and confused me for as long as it took to blink my eyes and understand what it meant.

At the top of my voice I called to my men, "To me! Here! To Frare!" and I gave six names. "The rest of you — secure the horses!"

As I formed the six-man guard and turned it over to Tor, the section leader Crask ran up to me and said, "We've got them all now, Isla Frare! All except one," and he pointed beyond the edge of the forest.

Well out in the bright, waist-high brush, a figure trotted and walked and ran toward a long arm running out from the mound of rock where the boar had made his stand. He was not far from the rocks now. "You can't catch him?"

"No. I'd have tried if I could. He'll have a horse there. All their horses will be there."

"Can you bring him down?"

He shook his head. "It would be luck."

But he hurried to his pony, took his bow and strung it and chose an arrow. Quickly he found good ground for footing, stamped on it, and nocked the arrow. With the bow held loosely across his knees, he leaned forward peering, judging the range. Then he raised the bow, drew, aimed, and loosed in what seemed one continuous motion. The rising arrow drew a black line in the white light against the steel-colored sky. Although I knew it did not, the arrow then appeared to pause at the top of its flight before it stooped like a hawk and struck the runner between the shoulder blades. He fell out of sight beneath the brush, but the tops continued to be agitated.

"That was a shot!" I said.

"Ha!" Crask remarked. "*Now* I can bring him in. I'll bring in the horses, too."

"Don't kill him if he isn't dead."

"He's dead," Crask said with no doubt. "That wound is mortal. At this distance anything is just luck. You can't even try to be choosy. Too bad, Isla Frare. He won't tell any secrets. There's one that *can't* talk." With that oblique reference to the secret he hadn't had to keep, Crask unstrung his bow and put it away.

I turned back to find Alwina conscious now, half-sitting, supported by Tor while her two young women tended to her. The horses were under control, but Trant told me several had knife cuts and two with slashed hamstrings would have to be killed. I told him to have that done, but first to see to Nyall at once. Then I hurried to Tenira, picking my way among the corpses of the assassins.

She was conscious and apparently not yet in great pain, but she was dead white and her eyes were not quite here with us. Of course she knew nothing. "Alwina is all right," I told her slowly. "Everything is all right. The boar is dead. So are all the assassins we've been afraid of for so long. Everything is all right. Alwina is all right. Do you understand?"

"Yes," she said, and some of the strangeness left her eyes. "Is that true?"

"That's true. Now, let's see about you. Do you feel it much? How much pain is there?"

"Some. Not so much just now. But I feel empty and at the same time as though I were all jelly."

She didn't try to raise her head when she spoke. She lay on her back, but with most of her weight on her right side slightly lifting her wounded leg and hip. I pulled aside the ripped, bloody cloth of her dress, cutting it with my dagger when I had to. The material was thick and sticky, but luckily not yet stuck. The wound had bled a good deal at the beginning — I thought it might better have bled more — and now was oozing in some places and crusting in others. Starting above her knee, the boar's tusk had ripped up the inside front of her thigh, crossed over her hip bone and then dug into her body again before sliding off to the side. The jagged cut safely missed the big artery on the inside of her thigh, but not by too much. The two deepest places were just below and just above the hip. About the hip itself I could be sure only that it was bruised and abraded. When I touched and tested gently, she winced and bit her lip. I couldn't believe she wouldn't have screamed if it was broken, but I simply didn't know.

There was little I could do. I sponged the long gash with water, almost hot, from my saddlebag, and then lightly tied a strip of dry cloth over it. Then I covered her with a blanket, also from my saddlebag. "There, that doesn't look so bad," I said — I thought it looked very bad, particularly because it was an animal wound and I was afraid — "but we can't avoid hurting you going back. Sleep now if you can." With her eyes closed, she nodded without speaking. I kissed her and touched her cheek with my fingers.

As I rose to my feet, I found Alwina standing beside me. She drew me a few steps away and asked, "How is she?" I told her what I knew. "And she did it to protect me," she said. "Tor will regret . . ." She pressed her hand to her forehead but brushed me away when I moved to support her. "I'm well enough. You'll stay with Tenira, Frare? It's a hard trip back for her. I'm leaving now."

She walked slowly to her pony and mounted with help. With her young women close at hand, with Trant's men before and behind, and the rest of the hunt company following after, she rode into the forest. Bodwin raised his hand to me in sad salute.

TOR DIDN'T WATCH the Queen leave. He was with Nyall and I joined him there. The ground nearby was drenched with Nyall's blood. Trant had staunched the flow with a cloth packed into the mouth of the wound and held there by wrappings. That seemed to work for the moment, but it might not hold against the stress of travel. The dangerous loss of blood was what we talked about, allowing ourselves to slide over what the deep stab and cut might have done to organs inside.

We were still bending over Nyall, joking gently and poorly, being as commonplace as we knew how, when Crask and three others came in with the assassins' horses and with the body of the man Crask had killed slung over one of the saddles. As the men lowered the heavy body, Nyall saw the dead face and said faintly, "That man! He was the one who spoke to me that day in the wineshop."

"Ah, that one," Tor said with casual interest, and stood up. "A long day, Frare. And we've scarcely begun yet. On with it."

At his direction we carried the eight dead men out of the forest and laid them on the nearest rocks, face-up to the sky. At the same time others made two litters from spears and saddle blankets. Placing Tenira and Nyall on them with perilous gentleness, we began the long, hot walk while the sun told us it was not yet midday. Those who were at any moment riding and not carrying led the extra horses. After a short distance we learned that teams of five men to a litter were easiest and smoothest — one man to each corner and a fifth alongside with a leafy branch to discourage the insects. Sometime during that interminable march, when both Tor and I were carrying, he smiled across at me and said grimly, "Remember going up the river, Frare? We must actually enjoy doing relay work."

At the edge of the moor, in fresh, gloriously brisk air, we stopped to rest and reorganize. The carts were here, and water, plenty of cool water. In different ways Tenira and Nyall both were suffering severely. She was feverish now, the flesh under the dried blood and the bandage proud and angry. The wound itself plainly was sending pulses of intense pain all through her. Nyall was gray, his skin clammy and his breathing light. For more than an hour he had been no more than half-conscious except when a pitch of the litter roused him and he called for water. We had not dared give him any.

Now we bathed them both about their faces, necks, and wrists and gave Tenira water out of sight of Nyall. Revived for the moment, however, he called us over and said in a quiet, cracked sort of voice, "I know the risk. Just the same, if my guts were ruptured, I don't think I'd be still alive. Anyway, if they are, you can't save me. You might as well let me have the water." I wasn't sure of this, but Tor nodded, went for a cup and held it to Nyall's mouth. He drank it eagerly, his Adam's apple dancing. Tor and I stood stock-still watching while something tugged at my memory. Then a smile crossed Nyall's face and he said, "That's a better philter than I gave poor Conyer. Let me have a little more."

We emptied two carts, made beds in them from soft, low growing plants and transferred our casualties. Looking down at Tenira, Tor felt her cheeks and forehead and said, "I know the Queen wants you to go to Islandia House so Sissona can look after you. She instructed Trant to tell me. Weak as you feel, you'll have to judge what I say now. I wouldn't say anything at all except that your life belongs to you and shouldn't hang on anger between Alwina and me. Animal bites, especially wounds from a boar's tusks, are likely to carry poison. I think yours are poisoned. They look it. If you go to Sissona, I believe you will be deadly ill and very possibly die. My mother is one of a few people who know how to treat these injuries. She can cure you if you go to her. I am going to send a messenger now. Tell me what you want to do."

Her eyes were brilliant with the fever, but she understood him. "I'll go to Attana. Thank you, Tor."

Attana was ready for us when we arrived at dusk. She had us put Tenira and Nyall in small rooms down a corridor from Tor's council room and then dismissed us. Filthy, weary, but temporarily relieved, I told Tor, "I'm going to the barracks and wash off the boar and the murderers. Maybe then I'll feel better."

"All right, Frare, but don't forget to come back. You know the day won't end this way."

When I had cleaned up and had something to eat I did feel fresher, but I was troubled by the recurring thought that Tenira and Nyall might not have been hurt if I had somehow done things I had failed to do. I had no idea what those things might have been, but I had the uneasy feeling I had allowed myself to be diverted. I had no doubt at all that Tenira had correctly foreseen calamity. The trouble was she connected it with Alwina's dinner, and I wondered if I also had been looking too hard in that direction. Second sight, I have been told, often mislocates what it sees. The futility of my feeling bothered me as much as anything. If there had been anything I could have done, I couldn't do it now.

I sent then for Nicking and he immediately told me the unfortunate boar — whose destiny I had forgotten — was at this moment on the jetty being butchered. The men felt he had cost too much to abandon and so had slung him between the two sturdy ponies originally brought along for the purpose.

Unknown to me, the boar, in state so to speak, had brought up the rear of our dreadful procession.

At first I found the notion very distasteful and my impulse was to order the carcass burned or buried, but at sight of the distress on Nicking's face I began to laugh instead. "Well, why not?" I said. "It's what we went for. Tell them I want a portion."

Nicking sighed in relief and smiled. "That will please them. This is important to them. They count on eating that boar."

"Magic?."

"Some, maybe. Mostly because they think it's fitting. Getting a boar isn't exactly what they went for. If things had gone right, they'd have had a token piece each and that would have been fine. But things didn't go well and they failed. In some complicated way the boar is the only thing to show out of a disaster. They don't want it to escape."

"They've got it wrong," I said. "They went to protect the Queen and they saved her life. Where's the disaster in that?"

"They don't see it that way. To them you and Tor saved the Queen. They failed."

"I'll have to do something about that," I said, "but after you and I have finished."

Without having any part in it themselves, the men were right in saying there was a disaster. What its consequences would be I was trying hard not to imagine. But in a backhanded way there had also been a triumph, one I would have been exultant about in other circumstances. The assassination danger was over. There might be other plots at other times and places, but this one was finished. Keeping that in mind, I talked with Nicking not only about disbanding the special force we had trained so lovingly, but also about the possibility of maintaining and even enlarging it for special war against the Karain. He thought that was a fine idea.

153

Then I went out on the jetty and called the men together. I didn't make a speech, but I explained exactly what happened — which even those who had been there didn't know because there had been too many trees in the way — and exonerated them from any failure. I praised their spirit and skill and said they had been trained to be resourceful and they had been. Finally, I pointed out to them that they'd won. The conspiracy was dead and it had been their job to kill it. They deserved the boar and I hoped he was good. I may have spread the jam a little thick for a few philosophers like Crask, but what I told them was certainly not undeserved and I had the feeling it worked.

With all my fatigue back again, I climbed the steps to Tor's place once more. It seemed unlikely, except in another life, that I had heard a bugle call here and run zestfully up this precipice. My inclination now was to think of the steps, rather than my feet, as being somehow heavy. The stars were not as numerous nor as bright as usual and for once there was no wind. I observed myself noting these things without interpreting them and I realized I was afraid to go into the house and ask about Tenira.

As I had really known she would, Attana told me there was nothing significant yet to say about either Nyall or Tenira. "His trouble is loss of blood. If he can survive a few days — perhaps. She is not in quite so much pain now because she is quiet and has been resting. I have forced her fever down a bit with wet cloths. But the salve cannot take effect before tomorrow. Until the poison is gone I can't touch her to learn if the boar's tusk did anything else. She needs fortitude and all the rest of us need patience."

"I understand. What is the salve you speak of?"

She smiled. "A mixture of things. It is mostly cobwebs from grapes."

Accepting this as a legitimate rebuke to aimless curiosity, I sat down with Tor at one end of his long table. Lighted candles were set about it, standing in holders with polished copper reflectors that amplified and diffused the light. I told him of my talk with Nicking about the future of the special force. He was interested but noncommittal and told me in turn how he thought the assassins had planned their ambush. That is, we marked time and waited.

Alwina came in quickly, followed inevitably by Sissona and Trant. There was no sound of an escort outside, so presumably that aspect of the day's events was understood at Islandia House. Tor and I rose and Tor gestured toward the table. Alwina hesitated and then sat down at the far end, with Sissona and Trant on either hand. Tor resumed his former place and I shifted to the conspicuous middle between them.

From the way Alwina moved it was plain her neck and shoulder were stiff and painful, but it was not so easy to read her state of mind from her face. The signs were not so much contradictory as not quite certain. Her eyes were angry, more angry than I'd ever seen them, and there was a sense of lightning playing around her head, but the rest of her face didn't seem quite convinced by all this. Her mouth presented so straight and thin a line one wondered what it might do on its own.

She chose a manner that was cold and quiet and spoke directly to Tor. "I told you to bring Tenira to Islandia House so Sissona might care for her. Trant informed you. Do you remember?"

"Yes, you did that." Tor's big voice was also quiet, but it carried an unusual amount of resonance. "I also sent you a message saying we were bringing Tenira here, with her consent, because we could give her better care."

"Better care? What makes you think that?"

"I don't think it," Tor said. "I know it. So does Sissona."

Alwina looked at me. "Isla Frare, I asked you to stay with

Tenira. I see you have. You must have heard any such conversation. Did Tenira willingly consent to come here?"

Her furious eyes and her cool, scornful voice carried her relentlessly on. She must know I could not submit to that question. "Tor doesn't need my corroboration, Your Majesty."

"You may think that. So then, he forced her consent when she was in no condition to give it. Better care indeed! Tor, why did you disobey me?"

Tor smiled and placed his wide hands on the table. "It's my pleasure to remind you, Alwina, that you are not Queen of Winder."

"Am I not? That from a renegade Isla. We shall see." She glanced from one side to the other, from Trant's square chin and sharp features to the melonlike roundess of Sissona. "Your bungling, Tor — your bungling and even cowardice — may have killed my dearest friend. You stood and watched — stood and did nothing — while the boar gored her. You didn't move a hand! Now you would conceal that by having her die here under *better care.*"

Alwina's voice had risen and Tor frowned, but his own tone was still low. "Do you mind telling me how you know all these unworthy things?"

"There were others there. Trant?"

"The matter was badly handled," Trant said and kept his eyes straight ahead.

"All right, Trant," Tor said. "I'll ask you the same question. How do you know that?"

"From what I observed on the scene."

"You observed? On the scene? The Queen at least was present. She was unconscious, but she was present. You weren't even there. Fortunately. The first thing you *observed* was Frare and myself standing over the Queen's body fighting off attackers and Frare's men killing them among the horses. The first thing you *did* was get in the way. Eight bodies

156

weathering on the rocks there and *my* friend next to death in this house are witnesses to what you didn't see and didn't do for your impatient Queen."

"Stop evading," Alwina said, and turned to me. "Tor doesn't dare call on you, Frare. Tell me what you saw."

I glanced from her to Tor and back and then spoke to the table in front of me. "I was the last to join the race for the boar. You led the way, Your Majesty. When you came near the thicket, your horse panicked at a dying dog and threw you. Tor dismounted and took position between you and the thicket. Then Tenira rode by both of you and dismounted at the edge of the thicket. She looked back toward you. Tor and I called to her to run, but she turned back toward the boar. He gored her and threw her aside. I was on the ground then and I speared the boar. While I did that the assassins came."

"But *you* killed the boar."

"I could do it because Tor was protecting you."

"Nonsense! Tor could have done it in time to save Tenira if he'd been man enough. He stood there and watched." She brandished her pathetic fact as though it were Alwin's great sword and she were slaying Demiji. "And don't confuse things by talking about assassins. They were laughable, or should have been. They could have presented no danger if they had been hunted down here by men who knew their own country. Nothing was done. It's all of a piece. Stupidity and brag deception. I have exhausted myself here trying to show Winder its own interest. I've offered a way out of this dog's life. Since the first day I've received nothing but humiliation and contempt for my trouble." Now she abandoned me as surrogate and spoke straight to Tor again. "Since I've been here you've done nothing but pose and posture as a King. You? A King? This is not even a province! Nor you an Isla! You come from a line of sea-robbers and pirates. Your people began your power by wrecking Islandian ships and increased it by blackmail. You're still doing it, but no more." She stood up abruptly. "Where is my friend? I want to see Tenira."

Tor said nothing and didn't move from his chair. I took one of the candles and led the way down the corridor and through a narrow door into a plain room with the shutters open onto the still night. A small oil dish with a lighted wick cast a dim light from a far corner. Walking around the bed, I set the candle down and stood waiting. Tenira seemed to be drowsing. She roused slowly and her flushed face and hot eyes turned first to me and then to Alwina. She managed a smile.

Alwina dropped to her knees beside the bed and bent over Tenira, touching her face lightly. There was a basin of water and a cloth on the table beside me. I dipped the cloth, wrung it out, and handed it to Alwina. She sponged Tenira's face.

"Oh, my dear! What have they done to you?"

"Not they," Tenira said unclearly. "The boar." And then with an effort, "Are you all right?"

"My neck is stiff. Nothing more. Thanks to you."

"Little thanks to me," Tenira murmured and closed her eyes.

Alwina went on with the gentle sponging, returning the cloth to be freshened. "We'll move you away from here," she said, "so Sissona can take good care of you and you'll feel better. We'll make a fine house on two horses and take you back to The City and you'll get well there."

That penetrated the drowsiness and the fever and Tenira said with alarm, "No. No litters. No horses. I'm here, you see."

"No?" Alwina asked. "Well, perhaps that is too hard. I know. I'd forgotten. There's the *Earne*. I'll put you on the ship. You'll sail straight to The City. It will be smooth all the way. That's the answer."

"Alwina," Tenira said now in her own full voice. "Listen to me! Understand me, please! I want to stay here. I am not going to leave until I am well and can walk."

Both women remained silent and motionless, Alwina with the damp cloth in her outstretched hand. Then she handed it to me and rose slowly to her feet. "I see," she said. "What can they have done to you?"

As she walked through the door I bent over Tenira to kiss her. She held me there with her fingers on my cheek and her mouth close to my ear. "She will order you to go back by land with her," she said softly. "I'm sure of it. She couldn't bear to leave us both here. You will want to refuse, but don't do that, Frare. Accept it. Please! Don't let her go alone with Sissona and Trant. Something will happen. I am afraid for her."

I said, "All right. I'll go if she orders me."

She dropped her head back to the bed. "Go on back now. You must be there."

In the other room Tor still sat as before, massive and powerful, his expression watchful and sardonic. Alwina, one shoulder held unnaturally high, stood at her end of the table while Sissona and Trant lined up behind her. "Tenira doesn't talk to me like the woman I know. You and your mother, Tor, have done something to her. Potions, I suppose. Philters. Nothing would be unlikely in a house where Conyer was a cook. There's nothing I can do now, but I'll not forget it." She tightened both hands on the back of the chair in front of her. "I have given up any hope of improving Winder's position. I have tried with all my power and I'm not going to try anymore. I am canceling my dinner tomorrow night. I am leaving Winder tomorrow. Frare, you will be in command of the party on the way back. Please arrange for us to leave as early as possible. You will instruct Nicking to assume command of the *Earne* and await orders. Is that clear?"

She watched me carefully while she was giving these instructions. My feelings were hard to sort out. I resented her blind vindictiveness and I blamed her for Tenira's injury, and yet my hostility was curiously blunted by the outcome of Tenira's earlier foreboding. Also I saw that if Tenira could still love and fear for this young woman, there could be something there for my sympathy. Formal loyalty was a lock with a different set of keys and that wasn't at issue now. I said merely, "Yes, that's clear."

"Very good. Is there anything you wish to say, Tor?"

"Why, yes," he replied, still from his chair. "Since you give me permission. You've said some endearing things to me this evening. I was willing to let them pass as long as I thought they were extravagances brought on by real distress at the misfortune of your friend. Now I perceive that your grief is real enough, but not all that great. What you can't stand is the shock to your conceit. It must be a conspiracy. You know perfectly well what you did today. I want you to realize that I know, just as well as you really know, that Tenira and Nyall lie badly hurt here entirely because of your irresponsible willfulness. There would have been no trouble with the boar, nor with the assassins either, if you had shown a decent regard for the people who were trying to protect you. That's one of several parts of your job you haven't learned."

Now he stood up and spoke down instead of face to face. "In spite of your touching protest, you haven't done anything to reconcile our two countries. On the first day you made a beautiful speech telling us we should all love each other forever and ever for the benefit of Alwina and Islandia. Nobody liked it and you were offended. But you put a pretty face on your sulks and wooed me with attention and submissiveness and melting looks. When you thought that must have done its work, you decided on something very silly and not at all nice." He gave the table an echoing slap and pointed at Sissona. "You sent this poor thing, got up like a she-pimp, to talk to my mother. Sissona offered you up in loving matrimony without political conditions — if I would make the proposal. Without political conditions? I make such a proposal? To hand my country to

160

Islandia's royal family tied up in a wedding knot? What did you take me for? History's fool? Did you think you had turned me into a calf? Or was it a pretty, girlish fancy held over from the time when you were the King's daughter? I'll wager you had the sense never to ask Tenira or Frare or Bodwin about it. The miserable Conyer had more idea than you of what it means to be Queen."

He crossed the room, poured wine into a goblet, and brought it back with him. "Here's to your pleasant journey back to The City. When you get there, reality in the shape of Cabing will intrude on your fantasies of vengeance. You will wake up because I don't believe you are always as demented as you have been here. You won't enjoy it. Cabing will ask you how you intend to go about building a fleet. And who will man it? You will want to know what to do. Remember then that we made an agreement and I gave a promise. I gave it in the name of reality, so you may trust it. In six weeks I will be at Shores. Be sure you are there. And be sure you send money here first."

Alwina turned her eyes to me, saying, "Frare, please settle anything about tomorrow with our host." Then she motioned Sissona and Trant to follow her and walked out of the house.

I DIDN'T GET the party away until late in the morning. There was a lot to do but even more to undo, all of it requiring tedious amounts of equivocal explanation. Only five people knew what had happened in Tor's room, and I was the one chosen to put a public face on it. All questions came to me and all lies from me, not so much out of a desire for deception as a wistful need for decorum. I expected Bodwin in particular to make my life miserable, but he accepted my inventions with a kind of wry sympathy and said, "It might have been better to have that dreadful dinner after all." He understood perfectly without knowing anything.

The weather signs I had noticed but not bothered about produced heavy clouds and a chilly southeast wind that could bring several days of rain. I told Alwina that if she wanted to send the main party home under Trant, I could take her and a few passengers by sea in the *Earne*. Forgetting her speech to Tenira, she said no, she'd go back the way she came, and if the weather turned bad it would be worse on the water than on land. Obviously her neck was still painful and I had the impression she was too preccupied even to consider changing plans once more.

At Tor's establishment there were no smiling faces either, but the air of order and purpose was tonic in contrast to the disarray at Islandia House, where Trant had not yet succeeded in assembling the baggage animals. Nyall I did not see. Attana told me his condition was very poor, he might not even know me and it would be better if he didn't have to try. I left my good will in her care for such time as it might mean something to him — if that time should come. Tenira and I parted in a reassuringly commonplace fashion by almost tacit agreement. One straight look and a few words told us we were in concert about what lay between us and also that we didn't want to tear up the fragile surface of things now just in order to manhandle our emotions. She looked better, considerably better, especially about the eyes. Her fever was down, not gone, but much reduced. Attana had already told me the inflammation had stopped its advance and showed signs of yielding to the salve.

"I'll get the Queen to The City," I said to Tenira, "and then, one way or another, I'll come back here for you."

"That would be nice, but I won't count on it. You shouldn't either. We can't tell what will happen in The City. Tor told me this morning he'll send me home when I'm well."

She touched on a question I had begun to have difficulty with the night before. What was mine and what was the Queen's? I said, "I'm not that important. Lon will bring me back. Very soon. You'll see."

"All right. I'll see. We'll both see. I can't think very well right now."

We kissed each other and put on smiles of a sort and I hurried out to say goodbye to Tor before we began to unravel. I thanked him for the trust and friendship he had given me and said, "You know how much I wish things hadn't come to this."

"Yes," he replied, "I think I do. It gives you troubles enough and you are generous to think of me. I hoped things would be different, too. For me and for Winder. I saw no good in this visit from the beginning and yet there was nothing I could do to stop it. Maybe I didn't really want to. Maybe I thought . . . Well, that's over. There are things to be done even if Alwina doesn't know it yet. In a week I will know how many ships are ready for service, how many can be completed or repaired, and how many new ones I can lay down each month. And there is the business of the crews. That's more complicated. It will take longer. But everything will get done — provided I get the money." He walked with me into the courtyard. "What are you going to do about the master assassin still alive somewhere?"

"I don't know," I said. "I admit I haven't thought twice about him since yesterday."

"He's not somebody to forget." Tor put his hand on my shoulder. "So, thank you, Frare. Goodbye. I'll see you at Shores if not sooner. Don't worry about Tenira more than you can help. We'll take care of her. We like her, too."

At Islandia House the pack horses had at last showed up and gear and supplies were moving from the rooms and the kitchen to the entranceway. The sight of trim bundles multiplying in orderly rows as they were supposed to do was visibly restoring Trant's sense of propriety, so badly injured the preceding day. He began to handle the loading with the efficiency he normally brought to such jobs.

Alwina was not so easily calmed. Ready to mount, as she had been for three hours, she paced the big reception room, striking her left hand with the short riding whip she held in her right. She paused now and then in the doorway to look angrily at Trant's proceedings and then each time turned away before she sctually interfered. When she caught sight of me, she knew of course where I had just come from and gave me a look that was unmistakably a plea for information. I thought I understood her difficulty. She was enmeshed in the charges she had made — against Tor of causing Tenira's injury and then spiriting her away to die, and implicitly of desertion against Tenira herself. She couldn't bring herself to ask me what she desperately wanted to know. Was Tenira better! I felt sorry for her, but not enough to want to extricate her and I didn't. Instead I went on to consult Drune and Halkon, the two Winderese of the special force whom Tor had suggested I take as guides as far as the border.

At last, under a dripping sky, hooded and swathed and indistinguishable one from another in gray parkas, we left Islandia House to whatever its normal name and use were, and took the trail to the east. We were as silent now as we had been boisterous the day before.

One's mind is an odd companion. You can tell it where to go and what to do and often it will obey you, sometimes reluctantly with poor result, very occasionally with enthusiasm and astonishing success, but mostly in a middling sort of way. Then there are other times when the relationship is reversed and your companion, your mind, tells you what it wants. When that happens, in your turn you may choose to go reluctantly, enthusiastically, routinely, or even not at all. As I looked between Lon's expressive ears and over his nodding head, in this private interval of travel I wanted to consider my heart's needs and return to the cove and the spring, to reconcile them somehow with Tenira's shattering misfortune and to think of contingencies. I asked my mind to indulge me in this, but it instructed me to see instead, framed still by Lon's ears, the face of the dead assassin, which had stirred Nyall from the edge of coma.

There was nothing remarkable about the face as I saw it now, floating in air much as I had seen it before hanging upside down from a horse's back. Pale, fleshy, neither bearded nor clean-shaven, there was nothing to suggest what it might have been like in life, urging subversion in the dimness of a wine shop. But surely the appearance of the face, dead or alive, was not the point. I was being obtuse to spite my companion.

I had never heard the dead man's name, so call him Ek, number one. Ek was one of eight who attacked the Queen, one of three Islandians, two Winderese, and three of the Karain. At least that's what the clothes of the whites told us. Ek was Islandian and so was one of the six who landed from the Sulliaban galley. He had accosted Nyall in The City. Was he also the killer of Woking? Possibly, even probably. There was time enough. And was he one of the men who attacked Cabing? Even more likely. We had picked up some evidence from the scene of that attack. Had Woking been killed because of where that evidence led him? Cabing had been at pains in his letter to say nothing about that, but it seemed almost certain. There had been no place else for Woking to begin. So then, as I had at first supposed, the man whom Tor called the master assassin was in The City, or had been, and I was back where I was when I saw the crows behaving strangely at the edge of the wood. No, not quite. There was the trail Ek must have left. And Woking had been able to make something out of two throw-darts, a pair of knots, and some tracks in the woods. So could others. Cabing must tell me what he hadn't written.

At a noise beside me I turned to see a shapeless, gray-clad figure pulling up on my right whom I recognized by degrees as Bodwin, from his posture and then his horse. "Hello, Cousin," he said. "Fitting weather."

I thought that required no comment and made none.

"I wanted to tell you," he said, "how very sorry I am about Tenira."

"Thank you, Bodwin."

"Did you learn anything this morning? I am fond of her myself, you know, even though she thinks I'm foolish when I'm most serious. And Nyall? He has an admirable ability to ignore his own hostility."

"I did find a few things. Nyall is very weak. I think they have little hope for him. Tenira, I believe, is not in danger of her life now. The boar's poison should recede, but what else he may have done no one can tell yet."

"I understand," Bodwin said. "Incidentally, the Queen did not send me to find that out and I won't repeat what you've told me." We plodded on for a few steps and then he continued, "I don't want to know the details of what happened last night. I can imagine well enough. It's too bad they didn't quarrel about something serious. That would be easier mended."

In no mood for Bodwin's provocative method of inquiry, I said without thinking, "None of it would matter if they weren't who they are."

"Cousin," he said, "in you we have a man unafraid to face the obvious. You are almost profound. Don't think about such things too long. Just the same, I'm glad you are in command of us now and not Trant."

As the afternoon wore one, the weather worsened and we moved very slowly, our heads bent forward. The wind picked up, blowing in gusts of increasing frequency and force. The clouds, which had formed a low-lying, dark blanket, now bulged irregularly downward, enveloping the shoulders of the hills and swirling in the upper ravines. From their lower edges hung curving veils of heavy rain. At this rate the wind and the rain would be nearly constant in another hour or so.

Although it had been my intention to reach the border that night, there was now no hope of doing that. Instead, the question was becoming how soon could we stop? I rounded up Trant and my two guides, Drune and Halkon, to decide on a place to camp. Our unanimous choice was the valley of the House of Quiet, where the House itself could serve as a shelter for the Queen and her women. Use of the Houses as refuges from storms has long been customary, whether it was part of their original purpose or not. Drune, who claimed to be familiar with the valley, said the stream there would flood quickly and we should find ground well above it. I then told Trant to take Drune along with half his men and all the pack train and push on ahead at his best pace. He could make better time than we could with one or two riders who were uncertain in these conditions. He was to make a camp and get fires going. There should be enough dry wood stored in the House of Quiet to get them started.

As I'd been forced to notice before, Trant's men were sometimes very good, and this was one of the times. Trant handled them confidently and they moved ahead of us in a briskly splashing column soon disappearing in the gloom and the mist. Sissona was the person holding us up. We sank our chins farther down onto our chests and squelched along, accommodating ourselves to the walk she could manage in this slithery going. Her slowness wasn't important any longer, just annoying, and she kept apologizing for it.

Bodwin, who I was beginning to realize could feel genuine malice and sympathy simultaneously for the same person, told me, "The old battleax isn't a good rider anyway, but she manages to struggle along pretty well in most circumstances. On the last day of the trip coming here, I thought the heat would kill her, but it didn't and she didn't complain. Earlier, though, we had a wet day or so — not as bad as this — and she was the way she is now. Something happens to her. It's her sense of balance. When the trail becomes slick and greasy, she is seized by a combination of vertigo and seasickness."

I laughed in spite of myself. "You're not making this up, Cousin? No, you can't be. What a pathetic infirmity!"

"Pathetic?" he said. "Perhaps, but I see I shouldn't have told you. You are already beginning to think of things it explains. There is a part of your mind that feeds on little plausibilities."

By the time we came up with Trant, the stream through the valley already covered its wide sand and gravel borders to a depth of an inch or so at the outside edges. On our side, because of the steep slope, it could now rise several feet without much more spreading. The horses were picketed well up the hill on a level with the House of Quiet, whose smoking chimney showed there was a fire there. In the angles of large rocks Trant had two other vigorous fires going, which were handling the rain at its present rate. We urged our horses up the slope. In a matter of moments we had the Queen and her ladies and their baggage out of the downpour and into the dry, musty room with its adjacent tiny cubicles intended for solitary meditation. I noticed that conversation stopped automatically at the door and I wondered if one or another of them might feel moved in the course of the evening to unburden her mind in public discourse, a customary privilege afforded by Houses of Quiet.

On a rock some distance away, out of the underbrush but with rain swirling around him, Trant watched his work details struggling with the slope and the weather. Some were cutting and hauling evergreens for firewood, some were hanging kettles over the big fires, and others in the distance were staking out a latrine.

When I joined him, Trant looked at me from under his hood and said, "Hello, Frare. Is the House all right?"

"It's fine."

He pointed toward the fires. "We may not have those for long. If this rain gets just a little steadier, they'll go out. I'm trying to get some hot food while they're burning. There's no sense trying to rig shelters or lay ground sheets now. Each man for himself when the time comes. Actually, a man will find his horse the best shelter in this."

"Where's Drune?"

"He thinks there may be caves in the hill up just below the crest line. He's gone to look."

"That would be good."

"Too good to be true. Things don't work out that way. When you're meant to be wet, then you stay wet."

I left him to see to Lon, say a few words to him, feed him,

and make sure he was on a decent piece of ground. I was finishing what I could do for him when I saw Bodwin making his way along the sidehill toward me.

He said, "Sissona wants to see you, Frare."

"Sissona? What is it?"

"I don't know. She's upset."

Hurrying toward the House of Quiet, I saw Sissona standing in the half-open doorway. She beckoned to me, but before I reached her the door swung all the way open and Alwina stepped out beside her. The bright, flickering firelight from behind them prevented me from seeing their faces clearly.

"Frare!" Alwina cried to me with alarming intensity. "I must not stay here! Not in this place! Om is too much here. Too much in me. I can feel Him like a fire. Like a roaring fire! Like all the bees in the world buzzing. I will burn up! I will burst open! I must not stay here! I cannot stand Om this way."

I could see her face now and I was certain she was another with a very high fever. I also remembered her description months ago — and she had been almost frightened then — about how the presence of Om felt warm like the buzzing of bees. I knew I must get her out of the House of Quiet, but where was I to take her? Out in the rain all night with a fever? In Sissona's face I read complete agreement, but not a hint of solution.

I said, "I understand, Your Majesty. I'm not sure what we can do. I'll find out in a few minutes. Until I come back you must stay here. You be sure she does, Sissona. She must not go out in the rain. I'll be back quickly."

I ran toward the place I had left Trant, found him still standing on the rock with the water curling around his feet, and shouted at him, "Drune! Where's Drune?"

"He's not back yet."

I started up the hill myself calling on Drune when some fifty yards above me I heard someone cry, "Who wants Drune?"

and a figure slid and stumbled its way down to a stop in front of me.

"Drune," I said, grasping him by the shoulder of his sopping parka. "What did you find?"

"A quarter mile from here at the top of the glen is a large dry cave. Just one. A half mile back along the ridge is a long chain of little ones. They are low and shallow, but they're dry."

"Will they hold Trant's men?"

"Well enough."

"Good," I said. No flames were coming from Trant's fires now, only steam. "I need the large cave for the Queen. Here's what you're to do." I gave him instructions for himself and his companion, Halkon, and also for Trant. "Off with you. Quick! Now, where has Bodwin got to?"

I found him near one of the drowning, hissing fires, drew him aside, and put the situation to him rapidly but in enough detail for him to understand it. "This may be a long vigil," I told him, "and I would like some help and support in it. You know the Queen and the circumstances and you can be discreet when you care to. I don't need to elaborate. So I've come to you. Will you join me?"

He slowly raised his head and shook it no. "I wouldn't be any use to you, Frare. I'm no good in a sickroom. Even so, I'd come if I thought I was necessary, but I'm not." Then he gave me an odd, apologetic smile. "You remember I once told you I meant to spend my life at the Queen's court? I still do. I'm sorry not to help you. Sometime you'll understand me better."

I didn't expect him to refuse, so my anger not only surprised me but I showed it. "I understand well enough right now. I'm sorry I suggested it."

Sissona took the news of the cave with relief but no enthusiasm and began gathering things together. I asked her, "Do you want to take one of the other women along? You can if you like. We don't know how long this will last and the nursing will be mostly yours."

She thought about this only for a second and then said in a way that was plainly intended to include me, "No. If I need help, I can send for it."

We wrapped Alwina heavily and set out with Drune on one side of her and me on the other, at times half carrying her. Just behind us came Sissona, followed in turn by two troopers with the baggage and supplies. Drune had already sent an additional pair ahead with some remaining dry pieces of wood to start a fire. If it weren't for the real danger of slipping and falling badly, I'd have done better to carry Alwina outright by myself. Her mind was a long way from the streaming hillside and she kept our pace miserably slow and uncertain. It was now dusk and, to avoid boulders and gain some shelter from the wind-driven rain, we abandoned the ridge of the glen for one of its sides encumbered wih vines and scrubby trees. During the final yards, however, we saw the light of a tiny fire in the mouth of the cave.

With messengers coming and going, it took about an hour and a half to resettle the whole camp. Trant got his men into the dry cramped caves down the ridge and posted sentries over the ponies and at the House of Quiet. The women were still there and so was Bodwin, whom they had certified harmless for the length of the emergency. During this, we arranged ourselves in our big cave and passed through our first crisis. The room was half again my height in the center, sloping down to four and five feet at the sides and back. All told, it was perhaps thirty feet across by twenty deep. The place was cleaner than I expected with a scattering of leaves and sticks on the floor along with a few bones left by cats or foxes, but no manure from bats or birds.

As I lifted Alwina over the cave edge past the fire and set her down with her back against one of the packs, I saw a look of awareness come into her eyes and then fade away. I knew at that moment what I hadn't had time to grasp before, that I had the choice of being frightened by her illness or unimpressed by it. My ignorance was complete enough to justify either attitude, but I was reasonably sure Sissona knew no more than I. It was up to me, and I decided then to be unimpressed. Even if I couldn't maintain the position steadily to myself, it was the only one that would give me any power.

Taking a blazing stick from the fire, I began to search the cave roof with it, hoping its smoke would find a fissure that would serve as a draft. Slightly to the rear and to one side of the cave the warm smoke suddenly veered upward as though drawn by a string. I told Drune to build a second fire directly underneath the spot. Then I noticed Sissona busy in a far corner, where the cave was lowest and the walls formed a sharp angle. She was making a couch there and closing it off with a fence of hoods, blankets, and packs.

I walked in that direction until my head touched the descending roof. "Sissona," I said, "if you are making that crib for yourself, that's fine. But we're not going to put the Queen in it."

As I spoke her face took on the Household expression of gentle, unquestionable authority, plus some of the weary patience of a children's nurse. "I've taken care of the Queen since she was a little girl, Isla Frare. I don't need to be told what she needs. I have to do what I know is best."

She did it well and it worked, making me sound wrong even to myself. I watched her serenity return with her incantation and felt resignation to the rules of the nursery creep through me. I said, "I mean what I say, Sissona. That corner is no good. It's dirty and crowded and the air is bad. Alwina won't get well there. I won't interfere with the privacy of your nursing. Put the bed out in the open air between the fires."

On her knees in the corner, her head bent forward under

173

the sloping rock, the firelight gleamed in her eyes, and she looked for an instant like some crouching animal. In the same soft, unyielding voice she said, "You are a man and you cannot cure. I know what is best for the child. Let us alone."

So our wills locked hard over everything that was suddenly summed up in the placement of Alwina's bed. "You don't know anything about this, Sissona. Alwina isn't a little girl now. She is a woman who is sick from stress and anxiety — and you don't even know you caused some of it. You can't intimidate me with the past. And not with the future either. If you don't agree with me about how we should care for her, I'll take you back to the House of Quiet and bring up the other women."

She stared at me, at bay in her corner, and I knew she was trying to estimate what might be gained or lost by testing my determination to evict her. My advantage at the moment was that I didn't care. I would do what I threatened. At last she said, "Yes, I see you will do that." Then all at once — too strong for calculation and too swift for pretending — her old, uncomplicated love for her charge surged up in her, her face crumpled, and she bent her head between her hands. After a moment or so she lifted her head again, wiped her eyes, reached for the blankets beside her, and asked, "Where is it you want all these?"

"Right over here," I said, and dropped to my own knees, helping her put the bed together between the fires near the middle of the cave.

After that we got on with our business. We moved Alwina, and Sissona put her to bed. Drune and Halkon built up the wood supply, again cutting only resinous pine and hemlock, which made a spitting, uneven fire but could at least be counted on to burn. By now nothing else could. We cooked a few things at the fires and Sissona made a broth for Alwina, of which she took a very little. I told Drune and Halkon to divide the night watches to suit themselves, but to be sure one was on duty and keeping up the outer fire. We didn't want a big cat, a wolf, or a bear calling on us. I would take care of the other fire.

All the while the rain plunged down and the wind whined across the cave mouth, whipped the scraggly trees, and shrieked and howled over the rocks of the crest above us. When Sissona needed to have me out of the way, I stood in the entrance watching the outer edge of the firelight, where the demonic water moved from the darkness and back into it again in twisting strands and braids. Now and then the wind dropped, suddenly and eerily, and then the sound of the angry stream rose up from the bottom of the valley.

I tended the inner fire at short intervals, trying to keep it from smoking and make it as steady as the unpredictable wood allowed. The warmth from the two fires from opposite sides became dependable enough so that Alwina, very restless and uneasy, did not have to be constricted with a great weight of blankets.

Sissona did not mention this, but once when Alwina was resting quietly for a few moments, she said, "You saw Tenira this morning. How was she?"

"She seemed better. The poison was leaving her."

"What did Attana do for the wound?"

Not knowing what to expect, I said, "She used a salve made from the cobwebs that form on grapes."

Sissona surprised me by nodding soberly and saying, "I've heard of such things, but those who told me always spoke of apples and pears. No doubt they're the same. I've never had such a salve or known how to make one. It seems to draw the heat and the pus right out of poisons. And I've heard that the web by itself is good to stop heavy bleeding. I'm glad Tenira is better."

That night I dozed only a few minutes all told, and I'm sure

Sissona did not sleep at all. Alwina's fever continued hot and, although she seemed to sleep a large part of the night, she was disturbed through it all, throwing her arms about, speaking incomprehensible words, crying out sharply and then muttering.

As soon as it was light, I set out with Halkon and made a tour of the scattered camp. Trant and his men were uncomfortable and stiff and some had pains in their joints, but there was no sickness. The ponies, most of them standing in pairs head to tail with the water coursing off their backs, presented a touching picture of quiet patience. When I spoke to Lon, he shook himself, drenching me in a cascade of rainwater, but had nothing else to communicate. At the House of Quiet, where I didn't see Bodwin, the ladies told me guiltily and gaily that they were in luxury.

The storm was not now reaching the furious peaks of several hours earlier, but in its steady severity gave every indication of lasting indefinitely. Below us the stream was rising up the hill as we watched and, on its other side, spread over the valley in a muddy torrent, carrying whatever it could uproot or dislodge. Trees still standing in its midst wore collars of grass, vines, and light debris formed against their upstream sides. Except for the grandeur of bursts of violence, the scene was desolate and dreary in the gray light.

On our return, Sissona told us quietly there was no change in Alwina's condition, and she refused my suggestion that she herself take a rest. At midday all readings stayed the same, but during the afternoon the rain slackened. At dark the rain stopped while the wind lifted itself off the ground to the level of the cliff tops. Alwina rested more easily now, and so at last Sissona consented to lie down for a while, insisting she would not sleep. She did, however, snoring softly in the corner she had intended for Alwina. I sat alone, feeding the fire intermittently, taking great pleasure in the freedom of being, save for

176

Drune who was now outside the entrance, the only consciousness in the place.

Then gradually I realized that this was no longer true. I
sensed that Alwina was awake and alert.

Soon, in a voice less than a whisper and charged with fear,
she said, "Frare?"

"Yes. I am Frare."

"Where am I?"

"In a cave up above the House of Quiet."

"Oh, yes." Her voice was almost her own now. "I'm not
surprised, so I must have known it. Is it night? How long have
we been here?"

"It is night. We've been here a little more than a full day."

"What happened?"

"You were taken sick and there has been a heavy storm."

"Why am I not in the House of Quiet? I think I remember
going there."

"Yes, we took you there, but you refused to stay."

"I see." There was silence as she seemed to think about this
information, and then she said, "Come here, Frare, and sit beside me, please. That way it will be easier for me. There's not
much time. I need to talk while I still remember what it was."

"Would you like some water first?"

"Yes. That would be good."

I brought the water and sat down on the edge of the blankets, noticing as her fingers touched mine in taking the cup
that her hands were cool now. The firelight showed me her
face now sharply and then again indistinctly, the moving
shadows constantly changing her expression to suit themselves. Recalling her outcries and the mumbled words I didn't
understand, I asked, "Did you go on another journey while you
were lying here?"

"I'm not sure. You will know when you hear. It was lonely

177

and I was terribly afraid. Maybe it was just silly and grotesque. It is all fading as I think of it. The connections are breaking and the words in my mind have no meaning."

There was nothing strange to me in what she was saying. Between the experience of a vision or a dream and the memory of it lies a realm through which meaning cannot pass before it is destroyed or mutilated. At the very least the sense is displaced and not where it seems, as with the straightness of a stick thrust slanting into clear water. The only thing that penetrates untwisted is the diminishing trace of feeling — often the frayed end of terror. So I did not know what Alwina thought she told me or tried to tell me. I did know what I made of it.

She was in Alwin House on a fine day ready to go somewhere. She started out, but whether she was riding or on foot, alone or with companions, she was not sure. The woods about the palace, the sparkling bay, the graceful hills enclosing The City were at their loveliest and best. (All through this adventure she stayed sharply aware of the looks and texture of her surroundings.)

Soon she was beyond The City and going north through rich country she knew well, the grain standing high in the fields and the cattle scattered along the green slopes of pastures above winding brooks half-hidden in turf and grass.

After another while she was climbing through a country of ledges, which must be in the Frays although it wasn't exactly like any part of the Frays she had ever seen. Now and then she stopped to touch the granite spotted with lichen that lay in orderly arrays all around her, and she noted approvingly, as something to be singled out, that the rough surfaces felt cool in the shade and warm in the sun. Whenever she did this, the sense of Om's presence swam strongly inside her and in the air around her.

178

Then, without having seen or climbed any mountains, she knew she was leaving great peaks behind her on either side. In front of her now, beyond a foreground of shallow craters, stretched a plain that she knew was endless and that she identified as the Sobo Steppes, a place she had never thought she would visit.

Here something said, very plainly and carefully, "Om is! Whatever is is Om!" The curious thing was that there was no voice and no sound, but she was aware of the words as though she heard them, although it might have been that she also saw them.

Then she marched out onto the plain in time to a noiseless chant, "Om is!, Om is!, Om is!", while the sense of Om's presence grew fainter with each step.

After a long walk she stopped in the exact center of the plain. How she was sure of this she did not know, because the plain was flat and completely featureless, its surface having a dull color and a rough nap that reflected nothing. Whatever was overhead was precisely the same, and consequently there was no horizon anywhere. It was now part of her awareness, however, that the vast carpet was receding toward her from its edges.

"Over there," came more words and did not indicate a direction, which was just as well because there was none, "is eternity."

Searching vainly for a horizon as a boundary, she asked, "Am I in eternity?"

"Some of you is."

"Is Om there?"

"No. Eternity doesn't exist, so Om can't be there. But eternity depends on duration, and all things must begin their lasting before or after other things. Once that is recognized, Om will be there."

"I see."

"And over there," the words continued, "is infinity."

"Am I in infinity, too?"

"Yes. All of you."

"Is Om there?"

"No. Infinity doesn't exist either. Infinity is based on extension and reduction, however, and these have limits, whatever the name says. Only words and names have power over what does not exist. When the limits are reached, Om will be there."

"I see. Is there anywhere else?"

"Yes. One more. Over there is chaos."

"Am I in chaos?"

"No. Not yet. Chaos is a little different. It doesn't exist any more than the others, but it is the material counterpart of eternity. It's full of stuff that was never trained by time. Unruly place. You may not go there at all. Some don't. Om would prefer not to."

Looking down, she knew without being able to discern anything that the solid patch on which she stood was now scarcely larger than her feet. "I'm about to fall," she said.

"Yes, you'll drop through any minute now."

"Why does Om keep growing weaker?"

"You forget. Om is. It isn't He who grows weaker. Sometime you may sense Him in one of those other places. Farewell."

That was the story, as it reached me, of what Alwina knew and did somewhere. She lay back watching me after she finished. "It doesn't sound impressive when I try to tell it, does it? I'll never be able to come even that close again. It's fairly ridiculous even now. Like a child's concoction." She smiled and shook her head. "But I assure you I didn't like it on that plain. The horrid joviality of it. But thank you for listening to me, Frare. Now I've told it I can go to sleep." She closed her eyes, turned on her side, and soon did go to sleep.

I got up after a while and walked quietly to the cave mouth.

Except for the steady rushing of the stream down below, the night was nearly silent now. Overhead, light from interrupted appearances of the moon showed the broken cloud stream pouring past. It made a lovely, preoccupying sight and I stood watching it for a long time. I wasn't thinking of anything except the bright edges and changing shapes of the clouds. Then I went back to tend the fire once more.

I had about finished when Alwina stirred behind me, and she said, "Frare," again, but more firmly than before.

"Yes?"

"You feel I behaved badly in Winder, don't you?"

Sitting back on my haunches, I turned my head to see her. "Badly? I wouldn't have chosen the word, but I suppose so — yes."

"You needn't fear," she said. "I agree with you. Or rather, that's what I feel. Now. I didn't yesterday. Not that Tor was altogether right, but that's not the point. And he was much more nearly right than I." She fell silent and the fire spat, taking hold of the new wood. Then she went on, "I've a lot on my conscience I must look at. Do you think Tenira will forgive me?"

"You've known her far longer than I," I said. "She loves you and fears for you. It doesn't seem to me that forgiveness comes into it."

"No, I suppose not. It's too serious. She would say that's not her affair. I must earn the ability to forgive myself. That won't be easy. My father put it differently, but perhaps he meant the same thing. He said a King must sleep well in both his beds or he will sleep in neither. Am I right, Frare? You love Tenira?"

"Yes."

"That's good. I hoped so." Again she was silent, less as if musing than examining a decision already taken. "There is a flood?"

"Yes. The stream is over most of the valley."

"Will we be able to travel tomorrow?"

"Probably by midday. The stream is small and drains only these hills close to it. It will go down overnight."

"Very well. Make everything ready to leave at noon. But, Frare, we will be heading west, not east. I am going back to Winder."

"Yes, Your Majesty."

The weather next day was delightful, warm and breezy but not hot, as though there were no such things as storms, the ugly story written across the valley notwithstanding. By daybreak the stream was down enough so that we could have started then, but everywhere it had left behind a cover of tan mud bearing every kind of scouring, from whole trees and their roots to withered oak branches with their dead leaves still clinging to them. The hill showed a tracework of raw gashes, where new gullies had been dug in its side. As soon as the sun came up we hung every cloth and garment to air and dry until it seemed some giant quilt-maker must have emptied his bag of patches over us. But at noon we were ready and I climbed to the cave to report to the Queen.

"Thank you, Frare," she said. "That was well done all round. Let's be off." But then she checked me, saying, "There's one change I haven't told you. We'll be going east after all. Straight to The City as fast as we can. What most needs to be done I can do best there."

"Yes, Your Majesty," I said, and turned back down the hill to form the troupe.

There was no harm done in any practical way, if indeed in any other. I faced no questions, had no confusions to untangle and no hurt feelings to assuage, except possibly my own. I hadn't announced the return to Winder because there was no need to make special plans for it. It's as easy to point horses in one direction as another. As for the surprise people would feel, the answer was similar. A surprise at noon is no harder to handle than one at breakfast. And certainly just one surprise is easier than two. Along that line, I wondered if part of my reason for keeping quiet was that I hadn't quite believed Alwina, and then I decided speculation wasn't worth much. Now there was no shock of any kind, and we lined up and set off at a good clip, all of us happy to be quit of the valley, horses as well as humans. That seemed a good way to leave the whole thing.

When we had been on our way an hour or so, Bodwin overtook me. I'd expected him sooner. Contrary to his usual custom, he didn't immediately open a conversation, but rode a while in quiet. I didn't help him. When he finally came to it he said, "Cousin, I'll regret it if our friendship is damaged. I'm sorry if I gave offense the other day. As I remember it, I was rude. The trouble is I can't apologize for what I did — or rather declined to do — because I meant that. I may have to do it again someday to someone else, and I will if necessary. Can you accept an apology for the manner and not the fact?"

"You gave two reasons for refusing," I said. "One was that you would be no help. As things turned out, you were correct in that. You would have been no help, although you couldn't have known it at the time. So there is something to your credit. The other reason I didn't understand and still don't."

"That I plan to spend my life as an observer at court? You don't understand the difficulty? It's not hard to see. In my position, you cannot let yourself get too close to particular events. If you do, you lose your balance and misinterpret what you see. Then you may go further and take not only a personal interest but a direct hand in the outcome. In that case you distort doubly. Either way you become worthless — worthless for what I want to do."

"That's acceptable as far as it goes," I said, "but there is surely more to it."

"More? There usually is — to anything — but here you will

have to make it for yourself. That is enough for me."

He was evading me, and intended me to know it. We were at our old game again and there was a certain feeling of companionship about it. If his pleasure lay in being subtle, mine came from perceiving that it didn't matter. I said, "Cousin, our friendship isn't harmed for me. I suppose it was in danger for a few moments when we almost took it seriously, but you've explained that mistake. Rest easy."

As we approached The City on the southern road from the west, we turned off toward Alwin House and sent a messenger to town calling Isla Cabing and Isla Mora for a midafternoon meeting, it being then midmorning. Alwina told me she wanted me to attend and then, straight-faced, placed me in Sissona's care. The joke, if it was one, was really at Sissona's expense, for the forced journey had been hardest on her and I knew she was weary, but she found me a room and had water, towels, and a fresh tunic brought.

She smiled as she left and said, "You should feel better about this room than the one in Winder you wouldn't use. Get some sleep, Frare. I'll see you're called in time."

"Thank you, Sissona. And you?"

"It rests me just to be home. I'll sleep tonight."

I washed, slept, woke, and ate, expecting to feel the weight of responsibility slide off me pound by pound. When I realized that it wasn't going to, I had to consider the possibility that I had misconceived the nature of what I was doing or that responsibility itself was different from what I had always thought. I had sometimes suspected I felt myself too big for my job. Was that true? Bodwin, who should find the subject crucial — as an observer of course — would resolve my dilemma as soon as he could think of an epigram. Finally, my companion, my mind, working unknown to me, had forced me to the place where I had already told it I didn't want to go. Turning into the road to Alwin House that morning, it came to me that I knew who the master assassin was, knew certainly but without any proof at all. Now that I had the knowledge, I had to decide what it required of me.

The meeting was small, only the Queen, Cabing, Mora, and myself. We sat in the garden where I had first met Alwina, all of us listening while she talked. That in itself said a great deal. Now and then, when called on, I supplied a detail or described an event at which she hadn't been present. The whole thing was Alwina's considered version of the mission to Winder. She wasn't easy on herself, and her severe editing I thought still left her conclusions sound. She told us the alliance was solid, but it had to be taken as an alliance, not as an agreement with an Islandian dependency. However improbable that might be, or unpalatable, it was a fact. Winder was in a touchy state and not ready now to listen to anything permanent Islandia could offer. It had to be talked to as an equal. With firmness, yes, but as an equal. Islandia would have to make up its financial arrears and a lot more — quickly. There could be no more punishment by withholding funds. Cabing and Mora would have to help her bring pressure on the Council.

All of that was good. What was not so good was her extreme sketchiness and her notable lack of candor. I understood her unwillingness to talk about her personal feelings, but they had caused a large part of what happened and when she described her bitter, wounding fight with Tor as nothing worse than a stiff exchange of formal differences, I couldn't help feeling she should be having some trouble sleeping in those beds her father mentioned. Naturally, she said nothing about the valley of the House of Quiet except that she had been sick there briefly during a storm. By now, of course, I knew very well why I was included in this gathering. Alwina was setting the limits for public discussion much as I, at her instruction, had justified our sudden departure from Winder. The same things, plus a few more, had to be avoided.

I guessed Alwina might tell somewhat more in private to Isla Mora, for he was an old, close friend. To Isla Cabing I thought she would also tell a little more, but less, for though just as old a friend he was not as close. I found it comic, but not laughable, to reflect that, when all was put together, I knew more about events in Winder than any other one person, including Alwina and Tor themselves.

When the Queen signaled the end of the meeting, Camian wine was brought and we sipped it once again out of silver cups I recognized, talking casually of matters of indifferent concern — the latest jests making the rounds of The City, a new strain of powerful mules being bred by Isla Dorn, a stubborn leak in the roof of the Council chamber that forced a pail to be hung over Isla Farrant's head. As Mora and Cabing prepared to leave, I asked the Queen's permission to accompany them and return to my own lodgings in The City.

She assented, saying, "Just when Sissona was beginning to say kind things about you. But I don't see why not, Frare. Just keep in touch with Isla Cabing in case I need you suddenly."

As we rode past the fields toward the woods, Cabing asked me, "What's this about Sissona?"

"Nothing serious," I said. "I got on the wrong side of her in Winder because I wouldn't move in and live with the Queen's party. I couldn't. The Household was offended for a while." When he made no comment, I asked, "May I come to talk to you tomorrow, Isla Cabing?"

"You should soon," he said, "but the next few days are bad, as you just heard." Then he looked at me and shrugged his shoulders. "I see you feel it's urgent. Well then, tomorrow evening."

The next day I spent re-establishing myself, paying visits and asking questions. Many of them I asked of Woking's younger brother, Atta, with whom Woking had lived and on whom I called to say I was grieved by Woking's death. Atta confirmed what Cabing had said in his dispatch. There was no information in Woking's room and probably none on his person when he was murdered. "That was his way," Atta said, partly in admiration and partly in annoyance. "He never wrote anything down and he expected everyone's memory to be as good as his. That made housekeeping difficult and my wife used to complain to him. No, what he knew was in his head. That made his enemies angry, I'm sure. It was hard on his friends, too."

We were sitting talking in what had been Woking's own room. It looked out not over the bay but north along the broad vale of the river toward the rounded hills rising on either side of it. I told Atta, merely stating the probability, that I thought his brother's killer had himself been killed, and he took the news with satisfaction but no joy of revenge or justice.

"I'm glad to hear it," he said, "but it doesn't seem to mean a great deal. I never saw the man. Maybe my brother never did either. He might as well have been killed by lightning or an avalanche." He smiled then and looked suddenly a lot like Woking. "What good is it to say an avalanche has been brought to justice?"

I might have said the killer didn't look much like an avalanche, or a bolt of lightning either, with Crask's arrow in him, but instead I asked if Woking had ever spoken of such things as throw-darts or knots, even if he never wrote anything down.

Atta thought for a moment and then said, "Yes, I think perhaps he did. Very early. It would be before he took things so seriously."

"You must have some of your brother's ability," I told him. "Can you remember?"

"I don't know," he said with irritation. "Isla Cabing's people didn't say anything about knots and darts when they were here. Anyway, you can't expect me to remember things I didn't hear. I just don't know. My brother had a way sometimes of speaking to you and yet not speaking to you. Mostly he was talking with himself, but you did try to listen just in case he wasn't. I don't call to mind anything about knots, but he did say something that might have to do with throw-darts. It was about heads. He seemed to mean points. He said some heads or other were a regular pattern and made of new iron. I'm sure that's all there was. No! Wait a moment. I do remember something about a knot. A certain knot was not common but not unusual either. Some hunters used it when they were in a hurry." Atta rubbed the thin hair over his temples and turned away. "That really is all. I never knew what he was going on about and I didn't ask him."

I left feeling depressed by Atta and reached home to realize I was thoroughly out of sorts. For one thing, I seemed displaced and disconnected. I had no proper job now and all my thoughts and wishes kept pulling me back to Winder and Tenira. For another, I was still hanging on my own dilemma. I thought action was necessary, but I had little stomach for pressing on with the ugly business of assassin trapping, particularly since I sensed that no one else was eager to do it either. The Queen hadn't raised the subject and Cabing was reluctant to see me. Perhaps there were times when an assassin foiled was better than an assassin apprehended. Cabing might think now that success, which we had, was more useful than public victory, a possible disaster. Reluctantly, however, I agreed with Tor. The killer should be found.

Cabing took me out into his small, walled garden, where we sat in the soft dark, the stars milky and indistinct overhead around the black outline of his big oak tree. There was no dew, but the moist night-fragrance of grass surrounded us and the leaves rustled on a faint breeze sliding across The City from the west.

After we adjusted ourselves to the quiet and the dark, Cabing said, "Go ahead, Frare."

Without overtly correcting anything in Alwina's account — she had said so little about the attack on her that the difficulty lay in not unbalancing the rest of her story — I gave him a complete account of the assassination conspiracy in Winder, including its bloody ending. Wanting him to have it for once as a whole, I did not spare him what he already knew from my dispatches. He listened without any interruption, his face a pale oval a few feet from mine revealing neither features nor expression. His fingers, however, plucked stem after stem from the grass.

When I finished, he said, "So that was what happened. I hadn't realized quite . . . It came much too close! And yet you wiped it out."

"Yes, we wiped it out — in Winder. And we collected no evidence to speak of. The Queen sees it in the light of other things and doesn't know the details. I'm afraid she very much underestimates it. Taken on its own terms, the attempt deserved to succeed. It very nearly did."

"No doubt," Cabing said. "It was a big effort and carefully planned. The plotters worked with determination and took great risks. Yet they failed and the mechanism was destroyed. Who remains? One, perhaps? Meanwhile, the situation changes. Do you think there can be another plot?"

"Can be? Yes, certainly."

"Then do you think there will be?"

"I don't know," I said, and I couldn't keep the irritation out of my voice. "What good is a guess like that? We have to assume there will be another one."

"Yes, we have to assume it," Cabing admitted, "but we also have to define the threat as well as we can. An intelligent guess is very useful. I know where all this is pointing and so do you. Straight at the Council. There's no other place. If I had proof, I could reach into the Council, pull out the man, and get solid support. But if I go there with your story and say, 'I know one of you is a murdering traitor, but I haven't anything against any one of you,' I don't need to tell you what will happen. I'll set them in such a fury with me and each other they'll do none of the things that absolutely have to be done. I don't dare provoke a mess like that now. No, like it or not, we've got to rely on defense for the Queen's safety and hope you hurt the killer enough to keep him quiet. He's bound to have some troubles of his own by now. I'm sorry, Frare, we can't go after him directly with what we know, but I'm not telling you to give it up either."

That was all. Cabing would hear no more on the subject. Alwina went back and forth from The City escorted by Trant and his men, and they were in charge of things at Alwin House. I thought briefly of talking to Trant, but I realized he would resent that justifiably and I would do much more harm than good. I told myself, with considerable truth, that my nose was out of joint and I could at least avoid making an unpleasant fool of myself.

Meanwhile, except for poking into odd corners — with no clue any longer as to what to look for — and pretending more or less seriously to be an Isla, I had nothing to do. Because the Queen held me at her disposal I could neither go back to Winder, nor could Admiral Lamas send me to sea. On general principles and also to observe the members in action, I did attend Council meetings and I very soon established for myself the truth of what Cabing told me. A session of the Council was a discouraging experience just then.

The members were restless and unsure, eager to escape the hard questions confronting them by pursuing trivialities and inventing phantoms. As happens when people are anxious and don't know what to do about it, they grew short-tempered and prideful, making a great show of their dignity. The news about Kilikash and his fleet was menacing and inescapably uncertain, but only a few tried to give the danger a recognizable size and face and confront it. For the rest, at this time, the threat of Kilikash's coming filled the chamber every day like a fog through which they peered at grisly shapes they conjured up to suit themselves.

In this atmosphere of prickliness and fear, many of the provincial Islar refused to contribute their complement of men to the national army. They thought of the Saracen Demiji tribesmen said to be ravaging Islandia province and said their men were needed to protect their own homes. In fact, the Demiji were sealed off and isolated in the upper Frays by Cabing's government soldiers and now represented only a nuisance, not a danger. The Islar, however, were hard to reassure and, once reassured, grew alarmed all over again at the prospect of doing anything. Slowly, very slowly, in response to the patient firmness of Isla Cabing and Isla Mora and the scornful comments of Isla Dorn, they found the clarity of mind to make their commitments. One afternoon, in tones that come naturally only to a Dorn, he said to his colleagues, "We are the bold men who questioned, asking whether a weak woman had the fortitude to wear the crown. It surprises me she doesn't summon our wives and daughters in our places. Let us get home to our firesides!"

Resentfully, looking askance at one another, they pledged the men to make an army around Cabing's nucleus. At the same time, as if to compensate for the frustration of mutual suspicion, they found a fierce and unreasoning unity in another issue — Winder. The Islar could always readily agree that the blame for all their troubles lay with Tor and Winder. Whenever they denounced Tor's infamy, the unpleasant weight of their own responsibility seemed to be lifted off them for a refreshing few moments and they stood up straight in the vigor of their indignation. Winder was still bound by the old agreements. She was not an independent kingdom with the power to make treaties. Outside her borders she did what Islandia told her. Tor was an Isla first and only then a courtesy King. He could not change that. He was a traitor, a betrayer. There could be no money for Winder until after she fulfilled her obligations in the traditional terms. And then no more money than had always been customary. There was unanimity, or near unanimity, on all these things, and there was also unanimous silence on what to do about them — except to pay no money.

Cabing and Mora struggled in public and private, but they could not handle the flood of righteousness that poured out by itself at the mention of Winder. The name became a signal for unreason and here Dorn was no help. His normally sure sense of reality deserted him and he talked as wildly as all the rest. Even the Queen, when she addressed the Council on the matter, was heard in rebellious silence. It was true that she still spoke them fair and refrained from spelling out the full consequences of their refusal. Perhaps she did not quite believe those consequences herself, and she had some reason for not believing them. Or perhaps she didn't want to shut off this emotional escape before she was sure of an adequate army. Whatever the reason, as the days went on and on, I finally decided the anarchy was too dangerous, the climate for killing too favorable, for me to sit quiet any longer. Using two small events as a pretext for myself, I forced myself on Isla Cabing once again.

"I've learned your lesson," I told him. "I understand why you can't say anything to the Council about assassination. But this state of affairs is an invitation to another attempt. I know I'm not in a position to say so, but something has to be done."

Because it was raining, Cabing was seeing me this time indoors in his study. In the clear candle light he looked worn and extremely tired. I expected him to be angry, but his legendary self-control did not fail. "I confess to the same thought," he said quietly. "What would you do?"

Instead of answering him, I said, "I have no proof at all, but I know who the master assassin is."

"So? Who then?"

"The man who said, 'It is her fate, the good fortune of the country, that she is the obstacle in our path right now.' Do you remember?"

"No, I don't."

"During the debate on the Queen's accession. A long speech. It was Sevin."

"Now I do — vaguely." He turned the recollection over in his mind and shook his head. "No, Frare. That's not much of an indictment."

"There's a bit more," I said. "Do you remember my report of Tor's suspicion that Sevin was smuggling iron into Vantry?"

"Yes. And I remember you didn't find any smuggling. And what has that to do with assassination?"

"I think we looked in the wrong place," I said. "There is a connection. Bear with me. Do you remember when we began putting steel heads on our throw-darts?"

"No. I'm not even sure I knew we did."

"I don't blame you," I said. "I didn't either until I went to the armory and asked. For at least six years all regulation darts have had steel heads. The darts thrown at you in the Alwin woods looked regulation in every way. And they were new. But they had iron heads."

"How do you know that?"

"Woking told his brother that. I talked with Atta the other day."

"But Woking told me those weapons were meaningless. We got rid of them."

"That's what he believed," I said. "He didn't see the significance of the iron. Why should he? You didn't. I didn't until I stumbled on it."

"Very well," Cabing said dryly, "what is the significance of it?"

"We know the Crown has the only furnaces that can make steel. Except for Winder we thought it had the only iron forges. But if Tor is right, there must be some in Vantry. Those darts must have been made there."

"That's thin, Frare. You couldn't even convict Kilikash with that argument. What do you want?"

"Sevin left The City this afternoon to go to Vantry. I overheard him talking about it in the chamber this morning. Said there was nothing more for him to do here for a while and he was going to see to things at home. He could mean anything by that. What I want is a set of innocuous orders instructing my to travel around the country anywhere I like."

Early the following afternoon Lon and I left The City on the road Sevin had taken to the northwest. My written orders told me to observe and report the progress of recruitment wherever I thought it advisable. Additional unwritten orders instructed me to return to Winder and join Tor on his trip to the rendezvous. Cabing had offered no real objection to my request and he had secured the Queen's consent on grounds he didn't mention. I was sure part of his reason was the understandable wish to get rid of me. Another part was that he found my mixture of odd facts and speculations unexpectedly persuasive. Also, as things were going, it would not be at all a bad idea to have a friend again in Winder. As for me, I was once more completely at a loss as to what cost Woking his life and fairly well convinced I would never know.

When Cabing handed me the written section of my orders, he said, "If you actually followed these, it would be a good idea. Please understand that these do not authorize you to take any action in the Queen's name."

"I know that," I said. "I'll try not to make you disown me. Thank you, Isla Cabing."

On the afternoon of the second day I overtook Sevin and a companion named Garit, who were traveling at a moderate pace leading a pack horse. When Lon and I drew up with them, Sevin returned my greeting civilly and asked my destination. I told him Vantry to begin with, explaining why, and he laughed.

"You'll find few soldiers in Vantry, Isla Frare, but if you're determined to go there, you're welcome to ride with us. It's a rough road."

Our way lay north of the one I had taken back from Winder, leading us at the beginning through Bostia and Tamplin, then over the first great mountains and down into the upper valley of the Doring River. All across the rich farmlands, where the trees wore the dark, heavy aspect of late summer, the first crops were coming in off the fields, and pickers were busy in the orchards of early apples. From Bostia past Tamplin, with the weather unwontedly clear over the mountains, the huge, pointed snow-dome of Mount Islandia floated in the sky like a motionless cloud, seemingly no farther away than the next line of trees. At last, well beyond Tamplin, lesser and nearer peaks to our right cut it off.

It didn't take Sevin long to shake my confidence in my own judgment, and after a day or so he had me nearly disarmed. What he thought of me then I don't know. I tried to behave normally, that is, like a man holding in suspension the hostility a supporter of the Queen would feel toward a man who had strongly opposed her accession. The countrified manner Sevin liked to use in the Council was not an affectation I discovered, but it wasn't the only one with which he was comfortable for he could be as urbane as Mora.

In addition to the border language current in Vantry, Sevin

spoke Arabic and regretted he had never learned to read and write it properly. Even so, he had read prodigiously and acquired some knowledge of the world outside Islandia from books I didn't know existed. He told me that the Catholic priests of two hundred odd years before had been happy to teach Latin to their noble converts, but were unwilling to translate from it. After the expulsion of Catholics, however, a few native Latinists remained and they did translate a number of Latin books, documents, and chronicles, including the Bible. These existed only in single copies, he said, some in Reeves and others in Dole.

Riding and talking with this thin, energetic, many-faceted elderly man, I found it hard to keep on believing that he belonged in either of my imagined categories of assassins — not that I had ever put much faith in them. It was true, of course, that the sentence of Sevin's I quoted to Cabing seemed especially revealing to me because it reduced, or elevated, the Queen to the level of an abstraction, but Sevin had said it in oratory and in a speech that was built around exaggeration and humor. Underlying everything and working most strongly in his favor was his continued openness about his attitude. He made the thought of conspiracy seem out of place.

He asked me on one occasion about Alwina's tour of the countryside, and I replied that I hadn't been with her but understood it went well. "I know she was pleased with it."

"She's been playing the Crown's hand well," he said. "As a woman she lacks some cards a King would have, but she also has some special ones. Witness the tone of the royal progress. She asked herself, so to speak, into the sewing room and the kitchen. A King has to stay outside the house. But intimacy can be overdone. Calling the Assembly over the heads of the Council was a bold, intelligent move. It's never been done before. Not by the Crown. It may be the handwriting on the wall — ah, that's a phrase you don't know — a portent. The alliance of the Crown and the people against the Islar. The people could come to regret it."

"Not a very strong alliance," I said. "The Crown's writ doesn't run very far now."

"No?" he said. "It would be nice to think so. The Crown gained a big advantage with the reforms after the League. I mean the power to appoint provincial Islar. You can destroy hereditary nobility very quickly that way. Only the tradition dies hard. It would still be impossible not to name a Dorn, a Mora, or even a Sevin, but the meaning of all this is plain to any Isla who wants to keep his position for his family. In normal times, he must not only smell sweet at court, but he must keep things happy in his province, where he has to be approved. That is what you see me doing now. Not that a King or a Queen is going to come all the way to Vantry to make trouble for me, but she could send someone to ask questions about recruiting — eh, Frare?"

I ignored that and said, "The Council isn't much concerned about smelling sweet in court these days."

"These are scarcely normal times."

I agreed they were not and asked, "From living in Vantry, what do you know about Kilikash?"

"A little, but not much," he said. "He's an easterner, so he isn't too familiar. An able man from what I hear. He wants to unite the Karain the way the Queen wants to unite us, but he has less chance of doing it. He uses us as a prize and we use him as a threat. It's a game he and the Queen can both win."

"Maybe it's not a game," I said. "Maybe we are a prize and he is a threat. But suppose you're right. Is there any way out of it?"

He looked at me and laughed shortly. "Yes, there is. Cabing should talk to the men in Sulliaba."

"They don't want to be united?"

198

"They don't want to be eliminated. Not any more than I do. And they don't want their people killed any more than I do."

That exchange took place while we were still in comparatively easy country in the foothills and I spent hours going over it along with everything else I knew. I made various sums out of the information from virtue to villainy — and sometimes they were the same thing — but it never seemed to add up to murder. It was his candor that defeated me, that and his shocking combination of wrong-headedness and insight. Solitary defiance suited him, and I could picture him in open rebellion or in partnership with discontented enemy chieftains, but underhanded killing still did not seem to fit. I suppose it was the idea of the mechanics of conspiracy, conspiracy as I had seen it in Winder, with which I wouldn't identify him.

The foothills changed without warning into the great mountains, the first of three ranges between us and Vantry, and I was somewhat uneasy about them because I am not mountain bred. The hills of Winder are often just as difficult, but there altitude itself is not a problem. I didn't know how I would fare for long periods at such heights. As it turned out, I suffered more from the thin air than Sevin but less than Garit. On the long, relentless climbs, during which we led our horses, I grew as breathless as I could bear but did not turn sick or faint. On the second night, however, just before we descended into the Doring valley, the height and my dinner combined to give me an uneasy night.

I had troubled dreams, many of them disturbing and some frightening. They weren't narratives, but mixtures of picture, color, and apprehension. I wasn't particularly aware of sounds, although there may have been some, and during a few of the dreams I was certain I was awake. At one point I saw, or dreamed I saw, Sevin squatting on his haunches on the far side of the fire. A single flame rose from something that had just blazed up among the embers. He was looking down between his knees and the light bathed his face, taking the age from it and removing any expression. It might have been a head carved from sightless stone. Watching him I received the oracular message to notice that he was different — not how he was different, merely different.

When I saw him in the morning I looked at him curiously, trying to discover what it was I'd been instructed to notice. I couldn't find anything. He looked and behaved just as he always did. Sometime during the day, however, I found myself thinking of him as a killer.

After crossing the Doring River, we moved into the mountains again, the wide range separating Doring from Dole and Farrant. It was on this stretch that Sevin finally asked me about Winder. I had been hoping for this, but I hadn't wanted to raise the subject. I told him much the same thing Alwina had told the Council, using different facts when I could, and then I gave him a full account of the assassination attempt. I was careful not to tell him that all of the killers died before they could talk, and I added, "Nyall recognized one of them, an Islandian. He came to Nyall in The City one night last spring and tried to get him to join a plot against the Queen."

"Of course the Queen said nothing about all that," Sevin said, and rode for a while in silence. Then he asked, "How did she feel about being attacked?"

"She didn't say, but I don't imagine she liked it. She behaved as though it was part of her job."

"That's too bad," he said. "It doesn't have to be part of her job. Being Queen isn't her job. And I'm sorry about Tor. I admire him, but I don't like what he's trying to do with Winder. If he succeeds, he'll end by making the Crown stronger than ever."

"That's too complicated for me," I said. "But you think the Queen will be attacked again?"

He looked at me sidelong, his lined face stretched into a

mocking smile. "In Vantry, when we put words into a man's mouth, we make sure first that he can't deny them. I didn't say that, Isla Frare. I don't know whether she will or not. Remember that when you report to Cabing about my recruits."

That night we were deep in the mountains again, and Sevin and I had little more to say to each other before we took to our blankets on opposite sides of the fire. Garit, who talked, and apparently thought, little at any time, was somewhat more on Sevin's side than mine. I didn't think it likely Sevin would set upon me during the night, for the risk was large. He knew I was alert. If he missed his stroke, I could easily do for him and probably Garit as well. I doubted he could depend much on Garit. Also I sensed some indecision in Sevin, as though he hadn't decided yet what kind of danger I represented. It might be better to leave me alone altogether. On the other hand, I hadn't reported my presence either at Bostia or Tamplin and hadn't been identified as being with him. So, if he decided to kill me, there was a good case for doing it before we reached Vantry. When the fire died down, I took my blanket back into the trees and lay down close beside Lon.

Next day we came close to the Karain border and turned west to keep from crossing it. This took us for some time along the grain of the range following the courses of high valleys and working along the flanks of mountains. We could now ride for there was little severe climbing up or down, although the trail was often dangerous. It followed natural ledges and slopes wherever they existed, but there were spectacular stretches, with cliffs above and below, where men had used hammers and chisels to widen and connect narrow setbacks and outcropprings. On these passages the mountains overhung us from above and dropped away from our horses' feet down and down through shadowed blue depths to the glinting thread of a river at the narrow bottom.

In the early morning the entire system of mountains and sky

was crystalline and taut, seeming to set up vibrations within our bodies. By afternoon, answering the sun, white clouds were flowing through the mountains, some above us, some below, and some enveloping us, changing as they passed from bright and shiny mist to gray, wet wool and back to mist again. These clouds were gentle and held no winds of their own.

We followed our usual marching order, Sevin in the lead, then me, and finally Garit with the pack horse. The arrangement had never been discussed, but it seemed to me as good as any. Sevin and I had dropped our hostility of the evening before, and he picked the way confidently, turning in the saddle now and then to call my attention to something I should not miss. In the faultless weather we rode on through the superb landscape, and I did not notice Death until he touched me.

We were following a slowly rising track across the granite side of a mountain, with its almost vertical face rising on our left and the shimmering chasm on our right. In the distance, at eye level, range on range of peaks stretched away toward the sea. Just ahead of me Sevin approached an outside turn to the left sharp enough to give no hint of what lay beyond.

He rode into the turn and then stopped suddenly. I halted Lon on Sevin's heels and leaned forward trying to hear what Sevin was saying over his shoulder. As I did this I felt Lon shift his back feet uneasily outward. Still askew in my saddle, I looked back and saw Garit almost on top of me. He was forcing his horse between us and the cliff and at the same time wrenching his horse's head to the right to ride us straight over the edge. As he saw me see him, he raised his dagger in his left hand and his face pulled back from his teeth in a grimace of fear and ferocity. I knew I was trapped and there was no time to get out.

Turning away from Garit, I snatched my own dagger and stabbed it into the rump of Sevin's horse in front of me. The animal screamed and sprang forward. I felt Garit's knife in my arm and I felt Lon lurch sideways and begin scrabbling desperately with his back feet. He hung there and hung there forever, his hoofs scraping and scraping and his neck stretched forward with me bent over it. Then, before Garit could shove us again, Lon's feet came under him and he took us around the corner.

I hadn't even thought of jumping off. It would have been more dangerous than staying. There ahead of us on the trail, Sevin had his horse back under control and was moving off at a pace too fast to hold. He would slow down. Looking behind me, I saw nothing of Garit and the pack horse. I guessed he had turned back and would not be seen again. So I pulled Lon to a stop and sat there stroking him and talking to him while we both stopped shaking. Then I tested my left arm. Garit had struck me in the muscle of the outer arm below the shoulder and I would be sore for some days, but that should be all. Sevin was small now in the distance, but I didn't worry about that. He wouldn't get away from me.

I overtook him sooner than I expected. Around just such another corner as the one he used to trap me, I found him leaning against the mountain wall while his horse, apparently none the worse for its stabbing waited quietly a few paces away.

When I stopped, he said, "I thought I might as well wait for you here as farther on."

Dismounting, holding Lon's bridle rein and keeping between him and Sevin, I said, "You had bad luck back there."

"What do you mean to do?"

I looked at him, the lined face, the wiry body, the intelligent eyes. "What would you do in my position?"

"Go on as before. See the thing for what it is. An act of insanity that fortunately didn't happen. Garit is deranged. Follow your orders."

"If you were me, I'm sure you wouldn't do that. You're not even trying hard to persuade me. Why did you trust Garit to kill me? He flinched, you know — just enough."

He shook his head. "Nothing I say here is evidence of anything."

"It's interesting though. I'd like the answers to some questions."

"Why should I give you any answers?"

"You might as well. Besides, I think you want to."

Looking out over the endless peaks, rocky intimations of infinity, he considered that and said, "What do you want to know?"

"Let's forget about Garit. I know why you tried to kill the Queen. Not because of a fault or a crime. You tried to kill her to satisfy a notion of yours. You told the Council this and they didn't see it. I saw it after a while, but I didn't believe it until a little while ago. How do you explain it?"

"You may call a principle a notion if you like, but a principle is the only justification. Not a crime. Not hatred. Not emotion. Only principle."

"There are lots of principles. Even I may have one."

"You're talking about notions again. A correct principle is self-evident."

"To anyone?"

"To those who can see. For example, not everyone can sense the existence of Om. And not all those who think they do, actually do."

"Then you can be wrong."

"No. One knows. I'm only inept."

"I see," I said. "Is there another plot on foot now?"

"That is a stupid question."

"So it was. Here's another. Do you have any accomplices in the Council?"

He smiled and said, "From what you've heard as a Council member, do you think that possible?"

"How do you manage your imports of iron from the Karain?"

He swung his head at that and spoke in a more matter-of-fact voice. "How did you get that idea?"

As I told him about the dart heads and our trip up the Trilla River, he walked to his horse and took a wineskin from the saddle bag. "Very ingenious. Too ingenious. Iron, you say? I think I'll let you puzzle over that." A cloud drifted across us, silvering and softening his figure as he drank. "Now answer my question," he said, and lifted the wineskin again across his elbow. "What do you mean to do?"

"You'll go with me to Dole. From there you'll go back to The City under guard."

The cloud was now a dense fog around us, dark and wet. I no longer saw him, but I heard him somewhat muffled. "That's too long a trip. You should have had some of this wine. It comes from Camia, of course."

The cloud thinned more quickly than it came, and left the trail slightly moist. Sevin wasn't there. I peered stupidly past his horse and even up the face of the cliff instead of down where I knew he had gone. When I looked over the edge there was nothing to be seen except the white top of another cloud and the dizzying, converging abyss. After a while, I gathered up the reins of Sevin's horse, mounted Lon, and set off again.

That night I spent in a small cup of a meadow covered with yellow and white flowers and short grass. It was good to have the horses with me. I felt lonely up there with the wind and the stars and the sharp peaks and the soft, sweet grass. Dawn looked very good to me when I was finally certain of it.

LEADING SEVIN'S UNSADDLED PONY, I came out of the mountains in Farrant, crossed into Dole, and rode straight to the town of Dole. There I called on the resident steward of the province, a man named Fell, who was Isla Ord's nephew. On him I practiced a deception, or at any rate I presented him with my alternate and lesser truth, for I needed his unwitting help. I meant Cabing to be the first to know what had happened to Sevin and I wanted to tell him in such a way that he could use the knowledge, withhold it, or destroy it as he saw fit.

I found that Fell was a friendly man with a round face and thinning hair, eager to answer all my questions about the contingent Dole was raising. He had only recently had word of my visit and was surprised at it, but thought it was a splendid idea. "It gives me and our people here confidence," he told me. "It means we're important and what we do matters. The Queen has had the time to think about us and send you here to see us. I tell you it makes a difference." He knew about the Queen's tour of parts of the country and couldn't praise it enough. "I'm only sorry she didn't come this far. It would have meant so much to our people. Something to remember for a lifetime. I understand why she couldn't. It is so far. And it takes so long. Still, I'm sorry. Ordinary people don't go anywhere. We've heard about The City, but we'll never see it. We probably wouldn't think about it if our young men weren't going to see it. We like to feel we're part of the country. That's why it's so good you came."

Not knowing quite what to make of Fell, I borrowed writing materials from him and composed a report for Cabing, which I sealed carefully and handed over. Fell volunteered to send a special courier with it before I could make the request and then took me out to show me off to the town. The man had no reserves of any kind and was virtually indecent in his enthusiasm, but I couldn't say no to him. He took me from square to square, street to street, and sometimes from house to house and, in spite of myself, I found that I was caught up in the birth and growth of an experience that undoubtedly would spread from here through most of the province. The ridiculous, embarrassing man was right. It *was* important that I was here. Unlike Fell, the people didn't grow talkative or expansive, but they showed me their pleasure in knowing their contribution wasn't anonymous. One man said to me in what seemed to be simple surprise, "We don't expect it, but it's nice to be noticed."

This was another aspect of things, one I hadn't seen for myself or heard of from Sevin or Cabing or picked up in talk from the Queen's party. Even the Queen let the people know what she wanted to hear from them. Tor came closest to getting an unprompted response. I'd been with him when he did. When I finally took leave of Fell after several hours, I was glad to be able to tell him truthfully that I had spoken highly of Dole in my report to Cabing. Although I felt like a fraud, I was delighted with my day in Dole and sensed an unfamiliar and welcome freshening of spirit as I turned south. Cabing, in his own grim innocence, had said my written orders were worth carrying out on their merits, and I wondered what he would have made of Dole. It would be very interesting to try my luck in other provinces, but there wasn't time.

Time, in fact, was now a problem. It had gone while I listened to the Council and while I rode and walked. If Tor kept to schedule, I could easily miss him, depending upon how fast

I traveled and on how many days he allowed for the voyage to Shores. Whether or not Tenira would go with him I couldn't guess. I wanted to think of her as being well, completely well, but I didn't dare.

Skirting the seaward edge of the mountains, I rode almost due south to the town of Thane. At the beginning I rode Sevin's horse from time to time, thinking to improve our pace this way. I was wrong. Lon did not like it. He liked it so little my arm grew weary and my back ached from pulling him. That other horse, he made it plain, was an inferior creature who didn't deserve the privilege of carrying me. Finally, I gave Lon sole possession of the honor, and Zero, as I was beginning to call Sevin's relict, had no objections whatever. We went forward quickly in perfect companionship.

From Thane I headed diagonally inland to Tory and then straight to Earne. There I decided to take the direct path through the hills instead of the longer, easier road that approached the coast not far from where we fought the Sulliaban galley. I was not wrong. The border hills with their familiar abrupt, chunky shapes gave us neither physical trouble nor bad weather. Near the end, I came onto the track I had traveled twice with the Queen. Lon recognized it before I did.

About midday we came to the small valley of the House of Quiet and I stopped to stretch my legs and rest Lon. Zero was as fresh as a spring morning. I noticed first that the stream had shifted its bed toward the far side of the valley. This was odd. When we left after the storm, the water of course was still far higher than normal, but there was no doubt the stream was returning to its previous channel. Now it was seventy feet from where it should be. Looking closely at the House of Quiet, I saw nothing wrong with the corner nearest me, but then I realized the building had no roof and the far end was a jumble of fallen stone and masonry. Very much puzzled, I climbed the hill toward the cave, leaving the ponies to themselves even though Lon was uneasy. The line of the ridge was not the same as I remembered it and the ravine was choked with new boulders. The scrawny trees that once dotted and held the upper slope were snapped off, uprooted or half-buried as they stood. I could not find the mouth of the cave. I could not find the cave or where it had been. It was evident there was no cave. The cornice of low cliff that had run along the ridge was still there in a fashion, but flattened and broken with deep saddles in it. I walked through one of these gaps and looked down the reverse slope into the adjacent valley. There were slides and uprootings there, too, but I couldn't see how far they reached.

Returning to the spot where the cave must have been, my memory now alive and accurate, I saw not one place on the old camp site or in the valley that looked wholly as it had been. From here the House of Quiet was two broken walls, forming a right angle. The scene of that turbulent day and a half no longer existed.

If Alwina wanted to forget the incident, she had help. I thought of Nyall's tale of the offense once given Cam and Bos in this place and the barrenness that followed. This time something far more powerful than they had been angered, and it shook the earth. Thinking skeptical thoughts but feeling decidedly queer in my stomach, I walked down the hill, mounted Lon, and rode quickly out of the valley.

As you approach Winder town, just beyond the empty guest house where the Queen spent the first night of her visit, there is a level place where the road tops a small rise and you get your first sight of the town and the harbor beyond. Here I pulled up and drew a great breath of relief. Spread out over the water in front of me I saw rank after rank of ships. Tor had not left ahead of me. Then a longer look brought surprise and the beginning of another anxiety. There weren't enough ships. Without actually counting them, I knew there were fewer than half the number Alwina stipulated. My thoughts went back to The City and I remembered the Queen speaking nicely to the Council about the problem of Winder. Without warning I found myself choking with rage at their combined folly.

Like Cabing, I do not lose my temper. The shock of doing it then, and of doing it against the Queen, brought me instantly back to myself. I rode on into town feeling sullen and somehow displaced.

Abstracted and paying little attention, I let Lon take us up the hill to Tor's house and into the stable. I left the horses there and walked to the front door. I'm not sure what I expected to find or how I expected to explain myself. I think my senses had temporarily stopped acting and almost stopped recording, doing no more than to lift my feet up steps and steer me through doorways. I entered the house and went into Tor's big room. This was empty and the great house was silent. I did not find this at all strange. For several moments it seemed inevitable that the house should be vacated, the town deserted, and the ships unmanned in the harbor. Like the cave, the whole place had ceased to exist. I wasn't meant to come back here. That was the message of the valley of the House of Quiet.

Then I rapped my knuckles on Tor's table, felt the sting and heard the sound. So I raised my voice and called, "Halloo! Halloo! Anyone here? This is Frare!"

The answer came from several rooms away. "Frare? Frare!" The voice was Tenira's.

She came into the room at the far end where there were heavy shadows and she seemed to limp slightly. I ran to her and took her outstretched hand, flexible and strong, and I felt the bones in them as she held on to me. There was a queer small smile on her face and her eyes were serious and surprised. After weeks of imaginings and rememberings, I found her wonderfully complicated and workmanlike. I put my arms around her and kissed her. Then she shifted so her head lay against my chest and shoulder.

"So you did come back here," she said. "I can guess it wasn't only good fortune that sent you. Just the same, *I'm* glad. It's been lonely, Frare."

"I know. Everything I've been doing has been half real, as though it had one dimension missing. How are you?"

"I'm well now, or nearly. But let's not begin on ourselves yet. There's so much. I don't want to nibble at it."

"All right," I said, and hesitated. "But just one thing. You are still lame?"

"A very little.'"

I nodded and held her closer. Then I asked, "Nyall?"

She stepped away from me, took my hand, and led me back toward the big table. She *was* limping, not much, but more than she had said. "Nyall is alive. No one knows how. Even Attana gave him up. He simply wouldn't die. He doesn't look well yet, but he's working and getting better."

"And Tor?"

"He is bitter and very angry. He doesn't tell me his affairs. He likes me, but I am the Queen's friend. He'll tell you, I think. Today he's prodding some shipyard to finish one more ship. That's what he's always doing."

"And Attana?"

Tenira smiled with great affection. "Attana is serenity itself. She lets nothing upset her. Not even her son, who does his best. Right now she should be in one of her gardens cajoling her simples. Now, let's get you settled."

"Settled? Here?"

"Where else? I'm not trying to be Sissona, but don't think

anyone is going to let you disappear onto the *Earne*. So get your saddlebags and see that Lon is happy. I'll find a room for you."

There was no doubt Tor was glad to see me, but the first thing he said was, "Did you bring money?"

"No. I wish I could have."

"I didn't really think you did. Alwina wouldn't have given you such an easy job."

Later, he listened quietly while I told him the story of the Queen's efforts and the panic in the Council. "Dorn was right," he said. "It's an insult to their mothers to call them a pack of old women. But Alwina is being cautious and this isn't the time for that. She has the Assembly behind her and that gives her a strong position. She should use it. One trouble is Cabing. He's enough on the Council's side to warn her not to. He's afraid of the Assembly."

I hadn't thought of that, but it seemed very likely indeed. Cabing would have been satisfied with a close, manipulated victory in the Council at the time of the fight over the accession. He had nothing to do with calling the Assembly. Changing direction, I said, "I saw the harbor full of ships when I came in."

"I hope you did," he said. "What would Islandia have to produce man for man to equal them? You also noticed there aren't enough."

"I didn't count them."

"You didn't need to," he said, smiling bleakly. "Things are so bad there's no use squeezing my people any harder. Alwina knew what would happen. She was certainly told. She talked of at least three hundred ships and that's not too many. Today I have one hundred and thirty-five. There are more than that number again I could use, if I could put them in shape and man them. There's not the money nor the credit in Winder to do it."

"Shouldn't the Queen be told there are so few? You can't leave for another day or so even with these ships. You'll be late at Shores as it is. I can go ahead of you in the *Earne* and explain what's happened."

"Yes, you could do that," Tor said, "if the *Earne* weren't careened for scraping. She won't be back in the water for a while."

"Why?" I asked sharply. "She didn't need it."

"I suppose any ship can use it after sitting at a dock for a few months," Tor said, "but I admit I was surprised myself. Nicking didn't go into details, but I think he did it to give the crew a job. They haven't had much to do since the Queen's visit. No excitement and no discipline either. I had the impression Nicking felt they were slack and unruly."

"Were they?"

"Maybe. Definitions of that differ. They wouldn't have been if you were commanding them, but Nicking isn't you, Frare. It's not worth worrying about. Tomorrow I'll show you the fleet."

In the morning we took a small boat through the rows of anchored ships, boarding one now and then for a quick inspection. They were good ships, all of them, and I would have been much surprised if they hadn't been. Varying greatly in size and power, none was as big as the *Earne* and none was new. While we rowed between ships, Tor talked of the fleet's capabilities and his prospects.

"I can't defeat Kilikash with what I'll have. Not a chance. Not in a straight naval engagement. But if I have the early autumn winds I can give him a lot of trouble. I can harass him and I can prevent him from making a major landing. With luck I can. It's not what I'd like, but it's not disaster either."

"I notice you say with what you *will* have. Are you getting more ships?"

"Twenty more."

"When?"

"Over the next two weeks."

"Two weeks! You're going to wait that long? If you sailed today you'd be about a week late. You're going to make it three weeks?"

"I'd wait longer than that for twenty ships. I need them. I'm very good at waiting. Alwina taught me. It's a skill she should learn."

"Tor," I said, "the Queen should know this. She may be at Shores now. What is she to think? What will she be forced to do? This is dangerous. Let me have a dispatch boat. Anything."

Tor shook his head. "No, Frare. I won't let you have a boat. Nor a horse. I didn't have anything to do with immobilizing the *Earne*, but I'm glad she's laid up. You will leave when I do. I'm not going to have this thing softened for Alwina. She can wait and worry and then see the results of what she's done. She'll find out she can't behave this way."

I took a sailing skiff and went out into the sound to the protected beach where the *Earne* lay on her side, ungainly and immodest. My impression is that ships dislike needless indignity and show their resentment in any way they can. At any rate, Nicking carried his left arm in a sling, his forearm broken when a malicious spar rolled on it for no known physical reason. The crew brightened noticeably when they saw me and even more when I told them we would be sailing before long. After talking with a number of them individually, I saw what their trouble had been — they felt they were deserted. They were right, and I couldn't blame them or Nicking much for that. Going over the work on the ship, I found that Nicking not only knew what he was doing but was doing it well. I also discovered that he knew nothing about the meeting at Shores so I discarded the dressing down I had planned for him.

I drew him aside as I was leaving and asked him the necessary question, why he had decided to careen and scrape and, as it now turned out, overhaul. He told me in explicit terms what Tor had suggested.

"Did you consult Tor?" I asked.

"Yes, sir. He told me the ship didn't need it in his opinion, but I was in command and it was up to me."

"I see," I said. "All right. I think I understand. Now then, you have enough unnecessary work laid out to take a month. Scrap all of it — that is, all you can scrap without leaving her unhandy. How long?"

"Two more days."

"Fine. Let's get her back in the water."

"A pleasure, sir," he said, his sharp face pleased and eager. "I didn't want to do this."

I smiled at him, failing to perceive the trouble I had just made for myself, and sailed home greatly relieved that what could have been a bad mess was so easy to handle. Tenira and I claimed the next day for ourselves and we planned it for our cove and spring. For this we had avoided personal matters beforehand.

In the weather now there were signs of coming autumn. The nights grew sharp and in the morning the dew lay white as frost. In the warm air of afternoon there was something invisible suspended that softened the outlines of roofs and hills alike. Single leaves on bushes and saplings began to show red and yellow. We spent a long, careless time playing with our spring, enlarging it, deepening it, lining its sides and edges with flat stones. As we worked and our muscles loosened with bending and rising and hunting and carrying stones, it seemed to me that Tenira limped somewhat less, but it may only have been that her movements were irregular because of what we were doing. Finally, splashed and muddy and laughing, all parts of us warm except our water-chilled hands, we went out to the bright sun on the beach.

There we opened our hamper and I began to tell my story first, all of it. When I came to Alwina's vision in the cave, Tenira smiled gently and shook her head. "She's still the girl who insisted apples are *not* alike. Poor Alwina. She must have been very frightened."

"I'm sure she's sorry now she told me."

"Yes, but better you than Sissona. She wouldn't have helped. At a moment like that you talk to anyone who's there and hope he understands."

"That's what Alwina may not like to remember, but no matter."

I went on then until I ended with Sevin's death. Tenira shivered and sat silent for a while. Then she said, "That's horrible, Frare. I remember Sevin in the Council. I liked his face. It was tough and humorous. He seemed like a man you could get along with even when you were against him. In times like this when we have to fight Demiji and maybe even Bants, I know people who find it easier to kill them by saying they aren't human, they're dangerous animals, pests. I never knew anyone before who could think of other people as things, stones in the road, or as functions. I suppose it's comforting to feel you are eliminating the idea of Queen and not killing a woman. Does Tor know this?"

"No. I haven't told him."

"Will you?"

"No. He doesn't need to know. This is a high card now in Islandian politics. Only Cabing knows. Maybe the Queen. They have a choice. They can destroy the information if they want. I rather hope they do. But if I tell Tor, they can't."

We ate a bit then and drank some wine — Camian wine as Sevin specified — and our talk began to turn toward Tenira's side of things. It began when she asked an unrelated question. "How did Sevin's men know where to attack?"

"We don't know, but it wasn't too difficult. There wasn't any secret about the boar hunt and they had two Winderese with them. I think they went into the valley the night before and took a position on the middle one of those little ridges. From there they could watch the hunt and get to the point of the kill as quickly as we could. They knew we would do a lot of milling around then. They didn't have to count on the complete confusion we handed them."

"Yes," she said, "that seems right. As you can imagine, I've done a lot of thinking about that day. Why did I keep standing there in front of the boar? I heard Tor and I heard you. I could have got out of his way. Or I could have tried. I don't think it was hysteria. It was more that queer singleness of purpose that comes with emergency — if that's different. Most of me was saying, 'You must protect Alwina. You can't leave it to anyone else.' I've been protecting Alwina from all sorts of things ever since I was a girl myself, so the habit runs deep. You know. You've seen it. That was the good part of me. Anyway the proper part." She smiled and looked down at the sand. "But there was another part of me. It was mulish and angry and it was saying, 'You will stand here and get hurt and show her at last what it costs to be heedless.' Now that wasn't so nice."

"Maybe not," I said, "but other people have had the same idea even if they weren't willing to stand in front of a boar to demonstrate it."

"She's a puzzle," Tenira said. "She's not unfeeling or ungenerous, but she doesn't always sense a connection between herself and what happens. And she's tremendously able when she can see past her impulses and inspirations. I've told you often my time of influence has gone. That's true. I can't teach her anything more. All I can do now is wound her. I'm sure that's what I did with the help of the boar."

"Don't talk like that!" I told her. "I was there, too. I saw a reckless young woman endanger her friends and get off with a bruised shoulder when she should have been killed twice over."

"Fortunately, she wasn't, but I know who agrees with you," Tenira said, and laughed. "Attana. You don't mean it and neither does she, but she received that unfortunate visit from Sissona. Her description of it is very funny but her opinion of Alwina is . . . unflattering."

"What's her opinion of you?"

"She's very fond of me. She's been so good to me. Oh . . . you mean her opinion of my health. Yes, we'd better talk about that now." For a moment she waited and I filled her cup. "Thank you, Frare. Attana doesn't claim to be sure of anything about me. She says she's too old for being sure. Her guess is I'll have some lameness always and I may have difficulty bearing children. Not in carrying, but in birthing. She doesn't like to guess even that much. There's so little to go on, I don't know what else to say about it. I think maybe I shouldn't have said anything."

What she was saying, it seemed plain to me, was that her injury made childbirth exceptionally dangerous for her and her baby. And she had a question she couldn't possibly ask. What difference did this make between us? She couldn't ask it because there was only one answer I could make. An answer like that, however truthful, is embarrassing to give, painful to hear, and essentially unbelievable.

I said, "When we were here last time, you might have had some such trouble for other reasons. If so, you would have brought it up and we would have talked about it differently then. I would have said there were plenty of people around to have all the children the world needed and we didn't have to risk your life or a child's life to be happy. And that's what I say now."

She smiled at me and took my hand. "You're nice, Frare. That was nice. You covered a lot of ground. A little too much.

I'm not willing to give up that much. I don't think things are that bad. Anyway, I'm not going to have them be that bad. We're not going to spend our lives being cautious and tentative with each other. I wouldn't marry you if I thought that's what I ought to do. And women do have some control over pregnancy. Not perfect, but some. You know that. It wouldn't have been right not to tell you what Attana said, but all I want is for you to let me be the judge of the risk. Is that fair?"

"I'm not sure I . . ."

"Oh, Frare! Frare!" She put her arms around my neck and pressed close to me. "Don't be silly! Don't be afraid for me. I'm young and strong and I love you. So, kiss me, please, and make love to me."

Going back through the harbor, I noticed ships at what seemed to be a new row of outlying moorings. Tor confirmed this, saying that four more vessels had come in during the day. As he was talking, something stirred in the back of my mind but stayed there unrecognized.

Next day I went out to the *Earne* and arrived just after the crew got her back in the water. We spent the day rigging her, getting the stores aboard, and filling the water casks afresh. When at last the *Earne* rested there offshore ready for sea, a sense of constraint seemed to lift from us all as though we had been secretly afraid we had done her some irreparable damage. For me, in addition, it meant freedom to go to Shores in my own ship and report to the Queen. Tor would not like it, and this I very much regretted, but it couldn't be helped. And it didn't matter. He could refuse me a boat, or even Lon, but he had no authority to stop me from leaving in the *Earne*.

During my absence from Winder, Tor had needed the wharf he lent us, and so Nicking moved the *Earne* to a mooring in the harbor out of the way of the fleet and within easy rowing distance of steps to the quay. We went there now and Nicking set me ashore while the crew made ready to resume living on board. I strolled along the harbor's edge and started up the staircases to Tor's house, pausing now and then to follow the subtly changing colors of the western sky. This was not a gaudy sunset.

At one of these stops I suddenly recognized, in all its simplicity and difficulty, the dilemma my mind and unreliable companion should have pointed out to me at least two days before. Now that I had the *Earne,* did I really intend to go to Shores? This question had nothing to do with Tor's consent. I thought of the Queen waiting and knowing nothing and of Tor filling his part of a broken bargain. I thought of other things as well. I reached no conclusion.

When there was an opportunity that evening, I took Tenira out for a walk in Tor's chilly, cliff-top garden. The moon in the clear sky was almost full, laying a silver track across the water. She knew nothing about the fleet plans and the rendezvous at Shores, so I gave her all the facts and then said, "I don't want you to make my decision for me, but I've been round and round this conundrum and I'm getting lost in the crannies. You're fresh to all this and you're good at picking out what's important. I know it would help me if you would set out what you think the issues are."

"Me?" she said. "In my state of confusion? You expect something disinterested? All right, I'll try." She put her arm in mine and we walked along the edge of the terrace until she was ready. Then she said, "This is going to be terribly simple. First, nothing you can do will put any more ships in Tor's fleet or get the fleet to Shores any sooner. Next, it's your duty to bring your information to the Queen right away, but your duty is to keep friendly relations with Tor. Beyond that, there is another choice. Suppose you go to Shores. You'll lose Tor's friendship and you'll increase his basic hostility toward Islandia. You'll give Alwina time to collect herself, to invent expedients, to find weaknesses in Tor's position. The result could be a temporary, suspicious, patched-up arrangement. Who knows? Then suppose you stay here. There will be an explosion. Tor says that's the only way to make things better. But there may be nothing left to be better."

"That's it," I said. "That's just about what I make of it. I hoped I was being too gloomy and you could show me matters would work themselves out either way. Duty cancels itself out. Unfortunately. It's a question of judgment."

"Yes," she said very quietly, "a question of judgment."

"All right," I said. "I've decided. I'll stay here."

She drew in her breath and stopped walking. Then she turned slowly and put her hands on my shoulders. "Frare, I don't think I could have made up my mind to that, but I feel you're right. Yes, you are."

"I'm very glad," I said, and kissed her. "I hardly thought you could feel that way. I tell myself this is a decision based on the facts. Nobody in Islandia is likely to think so."

"It is. I know the facts."

"But we don't know what will happen." I put my arm around her shoulders and laughed. "We're certainly going to be in a good position to find out." We turned our backs on the moon and moved toward the house. "And now we have time to do one thing that becomes very important."

"What's that?"

"To marry each other before we leave Winder."

ONE HUNDRED AND FIFTY-SIX ships are not three hundred, but they are a great many and I had never before seen such a fleet under sail. Nor, I think, had anyone else there, not even Tor. In midafternoon on the open sea, sails spread in every direction as far as the horizon. Two or three bow shots away from us on the *Aspara,* Tor now hoisted the red and yellow recall pennant and the signal was repeated from ship to ship into the far distance. To try out their crews and vessels, Tor had allowed his captains to sail at will all day, but the time had come to form squadrons and close up before dusk. All this time I had kept the *Earne,* faster as well as bigger than *Aspara,* carefully on station astern of her and under reduced sail. That was to reassure Tor about my intentions, but it also, I was quite certain, annoyed him as a fact to observe.

I didn't pretend to myself that I was now free of foreboding, but some of its symptoms, my gloom and sourness, disappeared the night I decided to stay in Winder, and the rest followed a few days later when I married Tenira on board the *Earne.* That turned itself into a happy occasion.

My crew approved of Tenira — some of them had helped carry her back after she was wounded — and they decorated the ship with late flowers, lengths of ground pine, and sprays of bright leaves. Attana, seeming for a time not quite serene, fussed over Tenira like a mother and then presided over the feast she had produced for the ship's company and the guests. It seemed for a while that all the fleet and all of Winder town were on our deck. At the end and at Tenira's request, Nyall, looking now like a healthy death's-head, played the lovely horn call that had wakened us on the morning of the hunt.

My last farewell was to Lon, but he refused to take the matter seriously. He let me know he appreciated my attention as always, but preferred grain to sentiment at that hour of the morning.

During the few days at sea, Tenira and I talked very little about what might lie ahead at Shores and a lot about ourselves, always in some indefinite future without dates or circumstances to constrain us. Then, too, the separation from daily concerns always imposed by the ocean and the vast scale of its indifference to us turned us to very simple thoughts about our enemies, childish things that would have embarrassed us on land.

"Here we are," Tenira said, nodding in the general direction of north without even any land in sight, "just across the mountains from them. We've been this way for hundreds of years. It astonishes me we don't know any more about them."

"I suppose that's what mountains are for."

"I wonder." She considered the idea and then laughed. "You mean we're better off not knowing? It could go on and on. If Kilikash drives most of us into the sea and makes the rest of us slaves and fills the country with his own people, then someday another Kilikash down there will tell his tribes it's time to conquer Islandia and kill all those rich, soft people up south. All because of the mountains?"

"It takes longer with the mountains. They've kept us from wiping out those barbarians over there."

"Maybe so. It's true we're always losing war parties in the passes."

"We're not very peaceable either," I said. "We can't afford to be."

"And yet the Mora family are all peaceable. More than most. It's said they have some Saracen ancestors."

"Yes, I've heard that," I said. "They look as though they might have. If that's what makes a Mora, then we all should have Saracen ancestors. But somehow I don't think that would help us with this Kilikash now."

"No," she agreed sadly, "not at all. Wouldn't it be nice if we didn't have to be as stupid as they are?"

Shores is not a good harbor for a fleet. It is small, poorly protected from southwest weather, and its entrance can be difficult. All this was known from the beginning, but it was never intended that the fleet should enter the harbor or even stay in the vicinity more than a few hours. The plan was that two or three ships would go in, exchange information with the Islandian commander, and come out promptly with the Islandian squadron. Now things were very different and Tor did not tell me what he meant to do.

In the early morning we made a good landfall near Shores, and Tor took the *Aspara* alone across the mouth of the harbor. Returning, he signaled for the *Earne* and two designated squadrons, thirty ships, to follow him in. The fleet was to stand off and on until further orders.

In a light westerly wind, under clear skies, I put the *Earne* in *Aspara*'s track and entered Shores bay with no difficulty. The other ships, leaving their formations one at a time, followed easily in a long, single line. In the bright morning air, details ashore stood out sharply against the background of sand and grass and trees — a trooper saddling his horse, a dog trotting along the beach, the smoke of a cooking fire. The bay itself was completely empty, not an Islandian ship, not even a skiff there. But back of the beach on a rise among pine trees stood a cluster of large tents, where Alwina appeared to be staying. To one side, separated by a stretch of low dunes, was the camp of a detachment of horsemen, certainly Trant's. Shores town was some little distance away and inland.

Tor dropped anchor near the middle of the small stretch of

open water and I moved on toward the east end to be out of the way of his squadrons. As I passed, he cupped his hands to his mouth and called, "Meet me on the beach as soon as you can."

Leaving the ship to Nicking, I called a boat crew, and Tenira and I landed within seconds of Tor and Nyall. Walking up toward the tents, we found ourselves following a well-defined path and I said, "They've had time to build a road. I wonder if they've planted crops."

Tor laughed shortly and shook his head. "Not that. That would be useful."

Trant met us at the edge of the trees, seeming squarer than ever in the chin and shoulders. "The Queen is waiting for you," he said curtly, faced about, and led us to a big, central tent where Alwina and Mora sat side by side at a cloth-covered table. Alwina rose, took Tenira by the hands, kissed her, and placed her in a chair across from her own. The rest of us she left standing except Trant, who sat across from Isla Mora.

Not a word had been said so far and the silence grew more hostile by the moment. At last the Queen spoke to Tor. "What have you to say?"

"What do you want to talk about?" Tor replied quietly.

"Why are you so late?"

"When there is no money, things take longer. You know that, Your Majesty."

"How many ships have you?"

"One hundred and fifty-five."

"You promised three hundred."

"No, Your Majesty. I said there would be as many ships as there were."

"Don't quibble with me," Alwina said, her voice growing thinner. "You know the figure. Frare? You were there."

"Yes, Your Majesty," I said, wondering why she risked calling on me once more for verification. "You said there must be at least three hundred ships. Tor then said what he has just told you."

"So you did hear me," she said bitterly to Tor. "There was no misunderstanding. I told you three hundred ships." She looked aside at Mora, as if to make sure that *he* did not misunderstand, and then turned back to Tor with her hands clenched. "I waited here a week and then sent Isla Cabing back to his duty in The City. I waited a second week and then ordered Admiral Lamas back out on patrol with my ships. I have now waited more than three weeks and you bring me half a fleet! One hundred and fifty-five ships to match Kilikash's four hundred and fifty! I've defended you against the Council. I've told them you were an honorable man devoted to Winder and Islandia and you would justify our trust. They hold you to be in rebellion. They say no terms have changed and none can change at your instance. They say further that no moneys may go to you while you are in rebellion, nor until you have performed the duties properly required of you. I am now forced to agree with the Council. You have shown me what your undertaking is worth. 'Be at Shores,' you told me. 'Be there on the day.' I was here on the day, and on many days since. To be failed and mocked. No more! Now I'll send no money until I see the ships. The Council is right. That is the only way to deal with you."

"Before you left Winder," Tor said calmly, "you agreed that there must be money before there could be ships. Nevertheless, while you and the Council are waiting for me to perform my duty, what is to happen meanwhile?"

"Can you fight Kilikash with your ships plus twenty-six of mine?"

"That's not the point. Do you expect me to? After what you've just said?"

"Of course. What else can you do? You yourself have said that if we fall, you fall."

Tor looked from Alwina to Mora and back again and shook his head. "That's a spirited attitude, Your Majesty, but I don't think Isla Mora approves of it. You keep returning to the comforting illusion that you are Queen of Winder and I am an Islandian Isla. I've explained to you before that these things are not so. Your writ does not run in Winder. You have no authority over me. Nor does the Council. I am King of Winder. While you were in Winder you made a flat, unqualified promise of money. Of that there is no doubt. The unfortunate Isla Frare can testify to that also. You broke your word and now you speak slightingly of a hundred and fifty ships. An equal effort by Islandia would come to more than a thousand. Islandia, where you can't even raise your own troops. Winder has more than kept its bargain and all it has received is bad faith. You count on my having no choice except to join you. You are wrong, Your Majesty. There are other things I can do. Before I decide on one of them, I suggest you spend an hour or so thinking over the rash position you've taken. The Council is not your best friend, as you should know by now. So take heed and consider until I come back."

He raised his big hand in a sign to Nyall and they walked out of the tent, leaving the rest of us to look after them and then at each other. The Queen spoke first and to me. Her eyes were angry and she was breathing fast. "What does he mean, Frare? There's no end to his insolence. What is he thinking of?"

"I have no idea," I said, and I had no idea whatever.

"Think, man! He must have said something you heard. Let slip some hint. That is, if he means anything."

"No," I said again. "We've all been over this problem in different ways, as you know yourself, Your Majesty. Tor has never suggested anything except that in the end he would support Islandia. I've heard him extremely bitter about having no alternative. I don't know what he means."

"It's bluster," Alwina said. "He's trying to frighten me. Wouldn't that be a pleasure to him! And what a success!"

Isla Mora coughed politely but with authority and interrupted. "Frare," he said in his light, surprisingly young voice, "how well do you know Tor?"

"Well enough by now."

"But how well?" he persisted. "In what way? As a subject knows a King? As an ambassador knows a ruler? As a man knows a friend? Can you tell me that?"

"I've fought beside him, worked with him, argued with him as man to man."

"That should do. In your opinion, would Tor make his own peace with Kilikash?"

"No. He wouldn't do that."

"Would he pretend to do it?"

"No."

"No," Tenira said. "I agree. He wouldn't do either one."

"I also agree," Alwina said. "He's too proud and too sensible."

"Very well then," Mora said. "In spite of what he says, it seems he has no other course."

"And neither have I," Alwina said. "There is no more considering to do. Ah, well. We've waited this long. We can wait another hour." She put her hand on Tenira's shoulder and smiled at Mora. "This is only a tent, Isla Mora. I would like a few moments with my teacher. Would you mind? You and Isla Frare?"

Mora rose, saying, "Come, Frare," and led the way out. We stopped briefly at the edge of the trees to look down at the bay. Tor's ships lay on either side of the *Aspara* by squadrons. Small boats were moving among the ships and a number of others were drawn up on the beach. There groups of sailors gathered around cooking fires, making themselves a change

228

from the food they got on board. For a moment we watched the scene, catching snatches of laughter and talk carried on the wind, and then Mora turned onto the path to the village. It made a pleasant walk, he told me, as he knew from doing it several times a day. It suited him better to stay there then at Alwina's camp.

Mora stepped out beside me with easy resilience, his walk casual and firm. Now and then he turned without apology to study me with his dark Mora eyes, which seemed at once to see everything and nothing. When he had satisfied himself, he said, "I wish she weren't in love with him."

"Do you think she is?" I said, surprised, but not pretending to misunderstand.

"At my age I've seen love too often to be mistaken about it. It seldom comes in moderation, but even so I've nothing against it. Nor against Tor. But it is bad for Alwina now. It makes her angry and hostile so she cannot see things for what they are. She could override the Council, but because she wants to do it, she won't do what she should do. She believes the Queen shouldn't give way in a matter like Winder. But she has made reconciliaiton with Winder a condition of her reign and someday she is going to have to reach agreement with Tor. More on his terms than hers, for I think he's been right in much of what he's been urging. She should do it now. But Alwina can't grasp this because she's in love with him and that makes everything suspect to her, particularly herself. It's a shame."

"It doesn't sound very much like love, Isla Mora."

"Ah, but that's just what it is."

"Tenira might agree with you," I said, "but she says Alwina doesn't listen to her anymore."

"She's right, and not only for herself. Alwina takes no advice now, except indirectly from the Council, and the Council is frightened and selfish at this point. They are still afraid for themselves and haven't risen yet to be afraid for the country. Tell me something, Frare. You didn't seem quite satisfied with the replies you gave me a while ago. Why?"

"It wasn't the answers," I said. "I'm sure of them. Tor won't go to Kilikash or pretend to. But I haven't known him to make empty threats."

"I understand," Mora said. "That is very troublesome." We walked on in silence until he broke out in exasperation, "But what can he possibly do?"

"Again I don't know," I replied. "Nothing, except go back to Winder."

"Yes, I suppose there is that."

Tor had not appeared for his answer when we returned, but Trant had been summoned and the five of us waited, sharing the kind of irritation that feels like boredom but is more nearly apprehension. Trant stood stiffly by himself and Alwina talked with Mora. Tenira told me some fragments of things to the effect that all the court ladies including Sissona had been sent home and that there had never been any quarters for Bodwin and that Alwina was not very good at making her own bed. Suddenly, through all the awkwardness and tension, the scene seemed funny to me and I winked at Tenira. At first she looked startled and then finally smiled.

Then Tor was with us. I'm sure no one saw him come in or heard him. He was simply there, very large and powerful, making our easy dismissal of him suddenly stupid and silly.

"You have had time now, Your Majesty," he said in a conversational tone. "I hope you have used it well. What have you decided?"

Alwina turned from Mora to face him, her head up and color in her face, her eyes sparkling. She was magnificently beautiful. "You needn't have left, Tor. There was nothing to decide. You are in rebellion and I will have no more to say until you have returned to your allegiance and your duty. I regret deeply that your people will suffer because of you. I have made you and them a fair and generous offer."

Tor stepped to the entrance, looked outside, and said, "Very well, Nyall."

Nyall entered the tent, instantly followed by a double column of armed sailors. He gave no word of command. Four men seized the Queen and two more took Trant, him roughly. Others pressed Tenira and Mora back into the corners. Five agile men swarmed around me, dropping me hard and neatly on my back. Some wrapped themselves around my arms and legs and one held a dagger to my throat. I recognized none of them.

All this was done in silence until Alwina cried out, "Your men, Trant! Call your men!"

"Yes, call them, Trant," Nyall said. "They are disarmed by now and prisoners."

Alwina's captors grasped her by the shoulders and elbows and marched her, more nearly carried her, out of the tent. Her queenly pose and dignity gone, her feet now touching and now missing the ground, she said nothing more. As she passed Tor, angry, helpless, and humiliated, he watched her with what seemed a mixture of pity and scorn. Then he turned back to the rest of us, looking down finally at me.

"I'm sorry to have done this to you, Frare," he said, "but I know you. I had to make sure of you. If I hadn't, there would be some dead on our hands. In a few minutes Nyall will release you all. You and Tenira may go back to your ship, Frare. Isla Mora with you, if he wishes. And Trant may go back to his troops. Don't feel too badly, Trant. They were well surprised. Just as you were." He paused and let his eyes run over us again. "The Queen, of course, goes with me. Goodbye."

Tor departed and my guards eased their weight on me without releasing me. Nyall took position at the entrance, where he could watch us and observe the progress of events on the beach. At last he was satisfied and nodded to his men. They let us go, stood back, and reformed their lines.

"You are all free now," Nyall said. "You may go where you like. I, too, am sorry about this, Frare."

I didn't answer him as I hadn't answered Tor. It wasn't anger or hurt pride that kept me silent. I felt neither. It was something deeper, and I think both Nyall and Tor shared the knowledge with me. A rock had been moved somewhere at the foundation of things.

Except for Trant, who ran to see to his men, we walked out into the trees, Tenira, Mora, and I, and stood at the crest of the little hill. Below, the *Aspara* was already moving into the channel at the mouth of the bay. One squadron was swinging into line behind her and the ships of the other were taking Nyall and his men on board.

"So that is that," I said. "So simple, and we didn't think of it."

Tor's flotilla steered for the cruising fleet, leaving two ships behind to block the passage out of Shores. We stood watching for a long, long time as the sails diminished and at last began to drop below the horizon. I suppose we all experienced much the same thing, for we all showed similar symptoms. There was a sense of desolation, as of a world and an order broken, coupled with a surprise so profound one was unable even to define what had happened.

Finally I said to the others, "I'm going out to the *Earne*. It's something to do. That is the necessary thing for me. Would you like to come with me?"

"No," Tenira said, "but I like your idea. I'll try to bring the household staff back to life."

Mora smiled and said, "You shame me, both of you. Perhaps I can save poor Trant's mind along with mine. On the evidence, there isn't much to save."

I don't know what the others did to hold themselves

together, but on the *Earne* I set up a watch on the headland to keep track of the two blockading ships and then I conducted a detailed inspection of the *Earne*. In the course of it, I determined not to incapacitate myself by wondering what might be different now if I had sailed from Winder on my own. That was over and done, or rather it hadn't been done, and to speculate about it was to mire myself in self-pity. When we all assembled later and sat outside the main tent, we were able at least to look at our predicament and talk about it rationally.

Mora said, "I have been forcing myself to consider what we may expect. In spite of Trant, who wants to ride and sail at once in all directions, it doesn't seem to me there is any action we can take now. But I realize I may be wrong about that. I yield to you, Frare. You are the man who knows about such things."

"We cannot pursue Tor," I said. "There is no point in talking about it. We *can* inform Cabing. I don't want to do this, but I think we must."

"Go on, Isla Frare."

"There is too much panic in The City now. The Council cannot be trusted. This crisis will be over one way or another before we can tell Cabing anything, but . . . we have to tell him because this is too vital for the country for us to keep quiet."

"I agree," Mora said. "We can write a message and send one of Trant's men. Not Trant. We can spare The City that. You have more, Isla Frare?"

"A little. I do not believe Tor will harm Alwina. She means too much to him personally . . . and otherwise. He is in love with her, too. I know that and you've probably seen it. He will not go to Winder. He will not go to The City. Nor will he stay at sea forever. His business is with her — no one else. It began here and, when it is finished, it will come back here. I can't understand this affair any other way."

233

"I think I understand what you are saying," Tenira said, "but I wish I were as hopeful as you are. I don't see any reason in the situation at all and I don't see how we can suppose what will happen. Alwina can be frightened, but only into stubbornness. When we talked about an explosion, I thought of something quick and sharp that would bring them both to their sense. Not more coils and coils of aggravation like this."

"You have pointed to the danger," Mora told her, "although I think Frare may be right. There is sense in what Tor has done. He has taken Alwina into a world where things have new shapes and meanings. The City doesn't exist. There is no Council, no Alwin House, no you, no me, no Cabing, no Sissona. With all her training, Alwina is ignorant in this way, but she is young and she knows how to see when she has the chance. She may well grasp a little of what Tor has pinned his life on. And a little will be enough for now. He will accept that. But if she blinds herself willfully, if she refuses to see anything at all, then there is the danger you fear, Tenira. In that case, if I were Tor, I would know I had to kill her or keep her a prisoner permanently. I would have gone too far to fail. I couldn't turn her loose on any terms."

Mora's was the last word. Neither Tenira nor I had any emendations of his verdict then or later.

That evening after dark my lookout on the headland came in to report that the blockading ships had put out to sea and the passage was now clear. Tenira spoke for all of us when she said she would miss their company. Their departure broke our very last connection.

Morning came to an empty sea, and all day long our eyes traveled back and forth along the smooth line of the horizon. Nothing came and nothing went and the earth, which had always seemed to me so marvelously full of life and motion, now stood frozen in this one binding intersection of water, land, and sky. The next day was like its predecessor except that our eyes now would not tolerate as much exposure to the brassy glare of the sun on the sea. Often we found ourselves looking down at our feet and they at least moved now and then. On this day, too, Trant needed rescue from himself. He came to each of us in turn, angular and manly, to explain new troop dispositions he had just made, but he would not leave until he had heard that his earlier dispositions were not the cause of the catastrophe. I should have been grateful for this distraction, but I wasn't.

And then one more day began things all over again. Emptiness filled the universe with a density one could feel as physical weight on one's shoulders. It tangled the mind, crushed the heart, and mingled time with space. When, near midmorning, the lookout cried, "Sail! Sail!" I did not know what he was saying.

The cry was taken up from the masthead of the *Earne* and then all along the beach. There *were* sails in the far distance. They multiplied and slowly grew larger, coming up from the sea where, so long ago, they had vanished. At last, one ship detached herself from the others, became the *Aspara,* slipped smartly through the passage, and dropped anchor off the beach. She lowered a boat and moments later Tor, Alwina, and Nyall stepped ashore and walked briskly toward us.

We gathered in the central tent and there were neither explanations nor, indeed, any acknowledgement that anything extraordinary had happened. I stared openly at Alwina and Tor, looking for outward signs of something inward, but faces do not readily reveal such things, at least not so quickly. Instead, I did notice that they both wore that air of confidence, almost of complicity, that comes from the private sharing of knowledge. This in itself was something new and very different. Alwina spoke for them and she might never have been taken from this place by force.

"I am happy to be back," she said, "and I am even happier

that our disagreements are over. Now Islandia and Winder can fight Kilikash together effectively. Tor will take the fleet to Arden on the east coast, picking up the ships of Lamas's squadron as he finds them. I will join him there in ten days. First, however, I will go to The City, give Cabing any military powers he does not now have, and make it plain to the Council what is going to be done to support Winder. By my promise to Tor I remain, in a manner of speaking, a hostage for the Council's performance. I will sail with Tor against Kilikash and we will keep him off our coasts this year.

"Isla Frare, I want you to go back to Winder and be my ambassador and fiscal agent. Tor wants you to serve him also as his minister. In this way you will have charge of the building of all Winderese ships, of all Islandian funds, and of the good name of Islandia in Winder. I don't like the thought of losing Tenira, but I know I cannot send you and keep her. These duties in Winder are the most important and difficult tasks we have to demand of anyone. You and Tenira are the only ones capable of doing them. Tor doesn't like giving up his ablest captain in you, Frare, and you know, Tenira, that I don't want to part with you, my wisest friend and counselor. Someday this war will end. Here, Frare, are your two commissions."

Tor said, "These are not small matters, as you know, Frare. You and Tenira will keep the promises the Queen and I make to Winder and Islandia."

Suddenly, just with that, affairs at Shores were over. The earth had opened, swallowed, and closed. Nothing remained to be seen on the surface except Tenira and me, and we not for long. The sour taste I felt in my mouth was somehow not entirely unexpected. I looked across at Tenira and saw that her face was completely guarded, as calm and smooth as the petals of a tulip.

I said, "I have little experience, Your Majesty, to justify your confidence and Tor's, but your joint support will more than cover my mistakes. I wish you a very successful campaign."

Tenira said, "You never lose the capacity to surprise me, Your Majesty. Tor knows how much I owe to the skill and kindness of Winder. I will do my best to repay it."

Within an hour Alwina rode off for The City with Trant, now restored to pride in his dispositions, and an escort of a dozen troopers. I walked down to the beach with Nyall and Tor, who said to me, "Goodbye again, my friend. Everything changes once more. When I come back I think you will be more a part of my country than I am. I wish you well. Wish me the same." I did that and then they rowed to the *Aspara* and sailed out to the fleet through the narrow passage.

I gathered my crew on the *Earne* and told them what our orders were. They heard me with what seemed to be a mixture of relief and misgiving. Then I went back to shore, where Tenira was supervising the last of Alwina's packing and Mora waited to lead the last section of the party. When he saw me, he told Tenira she had done enough and, taking us each by an arm, walked between us back to our boat.

"Are you surprised at Winder?" he asked.

"I'm not sure," I said.

"I think I know something of what you two are feeling," he said. "It's not nice to be shipped off and disposed of. The Alwins have always done a lot of it. It gives one sympathy for horses and dogs. Well as you know Alwina, my dear Tenira, I know her even better. You and Frare are too able, too knowing, and too forthright to be entirely acceptable at court, but that isn't the real trouble. Your crime and Frare's is that you stand to Alwina for some kind of lost integrity. That makes you much too valuable to throw away but intolerable to have around. Also I think you represent a pledge of good faith between her and Tor. All of this turns the pair of you into a fairly complicated object." We came to a stop at the water's edge, but Mora still held us by the arms. "When Alwina was describing the importance of your place of exile, she didn't say anything about the power you can acquire from there. Perhaps she doesn't see it herself. But the possibility won't elude you, whether or not you have any interest in it. Above all, do not despair. Alwina is a good Queen. Or she will be."

From the *Earne,* as we moved across the westering sun, the multitude of Tor's sails still showed as specks in the east. Standing beside me at the rail, Tenira reached into her cape and drew out a folded piece of paper with the seal broken.

"Let me read you this now," she said. "Alwina wrote it in the minutes before she left. She didn't sign it, but that's more or less usual. It's not quite honest, but she thinks it is. Over the years I've had a lot of notes like this.

" 'I find I cannot stop our habit of years without one last confidence. Treat it as you have all the others — with kindness, discretion, and understanding. I suppose you will show this to Frare. I do not mind. He has earned it and, so long as I do not see his knowledge, it does not matter. Tell him I sometimes still feel my piece of earth shrinking around my feet when my quotient of Om goes down.

" 'Now I have sent you and Frare to Winder. If this is not actually the price of my personal life — perhaps even so — it is certainly that of my useful life as Queen. Tor took me seriously only when I began to use you to bargain with.

" 'I have learned much in the last few days, but not enough. He loves me and hates the Queen. That I now know and the simple logic it sets up in my mind is too much for me. If he marries me, he will be the Queen's master. And yet, by some alchemy, whoever is the Queen's master must be the servant of her people. Unfortunately, this is not merely playing with words. Who sets the dance in the first instance, the Queen or me? Or has one of us already done it? I think I wish I were in Winder and you were here. I shall miss you.' "

I put my arm across Tenira's shoulders and kissed her. "I

remember how Bodwin explained why he couldn't help the Queen when she was ill. He said he didn't dare to because he wanted to spend the rest of his life at court. He told me I would understand what he meant someday. This is someday and I think I like the sound of Winder."

"Frare, dear," she said, "we already like Winder better than any other place. We know Attana. We have Lon. We've found our own spring and dug it. We couldn't do that in The City."

EPILOGUE - 1333

WINDER has become home to Tenira and me, who never really felt at home elsewhere. We would not now willingly return to court. Although we often visit our spring and keep it flowing, we did not build a house there. Instead we have taken the one Alwina used on her first visit here. It is large, but not too large now, and it seems to respond to some of my carvings and Tenira's drawings. Our relations with Alwina are cordial at this distance and there is no need to test them at closer range.

During the long years of war, the familiar difficulties with The City about money were often repeated here, but toward the end I had Winder producing ships as it never had before, and I still manage naval building for the united country. Aside from an occasional patrol, I had no part in the fighting except to command a squadron of new ships in Tor's climactic defeat of Kilikash in 1328.

Tenira grows more lovely every year. She is now physician to the countryside, as Attana was before her, and extends the magnificent herb gardens Attana created. We have two children — Ek, eleven, and Attana, nine. Their births were difficult and dangerous and without the older Attana's skill Tenira would not have lived. When she recovered the second time,

240

even she knew there could be no more, and we have been content with far more than we hoped.

Alwina did go to sea with Tor that autumn and for several weeks they searched unsuccessfully for Kilikash. Keeping him off the Islandian coast, however, was itself a victory for Tor's small fleet, and things continued to go reasonably for quite some time until a coolness began to fall between Alwina and Tor. The reasons for this estrangement have never been clear to us in Winder, but I have supposed it resulted from Alwina's idea that she and the Queen were different entities and her continuing unwillingness to pay the political price for Winder. In any case, she found herself fighting the Karain by herself and went from defeat to defeat to the edge of disaster when Cabing was killed. With this, she recognized at last that the single key to her policy and her person was to be found in Winder and invited Tor to The City. That move cut through all the problems.

The war was declared won on New Year's Day, 1329, the day Alwina and Tor were married. At the same time, Winder became an integral part of Islandia, not a foreign kingdom to be inherited separately. This was a great achievement for both Alwina and Tor, but for her it was merely a beginning, whereas for him it was an ending, as he had known it would be. There has been little place for him as consort. Since the birth of a son, ensuring the dynasty, Tor has spent increasing amounts of time at sea. Meanwhile, Alwina's court flowers and flourishes, and Bodwin, come into his own, sets the standard of cultural exchange.

Isla Mora was right when he told us that power could be built in Winder, but I have not tried to put the pieces together. As I once truthfully told Cabing, I am not ambitious. On one occasion, just after the war, Tor asked me to take the Islaship for Winder in the new order of things. I was eligible. I had resigned as naval Isla when we were sent to Winder, and at this point Alwina could not reasonably object. Tenira and I talked it over and I finally said no, but I suggested Nyall instead. He is doing the job extremely well and is popular here. He is also unmarried and says often that he hopes our son Ek will succeed him. The time for that is still far away, but, if it should ever happen, it would please me very much.